ALL MY ENEMIES

BY BARRY MAITLAND

THE BROCK AND KOLLA NOVELS

The Marx Sisters

The Malcontenta

*All My Enemies**

The Chalon Heads

Silvermeadow

Babel

The Verge Practice

*No Trace**

*Spider Trap**

*Dark Mirror**

*Available from Minotaur Books

ALL MY ENEMIES

A BROCK AND KOLLA MYSTERY

BARRY MAITLAND

MINOTAUR BOOKS

NEW YORK

ALL MY ENEMIES. Copyright © 1996 by Barry Maitland. All rights reserved. Printed in the United States of America. For information, address St. Martin's Press, 175 Fifth Avenue, New York, N.Y. 10010.

www.minotaurbooks.com

Grateful acknowledgement is made to Peter Watts and Penguin Books Ltd for permission to quote from Peter Watts's translation of August Strindberg's play *The Father*, published in *Three Plays* by August Strindberg, Penguin Books, 1958.

Design by Rich Arnold

ISBN 978-0-312-38400-5

First published in the United Kingdom by Hamish Hamilton LTD, a division of the Penguin Group

First U.S. Edition: September 2009

10 9 8 7 6 5 4 3 2 1

For Spats and Margaret

PART ONE

MADONNA WITHOUT A FACE

ONE

BY LUNCHTIME KATHY WAS reduced to the word-puzzle in the Sunday paper. *Form words of three or more letters from the title of The Grubs' latest hit single, "Claim to Dream." No proper names; target 130; include at least one 12-letter word.*

She had begun the day with good intentions. There were plenty of things that could be done before she started her new job: letters that could be written, bills that could be paid, housework that could be done.

Mad, ram, mat, tic, model, modal, rot.

She felt like a stranger in her own flat, hardly having been in the place in the past fifteen months. For a year, while she had been on secondment to the County force at Edenham, she had let the place to a tenant. Then, when she returned to London, she had had to leave again almost immediately for the staff college at Bramshill, in preparation for her new posting at the Yard. The result was that all of the little changes that her tenant's occupation had brought about were still there. The dining-table was in the wrong place, the curtain in the bedroom needed repairing, and his cigarette burn in the worktop of the small kitchen still glared like a fresh wound. Just to wash the whole place down would have been an act of reclamation, establishing that she was in charge again, and for an hour after breakfast she had plunged into the task, doing the easier bits—bathroom, kitchen, and windows—before running out of cleaners and sponges. She had turned to sorting an envelope of old papers, and come across things she was amazed that she still possessed: postcards, letters, fragments of the past. One piece in particular had stopped her dead, a forgotten scrawl, terse, imperious, on a scrap of pale blue notepaper. She'd given up at that point and made a cup of tea, overwhelmed by the feeling that she didn't belong here.

Tea, lair, meat, rice, tame, idle.

The weather was partly to blame, a hot late-summer spell that everyone had felt obliged to take advantage of, so that when Kathy had walked down to the corner shop to buy the paper it had felt as if she was almost the last person left in London. The city seemed evacuated, the few people who remained were suspended, waiting for life to resume. On such a Sunday morning, even the music coming distantly from the Meat Loaf freak's flat two floors below seemed to lack conviction.

Climate, micro, clear, air, clam, coma, melodic, time.

But mostly it was the unfamiliar sensation of having nothing to do. It had caught her off-guard and made her feel weak. Now she came to look at it, the paper seemed full of things designed to protect people from just this feeling, page after page of distractions and diversions to fill the awkward gaps between sleep and work. There were whole sections devoted to the problem—travel, sport, home improvements, the arts, gardening, food, entertainment, bridge, chess, crosswords. There was so much of it that you could occupy the day just reading about ways to occupy the day.

Everyone should have a hobby, the paper seemed to insist. Perhaps she should join something when she had settled in at the Yard. They were bound to have sports teams, social clubs. She turned the page and came to the personal columns. Better still, she could find a man, make a hobby of that.

Male, dream, date, admire, matador, idol, erotic, care, moral, laid, marital.

The words spun from her pen.

Lie, liar, immoral, malice, drama, rat, toad.

She shook herself and stood up. Clearly it was time to get out of the flat. Peter Greenaway's latest was churning stomachs at the cinema down the road. If she bought a sandwich first and took a walk in the park, she could catch the second performance, so that it would almost be dark when she came out and could avoid feeling guilty about having wasted such a wonderful summer day, her last free day before she finally joined Brock's team.

As she reached the door the phone rang and her heart gave a thump as she recognized the voice.

"Kathy! You're back from Bramshill."

"Yes. Hello, Brock. It's good to hear you. How's your shoulder?"

"Absolutely fine now." It sounded as if he was on a car phone, his voice fading and strengthening. "I expect you're busy, are you, just having got back?"

"Not really. I'm pretty much on top of everything." Kathy tried to sound convincing.

"Only, I know you don't officially join us until tomorrow, Kathy, but I've just got word of something that looks like a job for us. A killing. A rather nasty one by the sound of it. I'm on my way there now. If you were interested . . ."

"Yes! What's the address?"

"Petts Wood, South London—Kent."

"I know." She scribbled down the address he gave her, and as he went on, suggesting the best route for her to get there from North London, she wrote: *Mortal, crime, team, armed?*

When she put the phone down she took a deep breath and smiled to herself, feeling as if she'd just woken up from a deep sleep, although the twelve-letter word still eluded her.

TWO

THE DENSITY OF BUILDINGS cramming the sides of the road began to ease, and she came to dark woods, heavy with summer foliage swaying and billowing suddenly like green-black sails in the light afternoon breeze. She drove with the window down, catching glimpses of solitary figures weeding in flower beds, ponies on a shady bridle-path. Then across a railway cutting, and ranks of houses reappeared on both sides of the road.

She stopped to check the A–Z, then turned off the main road into a maze of quiet crescents and winding streets lined with identical houses submerged in gardens of endless variety. Another railway bridge, and semi-detached gave way to detached, the gardens growing larger and the trees more mature.

It was so quiet when she stopped again to check the map, with only the faintest drone of a lawn-mower somewhere in the distance, and the whiff of roses and Sunday roasts. And so familiar, although she had never been here before. For a moment she was a child again, knowing every paving-slab and lamp-post, every rockery and pillar-box, just as she once had been in another, identical suburb, miles away, years ago. It was so reassuringly ordinary, so nurtured, so secure. And in one of these cosy boxes, not far away now, something awful had happened, life had been thrown out of control, just as, in a different way, it once had in hers.

When she turned into Birchgrove Avenue it was clear which was the one, from the number of vehicles jamming the kerb. She stopped at the end of the line and walked back to number 32. As she passed the driveway of the house next door, a woman in a straw hat appeared suddenly from behind a hydrangea bush and waved a pair of secateurs at Kathy.

"Excuse me! Are you with the police?" she called.

Kathy paused. "Yes."

"Only, I just wondered if I could do something to help. Is it a burglary?"

"I don't know yet."

"Well, perhaps you could ask the Hannafords if there's anything I can do. I'm Pamela Ratcliffe."

"All right, Mrs. Ratcliffe. I'll tell them."

"Thank you. There's an awful lot of you, isn't there? For a burglary?"

Kathy turned down the brick drive of 32. The door was opened for her by a uniformed policewoman. Brock was standing in the middle of the panelled hallway, talking intently to a man dressed in a dark suit and dog-collar. Brock acknowledged Kathy with a nod and continued his conversation with the clergyman. "I'm only suggesting that, at this stage, it would be better to avoid speculation about motive, when you're talking to Mr. and Mrs. Hannaford."

The vicar appeared somewhat exasperated. Her eyes adjusting to the dark interior of the house, Kathy saw that he was a young man, rosy-cheeked, with rather stylish wire-framed glasses on his nose. He stabbed at them impatiently with his middle finger and said, "The fact remains, Chief Inspector, that we all have to share the responsibility when something like this happens. And the sooner they can accept that, the sooner they will be able to forgive, and the sooner the process of healing can begin."

"*We* have to share the responsibility?" Brock looked at him in disbelief.

"Of course. We have created a society based on selfishness and greed. People like the Hannafords have benefited materially from it. And now that the good times are over, it is others who are paying the price—the young who can't get jobs and who may, in their desperation, turn to theft. And when they are disturbed, a tragedy like this inevitably happens. Of course the act is theirs, but we are all responsible for the circumstances which brought it about."

Brock took a deep breath, then said, very quietly, "You haven't been upstairs, have you, Mr. Bannister?"

The vicar frowned and shook his head.

"Well, maybe it would be helpful if you could make a formal identification for us. I didn't like to press the point with her parents, the way they are at present."

"I see . . . well, of course."

Kathy followed them up the stairs, their footsteps silent in the thick carpet, air fragrant with Mansion House polish and Pine-o-Cleen. At the landing, Brock stopped them and went himself to an open doorway. He stuck his head in and exchanged a few murmured words with someone inside the room, then waved the Reverend Bannister forward. The vicar went to the door and stopped, adjusting his glasses again. There was a sudden dazzle of light from a photo flashgun within the room, and the clergyman recoiled abruptly from the doorway, as if someone had punched his chest. As Kathy went towards him she saw that his eyes were staring wide, the colour gone from his face. He looked at her for a moment without seeing, then brought a hand up to his mouth, looked around distractedly, and rushed across the landing to another doorway.

Brock stared after him, then turned to Kathy. "Perhaps I shouldn't have done that," he said. He nodded back over his shoulder. "You'd better take a look."

Within the snug, still house, a womb of Axminster and Liberty against an uncertain world, something awful had exploded in just this one room. A woman's belongings were scattered in all directions, slashed clothing mixed with broken things swept from the dressing-table and chest of drawers. Her blood was sprayed across the grey wallpaper, and her bedding was a turmoil of bloodstained sheets and pillows. In the midst of all this she was laid out, naked, as if by an undertaker, straight out on her back, arms by her side, palms upward, her body spattered with purple punctures. And at the very centre of the turmoil, the focus, the thing which had sent the priest reeling backward, was her face, a livid scarlet pulp, the flesh all torn away, surrounded by a halo of fair hair.

"My God!" Kathy muttered under her breath, and moved forward towards the remains of Angela Hannaford.

"Stop!"

The word was barked out like a military order, and Kathy froze immediately. She turned and faced a tall, dark man in pale blue overalls and plastic boots, who was staring at her, hands on hips. Behind him, a photographer and two other men were crouching on the floor, peering at a patch of carpet.

"I said, nobody in here till I give the word. Don't you bloody listen?"

Kathy flushed and stared back at him. "Sorry. I've just arrived. Kathy Kolla."

He stared coldly at her for a moment, then said, "Really? Well, clear off, Kathy Kolla."

Kathy glared back at him, reacting as much to the adrenalin shock from the scene in the room as to his rudeness. She swallowed, turned, and retraced her steps back out to the landing.

The Reverend Mr. Bannister was emerging from the toilet, wiping his mouth with his handkerchief. He avoided meeting Brock's eye. "I see . . ." he muttered, "I see."

They returned downstairs and went into the front room, where they sat at a dining-table, gleaming with fresh polish.

"Tell us what you can about Angela," Brock said.

"Ah . . ." The clergyman sucked in a deep breath and pushed his glasses back on his nose. "She was—" he swallowed, cleared his throat, the bile still burning "—a pleasant girl. Kind, obliging, pleasant. Yes . . . twenty-two, twenty-three." He shook his head abruptly, as if with irritation. "Why, then? I don't understand."

"Pleasant, you say?"

"What? Yes, pleasant. Of course. Umm . . . quiet. Dependable, regular church-goer, like her parents." He seemed to have difficulty finding things to say about her. "One of our Sunday-school teachers, popular with the kiddies." He looked at his watch, agitated. "That's where she should be now."

"You knew her pretty well?"

"Well . . . yes, yes. The family—Angela and her parents—are just about our most loyal parishioners. She wasn't at the service this morning. I remember that now."

"Where is that?"

"St. George's, C of E."

"So you noticed that she wasn't there."

"Yes. I knew that Basil and Glenys—Mr. and Mrs. Hannaford—I knew that they were returning from holiday this morning, and I thought she might be meeting them, or something."

Brock nodded. "I was a bit confused by Mr. Hannaford's account of all that just now. He mentioned that they flew into Gatwick this morning, from Frankfurt. And you think Angela was expected to meet them at the airport?"

"Oh, I've no idea. That's just what I assumed when she wasn't at the service. Adrian wasn't there either."

"Who's Adrian?"

"Her fiancé. Adrian Avery. He lives up near the station. Kingsway or Manor Way, I'm not sure."

"You'd have expected him to be at the service this morning?"

"Not necessarily. He's not as regular as Angela." He shrugged.

Brock looked at him carefully. "Would there be anyone else you can think of who was attracted to Angela sexually? A former boyfriend perhaps, or someone she knew, whose advances she'd rejected?"

The clergyman snorted. "Of course not!"

"She was unattractive, was she?"

"No, no." He corrected himself, a bit flustered by this. "I mean . . . God, what do I mean? I mean that she was . . . chaste. There was nothing sexually provocative about her. Do you know what I mean? I remember my predecessor telling me that she always used to take the part of the Virgin Mary in the Christmas nativity play when she was a girl. She loved the part, and she was perfectly suited to it."

Brock nodded. "And there's no doubt in your mind that that *is* Angela Hannaford upstairs?"

"Chief Inspector . . . I couldn't say. I really couldn't. The hair . . . it looked like hers. Do you want me to . . . to look at her again?"

Brock hesitated. "Would you be able to identify her wristwatch, say, or her rings?"

"No . . . I wouldn't have any idea."

"Well, we'll leave it then. Will you stay with the parents for a while? They seemed anxious for you to be here. I believe they rang your house immediately after calling the police?"

"That's right. Actually, they asked for my predecessor. They weren't thinking straight, of course, with the shock of finding Angela. They would have got more comfort from him than from me, I'm afraid. He'd known them for a long time, you see, and he was more their age. But I'll do my best. I'll steer clear of motive,

Chief Inspector, but, dear Lord!" He shook his head helplessly. "What could have possessed anyone?"

Brock got to his feet and showed him to the door. "We'll come through and speak to Mr. and Mrs. Hannaford again in a little while." He followed the vicar out into the hall and returned a moment later with a woman, whom he invited to sit at the table. Kathy judged her to be in her early thirties, not much older than Kathy herself. She looked preoccupied.

"What can you tell us at this stage, doctor?" Brock asked.

"Death appears to be due to stabbing." Her voice was low and very quiet, so that Kathy found herself leaning forward to catch the words. "There are more than forty stabbing cuts to various parts of her body, done with a blade perhaps half or three-quarters of an inch in width, I'd estimate. Any one of a dozen of these might have been the cause of death. There are other injuries too—extensive bruising and a couple of possible fractures . . . a rib and a finger."

She paused.

"So he continued stabbing her after she was dead?" Brock prompted.

"Yes."

"Was there a struggle?"

"There was a lot of activity, obviously, but whether she resisted him . . . I couldn't say."

"Was she restrained in some way?"

"I think her thumbs were tied together—there's deep bruising and tearing of the flesh of one thumb and the remains of a thin cord round the other."

The thick curtains and carpets in the room seemed to absorb all sound from outside, so that a heavy silence filled the pauses in the doctor's account. Kathy was conscious of a ringing in her ears.

"Was she sexually assaulted?" Brock said.

The doctor nodded. "There is extensive vaginal and anal

bruising. But hardly any traces of semen. They're still working with the UV light, but I couldn't be sure there was any at all. He washed her, afterwards."

"Washed her?"

"Yes, that's how it looks. There was a wet face flannel in the bathroom, and the sheet beneath her is wet."

Another pause, longer, as if the doctor were becoming increasingly reluctant to go on.

"What about time of death?" Brock asked.

The doctor shrugged. "Maybe twelve to fifteen hours . . . say between midnight and dawn."

"And her face?"

"That was done after she was dead. He made a cut from ear to ear, under her chin, then pulled the skin back up to her hairline. He didn't do it very neatly. Possibly the blade wasn't very sharp— all the other wounds are stabs, rather than cuts."

"Any ideas about the mutilation of the face?"

"None whatever. I can't imagine that he was trying to hide her identity."

"No."

"There was another odd thing. Her jaw was propped open."

"Eh?"

"With a piece of matchstick, jammed between her back teeth, here." The doctor opened her own mouth to show them, then closed it and began to get to her feet.

"I think that's about all I can tell you for the moment. I had a look at the parents. I think we should get their own GP to see them. He should be familiar with their medical history. This is the name they gave me."

She gave Brock a note and he said, "We'll organize it. Are you happy with the way they're going upstairs?"

"Oh yes, Desai's very competent." She hesitated, then went on, "The father took me to one side and asked me why this had happened to his daughter. I said I couldn't tell him." She looked Brock in the eye. "I could have given him some medical terms, but what would that explain?"

Brock nodded.

"Also, he asked me if she had died quickly. I lied to him. I said yes."

ANGELA'S MOTHER SAT CROUCHED in an armchair in front of the fireplace, her head bowed towards the tapestry screen which was used to hide the grate during the summer months. She was sobbing quietly into a tiny handkerchief clutched in her hand, and a policewoman sat in the inglenook beside her, holding the cup of tea which Mrs. Hannaford had accepted, but not touched. She appeared older than Kathy had expected, and made no attempt to hide the silver in her hair. Her husband rose to his feet from the chair opposite her when he saw Brock and Kathy come into the room, and followed Brock's nod towards the bay window, where the three of them sat down, out of earshot of Glenys Hannaford.

"This is Detective Sergeant Kolla, Mr. Hannaford," Brock said. "She'll be part of our team working on this case."

Basil Hannaford looked at Kathy through his horn-rimmed glasses without seeing her. He sat stiffly upright, his heavy features expressionless. Kathy had the impression of someone mentally hanging on grimly to the rail of a ship during a hurricane. In the light of what they had come home to, his carefully casual travelling clothes and the glow of his holiday tan seemed incongruously frivolous.

"I'd just like to check again with you the sequence of events this morning, then we'll leave you in peace for the moment. We've asked your GP to come round, and he says he'll be here within the hour."

Hannaford didn't respond. Like his wife, Kathy took him to be at or near retiring age. There was a pugnacious set to his mouth and chin, temporarily softened by shock.

"You and Mrs. Hannaford were in Germany on holiday, is that right?"

It was a moment before he nodded. "We . . ." He cleared his throat and tried again, speaking in a low monotone. "We were on a tour. Four days on the Rhine, and then four days on the . . . the Romantic Road . . . in Bavaria. Got back to Frankfurt last night and caught the plane to Gatwick this morning."

"What time did you get in?"

"10:53 was the scheduled time."

"Were you expecting Angela to meet you there?"

Hannaford shook his head slowly. "No . . . No. We took the car to Gatwick. Left it there. Airport car park."

"So this morning you collected the car from the airport car park and drove back here, arriving when?"

"Soon after midday. Gardening programme . . ."

He stopped, jaw clenched, and they waited.

"On the radio?" Brock murmured after a moment.

Hannaford nodded. "Radio Four. Hadn't long started."

"Now when you arrived home, you drove into the drive, where your car is now?"

A nod.

"And was there anything at that stage that you noticed? Anything out of place?"

He thought a moment and frowned. "Only . . . only that Angela didn't come to the door. She'd have heard the car arrive, if she'd been at home."

"What did you think?"

"Thought she must still be at church. The service runs from 11:00 to 12:00."

"Would she have gone to that in her own car?"

"Doesn't have a car. It's a ten-minute walk to St. George's."

"So there was nothing to alarm you at that point?"

"No. I went to the front door, to open it before I got the bags out of the boot."

The expression on his face changed.

"You noticed something?"

"Not at first. I called Angela's name, but the house was so silent. I knew . . . she wasn't there. Then I noticed, on the hall floor, her bag."

"Describe it, please."

"Just thrown down. The clasp was open and some of the things inside had spilled out."

"You didn't think she would have left it like that?"

"No, of course not. Not just lying there, on the floor."

"What did you do?"

"I picked it up—put the things back inside. Then I started checking the rooms, down here first of all, then upstairs. And then . . ."

"Were there any signs of a disturbance in any of the other rooms? Anything at all that you noticed as being odd in any way?"

"Nothing, no. Not until I got to Angela's room . . ."

They waited in silence for a moment, then Brock murmured, "Was her door closed when you first saw it?"

He nodded.

"And Mrs. Hannaford, has she also seen Angela's room?"

"Couldn't stop her. She'd followed me into the house. I was standing just inside the doorway of Angela's room, trying to . . . comprehend. Glenys must have come up behind me. I heard her ask what the matter was. Then before I could turn round she passed out—just fell to the floor. I carried her through to our bedroom. Rang you from the phone there."

"Did you go back to Angela's room after that?"

"No."

"So neither you nor Mrs. Hannaford stepped more than a

couple of paces into the room? You didn't go over to the bed, say, or move anything?"

"No, no."

"All right. And where is Angela's bag now?"

Hannaford pondered. "I think I put it down in the hall before I started looking into the rooms. On the settle, I think."

"Could you show us?"

They got up and made for the door. As they passed Mrs. Hannaford she looked up and whispered, "Basil?"

"It's all right, Glenys. I'll be back in a moment."

The black shoulder bag was still lying where Hannaford had laid it.

"Ah," Brock said. "We assumed that belonged to Mrs. Hannaford. Kathy, would you ask Desai upstairs to check this for us, please? Tell him we'd like to have a look inside as soon as possible."

Kathy went quickly upstairs to Angela's room. This time she stopped at the doorway and spoke to the back of the man who was crouching beside the bed.

"Are you Desai?"

He looked back over his shoulder at her. He had a lean face, dark good looks, Indian she assumed, and the same arrogant expression in his eyes.

"Chief Inspector Brock asks if you would check the dead girl's handbag for us. It's lying on the hall settle downstairs. As far as we know only the father has touched it, although it's possible the mother did too. They found it lying, open, on the hall floor when they arrived this morning."

"OK." He turned back to his inspection of the carpet.

"He says we'd like to get at the contents as soon as possible."

This got no answer. Kathy stood for a moment staring at the woman's body on the bed, then clenched her jaw and hurried back downstairs. Brock and Hannaford had returned to the window seats in the bay.

"Why do you want to know the name of her dentist?" Angela's father was asking.

"Sometimes it's useful."

Hannaford shook his head and gave a name.

"Did your daughter have any particular physical distinguishing marks at all, Mr. Hannaford? A birthmark, a tattoo?"

The man looked at Brock as if he were mad. "A tattoo?"

Brock shrugged apologetically. "These days, quite a few young people do."

"Really? Well, perhaps the sort of people you . . ." He stopped himself. "No, of course not. It's inconceivable."

"And have you any idea what she might have been doing yesterday evening?"

Hannaford shook his head.

"Were you in touch with her at all during the past week? Did you ring her from the Continent?"

"Yes, once. It would have been last Tuesday, I think. We had reached . . . what was the name of the place?" He looked for a moment towards his wife as if to ask for help, then remembered. "Lindau, on Lake Constance. We rang her from the hotel at about 6:30 that evening. Everything was perfectly normal. She didn't mention any plans for this Saturday, as far as I know. I would have expected her to be with Adrian if she went out at all."

"No, dear."

They looked up to see Mrs. Hannaford standing a few paces away. The vicar was holding her arm, awkward. Brock stood up to get her a chair.

"Adrian was going out with his friends, don't you remember? One of them was having a stag night. He's getting married next Saturday."

Hannaford shook his head. "No, no, I don't remember, Glenys. Shouldn't you be lying down?"

"Dr. Pollock will be here soon, dear. I'll wait till then." She hesitated, then continued. "She said she was going out on Saturday evening too. She'd got tickets . . . for the theatre."

"Tickets, Mrs. Hannaford?" Brock asked gently. "There were others going?"

She bit her lip suddenly and began sobbing once more. After a moment she whispered, "A friend from the office."

She turned away and blinked out through her tears at the garden. "The grass needs cutting, Basil," she mumbled distractedly. Kathy followed her gaze. A lush lawn framed by beds of annuals and banks of shrubbery led to a huge, shady ash tree at the far end. A plump squirrel was scurrying across the lawn, its fluffy grey tail held high.

ANGELA'S HANDBAG CONFIRMED WHERE she had been the previous evening.

"You've met DS Leon Desai then, Kathy? DS Kathy Kolla."

"Yes, we met upstairs," Kathy said coolly.

Desai nodded briefly in acknowledgement and turned to the handbag on the dining-table in front of them. Brock let him empty it with his gloved hands, carefully bagging each item as he brought it out. The first of these was a glossy theatre programme, folded to fit into the bag, for a performance of *Macbeth* at the National Theatre. Later, when they came to her purse, they retrieved the theatre ticket, for the evening of Saturday, September 8.

Kathy made her own list of the items in the bag as Sergeant Desai brought them out. They included a current season ticket on Southern Rail from Petts Wood to Blackfriars in the City of London, an Access credit card, a cheque card and a blood donor card. There was no driver's licence.

"All right, thanks, Leon. How's it going upstairs?"

"Slowly. We'll be some time yet. He seems . . ." He hesitated.

"What?"

Desai shrugged. "I was going to say that he seems to have been remarkably careful. It sounds an odd thing to say, looking at all that mess. But it's not as easy as it should be to find his traces among it all." He pursed his lips with frustration. "What I would appreciate, sir, is if you could keep people downstairs. You know what it's like. Every new person is just another contamination to eliminate. Somebody threw up in the toilet upstairs not long ago, and we hadn't even started in there yet."

"Oh dear." Brock frowned, avoiding his glare. "Yes, of course, Leon. Just give us a shout when you can let us back up again."

The man got to his feet. "Any idea how he got in yet? We haven't been able to find any traces of a forced entry upstairs."

"No," Brock said, "nor down here either. That's one of the worrying things."

Desai nodded and left.

"Who is he, Brock?" Kathy asked when the door closed behind him. "I thought he was with Scene of Crime."

"He's our LO, Kathy—Laboratory Liaison Officer. He's with the Met Forensic Science Lab in Lambeth, coordinating the scientific blokes, advising us on scene management and so on."

"Well, when I went upstairs he made it pretty clear what he thought of liaising with *contaminants* like me."

Brock smiled. "The more refined their equipment gets and the more subtle the traces they can pick up, the more of a headache the rest of us become for them. What they'd really like when a crime is discovered is for the whole neighbourhood to be evacuated and sealed off, and for them to be given a month or two to sift through it in space suits. You can understand their frustration with what happens to their evidence when we barge in. It's bad enough for them trying to make sure that they don't themselves provide some opening for the defence—you know, inadvertently picking up a hair in the toilet and transferring it on their shoe to the bedroom, or something."

"Yes, I know," Kathy said. "We spent quite a lot of time on that at Bramshill. But it's also important that *we* get a good look at the scene."

"Of course. Look, Kathy," Brock said, changing the subject, "I didn't get a chance to say it earlier, but thanks for agreeing to come out today. I could have called Bren, but he's had quite a bit on his plate recently. And of course, I'm really delighted you're joining us tomorrow."

Kathy beamed. "You know it's what I always wanted, Brock. I was a bit worried that there would be some . . . well, embarrassment at what happened at Edenham—that it might stop them transferring me to Serious Crime."

"It is true that, on the whole, young aspiring officers are discouraged from stabbing suspects to death. I dare say that it would be regarded as unduly colourful, on a personnel file. On the other hand, you did save my life, which would probably count on the plus side, marginally. At least, it does with me."

He smiled at her. "On the two occasions we've worked together, Kathy, you've managed to cause quite a bit of physical damage, to yourself as much as anyone else. This time, let's just track down the animal responsible for what happened upstairs, and then arrest him in an orderly fashion, shall we? For the sake of your file."

"You don't want me to become type-cast, is that it?" Kathy smiled back.

"What I'd particularly like is for you to concentrate on the girl. Find out what you can about her. It's beginning to look as if the physical evidence may be a bit sparse, in which case the connection between Angela Hannaford and her killer will become all the more important."

"Perhaps there is no connection. Perhaps it could have been anyone."

"No. We're surrounded by five million houses very much like this one. There has to be some reason why it was this house, this girl, this time. How did he know there was a young woman here? How did he know she was on her own? How did he know that he had time to spend on her? I don't mean that he necessarily *knew* her, although we'll begin with that as a possibility. But even if he didn't, there was *some* connection between his pattern of life and hers."

Kathy nodded. "Where would you like me to begin?"

"The boyfriend, I think. I've got people from the local Division starting on house-to-house interviews in the street here, with the neighbours and so on. But you might see where you go with her social life. Keep in touch with me here. This is the phone number."

As Kathy got into her car, she looked back and saw him come out of the porch at the front of the house, talking with a couple of local CID detectives. He was a big man, and his mop of grey hair stood out above their heads, framed by a trail of yellow honeysuckle blossom growing around the framework of the porch. He seemed to be only half listening to the other two, his eyes straying over the windows in the upper part of the house. He scratched his beard, pondering, then hunched his shoulders and said something, and the little group dispersed.

KATHY RANG THE FRONT door bell and waited while the chimes died away inside. Eventually the door was opened by a small girl, barely tall enough to reach the latch. She stared up at Kathy silently while the smell of roast lamb and scorched ironing drifted out of the interior of the house.

"Hello," Kathy said. "Is Adrian at home?" The little girl just stared at her, saying nothing. "Adrian Avery?" Kathy repeated.

"I'll need a fresh shirt tonight, Mum," a male called from somewhere upstairs.

"Well, I can't help that," an exasperated woman's voice replied faintly.

"Just tell him there's someone to see him, will you, please?" Kathy smiled encouragingly at the girl, who abruptly turned and ran away down the hall. After a couple of minutes a middle-aged woman bustled out with the small girl in tow.

"Yes?"

"Mrs. Avery? I wanted to see Adrian, if he's at home."

The woman looked at Kathy with interest. "Are you a friend of his?"

"No, Mrs. Avery, I'm with the Metropolitan Police."

The woman's face dropped. "Oh. Is something wrong?"

"Yes, I'm afraid there is. May I come in?"

The woman showed Kathy through to a plumply furnished living-room.

"What is it?" she demanded anxiously.

"You know Angela Hannaford, do you, Mrs. Avery?"

"Angela? Yes, of course. Has something happened to her?"

"I'm afraid so. She died last night."

All over Petts Wood, Kathy knew, the same message, in all its variations, was being met with the same stunned look, the same moment of disbelief followed by the same hushed question, "How?"

"She died at home, Mrs. Avery. We are treating it as a suspicious death." Kathy waited a moment while this sank in, then continued, "When did you last see Angela?"

But Mrs. Avery didn't hear her. She was staring at the carpet. "How awful. Her poor parents! Do they know? Are they back?"

Kathy nodded.

"Should I speak to them?"

"Are you close friends?"

"No . . . not really, but . . ."

"I'd leave it for a while. When did you last see Angela, Mrs. Avery?"

"Oh . . . well, Friday night, yes, of course. She had dinner with us, here, on Friday evening." She shook her head.

"Did she speak at all about her plans for Saturday? How she intended to spend the day?"

"I don't know . . . Adrian will know. I think she said she had to get some shopping in for her mum and dad coming home."

"What about yesterday evening, did she talk about that?"

"Oh, yes, that's right, she did. She was going up to town, to the theatre. She was very keen on the theatre."

"Did you see her at all yesterday?"

"No, no, I didn't. But Adrian did. He'll tell you."

"Yes. What time did he get home last night, Mrs. Avery?"

"I'm not sure . . . Why? Why do you ask that?" A note of alarm had crept into her voice. "There's no . . ."

At that moment her son appeared at the door. He was wearing jeans and a T-shirt, and his feet were bare. He hadn't shaved, and his face was puffy, as if he'd only recently woken up.

"What's going on?" He looked tentatively from his mother to Kathy. "Lizzie said . . ."

As Mrs. Avery rose to her feet, staring at her son, Kathy broke in, "Perhaps I could speak to Adrian alone now, Mrs. Avery. If you don't mind."

The woman shook her head slowly. As she left she whispered, "Oh Adrian, darling. I'm so sorry."

Her son stared at her in surprise, then turned to Kathy. "What's this all about then?"

He too seemed stunned by what Kathy had to tell him, but, as with his mother, there were no tears.

"I can't believe it . . . can't believe it . . ." What little colour there had been in his face had drained away. "What . . . happened?"

"We're still trying to find out. I'm very sorry, Adrian. You were engaged to Angela, I understand."

"Yes . . . well, sort of."

"Sort of?"

He blinked, having difficulty focusing on her words. "We haven't named the day or anything."

"Right. Did she wear your ring?"

He shook his head numbly.

"How long had you been going out together?"

"What? I dunno. Years. Christ . . . are you sure it's Angela?" He peered at her doubtfully, puffy eyes narrowed to slits. "Are you really sure it's her?"

"Yes, we're sure. I'm sorry. You saw a lot of each other, then? Went out regularly?"

He shook his head, and at first Kathy thought he was saying no, then realized he was still grappling with the question of whether she could really be dead.

"Did she go out with other men?"

That stopped him short. "No." Surprised by the idea, rather than offended.

"And you, do you sometimes go out with other girls?"

"No, I do not!"

"I'm sorry, Adrian, I have to ask these questions. It's so important that we understand Angela's background. Please don't take offence."

He stared at the floor. "Six years, right?"

"What?"

"How long we've been going out. Since her sixteenth birthday."

"I see. What can you tell me about her movements yesterday?"

He ran a hand over his head, the hair greasy, sticking out in tufts, half his mind still catching up with the start of their conversation. "What do you mean that you're treating it as a suspicious death? Can't you tell, or something?"

"There doesn't seem to be much doubt, Adrian. What did she do yesterday, please?"

He stared at her, puzzled, then his shoulders sagged.

"She went to the supermarket in the morning," he said in a low voice, subdued by the certainty he had seen in her eyes. "Get some stuff for her parents coming home today." He shook his head. "Do they know?"

Kathy nodded. "Go on."

"I went round there in the afternoon."

"What for?"

"Just to see her, you know. We'd arranged it."

"What did you do?"

"Oh . . ." he shrugged. "Just chatted and that. Nothing special."

"When did you leave?"

"About 5:00, I suppose. She was going to get something to eat and then get ready to go out. She talked about this play she was going to see."

"Yes, tell me about that."

"Well, she got a couple of tickets for this production of *Macbeth* that everyone's raving about."

"Two tickets?"

"I think so."

"You weren't interested?"

Adrian shook his head. "Not me. Anyway, I was already going out, see."

"So who was the other ticket for?"

"One of the girls at work, I think," Adrian said vaguely. "Rhona, I think. Yes, I'm pretty sure it was Rhona. She works with her. I don't know her other name."

"Did Angela often go out without you?"

"To the theatre, that's all."

"You weren't jealous, anyway." Kathy smiled as if it was a joke.

Adrian shook his head and said "Nah," as if the idea hadn't occurred to him.

"Oh, one thing I have to ask, Adrian. Did you and Angela have sex when you saw her yesterday afternoon?"

Adrian stared at her. "What . . ." Then the significance of the question dawned on him. "They didn't . . . ? Did they . . . ?"

"We don't know what happened, Adrian," Kathy said. "This is just one of the questions I have to ask."

"Well . . . we didn't."

"I take it you were lovers, though?"

Adrian nodded, still searching her face for what she might be keeping from him.

"You must have thought about it, yesterday, didn't you, alone in the house together?"

"I might have suggested something. But she wasn't interested."

"Did you have an argument about it?"

"Nah." He gave the impression he lacked the energy or passion to have much of an argument about anything. Kathy felt sad, looking at him, slumped forward in his armchair, trying to keep up. *This was Angela's love-life*, she thought. *From her sixteenth birthday to the day she died. Kind, obliging, pleasant Angela and Adrian the slug. Held together by her loyalty and his lethargy, probably. If she'd lived, she might have moved on, been able to look back with some fondness at dear old Adrian. But, as it turned out, Adrian was all there was ever going to be. How bloody sad. No wonder she had a passion for the theatre.*

"She had to hoover the house for her mum and dad getting home. Didn't have time."

"What are they like?"

"Glenys is all right, fusses a lot. Mr. Hannaford . . . he tends to be old-fashioned."

"In what way?"

"Oh, his tastes and opinions and that."

"Could you give me an example?"

"Well . . . for instance, Angela didn't want him to know she was on the pill. I mean, that's a bit pointless these days, innit?"

"But her mother knew?"

"Yeah, yeah, I expect so."

Kathy nodded. "I get the picture." She closed her notebook and put it firmly in the pocket of her coat, as if she'd finished her questions. "You look as if you had a heavy night with the lads last night." She smiled sympathetically.

"Yeah." Adrian sagged back in the armchair and passed a hand across his face.

"They say a couple of raw eggs and Worcestershire sauce helps."

"No thanks."

"Big crowd?"

He sniffed. "About twenty."

"I expect the future bridegroom is suffering this morning too."

"That's for sure." Some recollection brought a little smile to Adrian's mouth. "He was paralytic."

"And I suppose somebody ordered a strippergram for him?"

"Yeah . . . yeah, you're right. We all chipped in."

"Was she sexy?"

"Not bad."

"That's a job I wouldn't like to do. They're usually pretty smart at winding the blokes up, though, aren't they? Especially after the boys have had a few."

"S'pose so."

"Whereabouts was this party?"

"We hired a room upstairs at the Daylight."

"Handy. What time did they throw you out?"

"Oh, I dunno . . ." He rubbed his eyes. "About one o'clock, maybe."

"Then what?"

He shrugged. "Some of us went back to one bloke's house for a nightcap and that."

"Where was that?"

"Willett Way—does it matter?"

"How did you get home from there?"

"Well, I didn't drink-drive, if that's what you mean." He was becoming belatedly unsettled by Kathy's questions.

"Did you get a taxi?"

"No, I walked, s'matter of fact."

"I'm surprised you made it."

"I wanted to clear my head, like. I wasn't that bad."

"What time did you get home, would you say?"

"About 4:00, probably. What are you getting at?"

"You didn't detour by way of Birchgrove Avenue, did you, Adrian?"

"No, I did not."

"The thought must have come into your head though, that your girlfriend would be at home, lying all alone in her bed, the last chance before her parents came back."

"No way." He shook his head, looking at Kathy warily. "I came straight back here."

"And you'd had quite a skinful, but not so much you couldn't walk, and maybe you had the stripper on your mind, the way she'd wound you all up, eh?"

Adrian's face was grey, his upper lip damp with sweat.

"Did anyone see you on the way home? Did any of the family wake up when you came in and got yourself to bed?"

"No . . . nobody."

"I'd like you to take me to your room and show me the clothes you were wearing last night, Adrian. OK?"

"I . . . I dunno." He looked alarmed.

"Why not? Why wouldn't you want to help?"

"I do, but . . ."

"Come on." Kathy got firmly to her feet and headed for the door. She turned. "Coming?"

He got up reluctantly and led her upstairs, past his mother in the hallway, ignoring her anxious look with a shake of his head.

Another pair of jeans, a casual summer shirt and various other bits of clothing were scattered across the floor of the bedroom.

"You wore these last night, Adrian?"

He nodded.

"Have you got a suitcase or an overnight bag here?"

"Overnight?"

"Just something to put these in. We'll need to look at them."

"But why?" Adrian finally yelped at her. "What the bloody hell are you trying to make out?"

"Adrian," Kathy rounded on him, speaking quietly, intently, "your girlfriend was murdered last night by someone. We are going to find out who. We begin by eliminating as many people as we can, people who were close to her, or knew her movements. It's up to you how quickly we can strike you off the list. OK?"

She watched him pack, and then made a quick search of his cupboards and drawers while he looked uneasily on. On the way out she phoned Brock.

"Take him to CID at Orpington, Kathy. Get them to take a statement from him. I'll phone them and tell them you're coming. I'll get them to hold the lad's clothing until Desai can arrange to pick it up for tests. What do you think?"

"Talk to you later, Brock," Kathy replied, conscious of Mrs. Avery hovering in the background.

BY THE TIME SHE had finished processing Adrian Avery at Orpington, Kathy only just had time to get back to Petts Wood for the six o'clock evening service at St. George's. She had a brief word in the vestry with the Reverend Mr. Bannister, and took her place in a pew towards the back of a fairly thin congregation.

The church had been built just before the outbreak of the Second World War to serve the surge of development which had occurred in the area during the thirties. It was in a simplified

Gothic style, built of brick, and pleasantly cooler than the still hot evening outside. A few of the windows contained stained-glass figures, the Virgin Mary in the one nearest Kathy. Draped in an electric-blue gown, she gazed heavenward with a look of pained resignation, as if waiting for the next blow to fall. She reminded Kathy very much of Angela's mother.

The vicar ended his sermon with a reference to Angela, "tragically taken from the bosom of her family and the community of her friends." The congregation was very still as he told them that a police officer was among them, and would like to talk after the service with anyone who knew of the dead woman's movements during the previous few days, and in particular Saturday, or who could offer any other information which might assist the police with their inquiries. Then he led the congregation in prayers for Angela's soul, and for the comfort of her family.

Half a dozen people stayed behind to talk to Kathy. Most were of an age with Angela's parents, concerned for them and shocked by such an inexplicable atrocity so close to home. Most had seen Angela at the shops on Saturday morning, and had exchanged words with her there. They stressed what a pleasant, helpful girl she was, how she was the last person to whom such a thing should have happened. One was younger than the others, a woman of Angela's age who had apparently been a longstanding friend, and she was able to give Kathy some background on her character and habits. But none had seen her after midday on Saturday, or could throw any light on who might have attacked her.

THREE

KATHY GAVE HERSELF PLENTY of time to get to work the next morning, relishing a moment she had long anticipated. She took the Northern Line tube down to Charing Cross, then walked across Trafalgar Square, through Admiralty Arch and slowly down the east side of St. James's Park along Horse Guards Parade, enjoying the bright summer morning. She paused when she came to Birdcage Walk and sat for a while on a bench, still too early for the time she'd been told to report. Through the trees she caught glimpses of office workers in short-sleeved shirts and lightweight suits, hurrying to start another week. A couple of nannies walked past her, pushing prams side by side down the shady path. She thought how absurd it was that she should be nervous, when she already knew several of her new colleagues quite well, and in particular the most important one, Brock. But this was more than just another job shift. She felt like a child presenting herself for adoption by a new family.

At 8:50 she got to her feet, made her way down Storey's Gate, and so into Broadway and the modern office building with the rotating stainless-steel prism outside: her new place of work.

After a moment's confusion with the man at the reception desk inside, she discovered that it wasn't.

"If it's DCI Brock's outfit, you want Annexe Q, love."

"Do I? It is in New Scotland Yard though, isn't it?"

"But not in this building. It's a couple of blocks away, over towards St. James's Park. Look . . ." He showed her on a photocopied street map. "Queen Anne's Gate."

"Oh, are you sure?"

"Course I'm sure. He used to be in here. But he managed to escape." He grinned at her. "You joining them permanently?"

"Yes."

"Good. 'Bout time they had a woman. You'll probably have to come back here later to check with Personnel and Training." He looked over at a large board on the wall. "PT4, Career Management. They'll see to your headquarters officer's warrant card, and so on. Give 'em a ring when you get to Brock's place. The internal number is 5771."

Kathy wrote it down. "Thanks. See you later."

She followed his directions back towards the park and found Queen Anne's Gate, a quiet street of Georgian terraces, originally homes, which had long been converted into offices. She walked down the row of identical front doors on the south side until she found number 9. There was no nameplate outside, and when she rang the doorbell the door clicked open automatically. She stepped inside into a small reception area, with a clerk sitting at a desk. Kathy told him who she was, and waited while he made a phone call. A couple of minutes later she heard her name called.

"Kathy!"

She turned and smiled at the familiar figure. Bren Gurney had been a detective sergeant in Brock's team on the first occasion that Kathy had come across him, and she had hoped that he would still be there. As tall as Brock, he looked like a younger version of his boss, so much so that Kathy had imagined at first that they could be father and son. He spoke with a soft, reassuring

West Country accent, and he was beaming with genuine pleasure as he shook her hand with a paw twice as big as her own.

"We've been expecting you, Kathy. It's grand to see you again. It seems ages since Jerusalem Lane."

"I finally made it, Bren. I was hoping you'd still be here."

"Of course I am. Where else would I be?"

"You haven't got bored and been tempted back to flying helicopters?"

"You've got a good memory, Kathy. No, I'm too old for that now. But I certainly haven't had time to get bored."

The shadow of something—fatigue or worry—passed momentarily across his face. Looking at him closer, Kathy thought he had aged more than the eighteen months which had passed since Jerusalem Lane, and she recalled Brock's remark about him having a lot on his plate.

"You found us all right, then," he said as he led her off down a narrow corridor.

"Yes, eventually. I went to Broadway first."

"Brock prefers it over here, tucked away out of sight. This place is leased as overspill space. I don't know how long they'll let us stay here."

As they made their way through the building, Kathy realized that the original terrace of individual town houses had simply been knocked together, so that the old staircases, front doors, and corridors were now all linked internally into a confusing three-dimensional maze.

"We're in the basement," Bren said. "Brock had to fight hard to get it."

"Why did he want it?"

"I'll show you."

They descended to the foot of one of the stairs, and made their way along a tight, low-ceilinged passageway until they reached an arch. Bren switched on a light and Kathy was surprised to find herself in what appeared to be the tiny snug bar of an ancient pub. A huge stuffed salmon in a glass case dominated one wall, and a variety of other trophies and mementoes covered the others. The bar was jammed into one corner, barely large enough for three stools to cluster in front of it.

"The Bride of Denmark," Bren announced proudly. "Until we took it, this building belonged to an architectural publisher, who'd had it since before the war. They made up this bar from bits and pieces they collected from old pubs that had been bombed or demolished. Not surprisingly, the Bride is the only pub in a Metropolitan Police building in London, and Property Services were stumped what to do with it. They thought they'd clear all this out, to make a file store, but Brock wouldn't have it. He threatened to go to the National Trust."

"What do you use it for?" Kathy smiled.

"It's officially designated a conference room. We quite often have conferences, usually at the end of the day."

"I can imagine. It's wonderful."

In the distance they heard Brock's voice. Bren looked at his watch. "I think we're having one now, as a matter of fact."

Brock arrived with a greeting for Kathy, and squeezed round behind the bar, on which he began to lay out the pile of documents he'd brought under his arm. He was followed by a detective sergeant Kathy recognized from the Jerusalem Lane case.

"Did you ever meet Ted Griffiths, Kathy?"

"Yes, yes, I did. Hello, Ted." They shook hands. He was a little older than Kathy, quite good-looking, and with enough attention spent on his hair and clothes to suggest he was aware of it.

"You'll have to excuse Ted if he seems a bit preoccupied, Kathy." Brock spoke as he peered through his half-lens glasses at the papers he was sorting. "His wife has just produced their first baby. Couple of weeks ago."

Ted Griffiths nodded, his grin a little smug, Kathy thought.

"But since the same thing happens somewhere around the world about five hundred times every minute, we're not going to let it distract us from our work, are we?"

Ted smiled some more and sat down below the salmon, on an oak bench as black and worn as an old church pew. As Kathy and Bren took their seats on the stall facing Ted, DS Desai arrived and, with a brief nod, sat on a spindle-backed chair at the far end of the small room from Brock's bar counter.

"Right," said Brock, apparently finally satisfied with the layout of his papers, "the murder of Angela Hannaford." He began to pass photographs and pages of summary information across to Ted to circulate to the others.

"Aged twenty-two last month, single, lived with her parents at 32 Birchgrove Avenue, Petts Wood, and had done so since 1971. Kathy might tell us what else we know about her in a moment."

He tilted his head and peered down through his glasses at another piece of paper which he drew out of the pile. "Last Saturday night, while her parents were abroad on holiday and her fiancé was out with friends at a stag night, Angela is believed to have come up to town to see a performance of *Macbeth* at the National Theatre on the South Bank. She had apparently bought two tickets for the play, the other being taken by a girlfriend from work called Rhona. Angela didn't possess a car, and probably travelled up to town on the train, using her season ticket. The performance began at 7:30 and finished just before 10:30. That would have given her plenty of time to walk the 500 yards or so to Waterloo station to pick up the last reasonable train home that night, the 11:05 from Charing Cross to Sevenoaks, stopping at Waterloo at 11:08, and reaching Petts Wood at 11:40. From Petts Wood station it was a fifteen-minute walk to her home, so if she did come home that way she should have arrived at 11:55."

He paused, took off his glasses, and looked around the room.

"Which happens to be precisely the time when the boy next door, one Warwick Ratcliffe, aged fifteen, says he arrived home, on foot, from a party. He doesn't remember seeing a light on at number 32, and heard nothing, either then, when he arrived, or when he went to bed soon after.

"She could have returned some other way, of course. Maybe Rhona had a car and gave her a lift home, in which case they might have got to Birchgrove Avenue soon after 11:15, if they came directly there, or any time later if they stopped along the way. Again, she could have come back to Petts Wood by train, then accepted a lift home from the station, perhaps from someone she met on the train, who'd left their car near the station. But, again, Warwick didn't notice any car parked outside Angela's home, nor anywhere else in the street.

"At any rate, some time after arriving home, Angela was sexually assaulted and murdered in her bedroom on the rear first floor, by someone who apparently didn't need to force an entry into the house. A preliminary schedule of injuries is given on one of the sheets I've copied for you there, although we'll have to wait for the post-mortem this afternoon to confirm these. As you see, they are quite extensive, and there are peculiarities about the way the body was left. I particularly don't want to publicize these features—the matchstick in the mouth and the way she was laid out. I don't want these appearing in the newspaper accounts. Obviously they are things that only the murderer could know, and for the time being we'll keep them to ourselves."

"Or murderers," a soft voice said from the other end of the room. They all turned to look at Desai. "It's possible there was more than one, sir," he added.

"Is there forensic evidence of that, Leon?"

Desai nodded. "Possibly. I can't be sure at the moment, but there may have been at least two men involved."

"I see. Is there anything else you can tell us at the moment?"

"It's too early for any results from the scientific tests, of course. Only an impression, really, of the style, the way it was done."

"Go on."

"Well, you know more about this than I do, sir, the psychological side. But there's something odd about it. It's not like anything I've seen before. Usually the scene of a murder is just a mess—there's been a fight, someone was drunk, in a rage, high, or just couldn't put up with something any more, and they've exploded and killed someone. Much less often, there's preparation, premeditation. What you see isn't so much rage as a kind of blind panic to get the job done—usually fumbling, taking three or four attempts to get the carving knife in to the right spot, or getting bitten and scratched, desperately trying to keep the victim quiet until they finally choke or drown or whatever."

Brock nodded. Kathy listened intently to Desai's words, which were delivered, she thought, with a great deal of preparation and premeditation. She noticed that Bren's foot was tapping impatiently. His shoes were in need of cleaning and repair, unlike Desai's which looked brand new.

"Call me Brock, for God's sake, Leon. You're part of the team. So, what's different about this one?"

"There was certainly a great deal of rage, or passion of some kind. But it was also very . . . calculated. He—or they—seem to have been in control, of the girl, of course, but also of the sequence of events, and of the traces that they left behind."

"Yes." Brock raised a hand to his face and clawed at the short grey beard he wore. "Murderers display two basic kinds of behaviour. The Americans call them organized and disorganized. You're saying that this one was organized. He wasn't acting impulsively. He wasn't carried away by a sudden fit of uncontrollable emotion. He was carrying out a plan he had thought about very carefully before he ever got to Angela's house. He was in control, and he was enjoying himself."

Kathy lowered her head, feeling sick.

"So," Brock sighed, "Kathy, what can you tell us about the young woman?"

"She . . . she seems rather colourless, at this stage, Brock. Everyone says how nice she was. She was a very dutiful daughter, a faithful member of her church. She'd been going steady with the same bloke, Adrian Avery, since they were both sixteen. I don't think she'd ever been out with anyone else, and my impression was that he'd pretty much come to take her for granted. She did reasonably well in her A-levels at school, and could have gone to university, but apparently decided not to. Instead she did a one-year secretarial course and then got a job in the City. She's still in the same job, a clerk-typist with a finance company called Merritt Finance, near Blackfriars Station.

"Perhaps 'colourless' isn't the right word. Maybe it just all sounds a bit old-fashioned, somehow. Rather tidy and static. I'm not sure that she even had a driving licence. She certainly didn't own a car. The only corner of her life that seemed to arouse any passion, from what people told me, was the theatre. She belonged to a church theatre-goers' club which regularly does the local shows and the West End. It was about the only thing she did without her boyfriend or her parents."

Brock nodded. "We found a collection of old theatre programmes in one of the drawers in her bedroom. Any thoughts?" He looked at Bren, who shrugged and reeled off a number of suggestions. "Who saw her at the theatre? Who else was on that train? Who else got off the train at Petts Wood? Who else walked down Birchgrove Avenue that night?"

"Mm. Well, you and Kathy might begin up here in town, Bren, while Ted goes down to Orpington to set up an incident room with the local CID there. That way your wife will know where to get ahold of you."

"Thanks, Brock." Ted smiled.

"You'll be at the post-mortem, Leon?"

He nodded.

"Well, I'll see you there, and then I'll join you down in Orpington, Ted. I'll hold a briefing for the local CID, and then I'd like to talk to the boyfriend. Do you know what he does, Kathy?"

"He's unemployed."

"Well, line him up for me, will you, Ted? We need to check up on the crew he was out with on Saturday night."

"To confirm his alibi, Chief?" Ted said.

"And theirs. It's possible they all knew that Angela would be returning to an empty house that night."

"Was she in the church choir?" Bren turned to Kathy.

"I'm not sure. Nobody mentioned it. Why?"

"The way she was set out, with her mouth jammed open, arms by her side, like she was singing or something. If it was one of those blokes who knew her, if maybe they paid her a visit that night and she refused to co-operate, could that be some kind of sick joke? The choir girl singing her last hymn?"

Kathy frowned, but didn't reply.

Brock shook his head, shoving his papers together, the meeting over as far as he was concerned. The others recognized the signs and began to get up. But Kathy said, "Brock, can I ask something?"

"Of course." He stopped what he was doing and looked at her, while the others sank back down on to their seats.

Kathy suddenly felt that she should have kept quiet, but she ploughed on anyway. "Yesterday you said that there had to be some pattern linking Angela's life and the killer's. Fair enough if, as Bren suggests, it was someone she knew. But if it wasn't. Where would we begin?"

He seemed disappointed by the question. "It's far too early to say, Kathy. We don't want to start with preconceptions. We need a lot more information."

She winced and muttered, "Yes, yes, of course," and to herself thought *Great start, Kathy*.

"But . . . one inevitable thought . . ."—Brock stared at the salmon as if its gawping mouth might tell him something—"is the railway."

"The railway?" Kathy wondered if she'd misheard.

"Mmm. Angela lived in Metroland, Kathy, the great suburban territory sustained by the intricate web of its electric railway system. There are more passenger trips made each year on the Southern Region railways around London than in the whole of the United States. But, more to the point, Londoners understand London in terms of its railway system."

Kathy still looked frankly puzzled.

"Remember John Duffy, a couple of years ago?"

"The serial killer?"

"Yes. The papers dubbed him 'The Railway Rapist' because he seemed to have a preference for committing his crimes near a railway line. And the reason for that was that his mental map of London, the way he could navigate within it, was built around the railways he travelled on. From that it was possible to identify the area he lived in.

"For Angela, London was what you see from the Petts Wood to Blackfriars line. She got on it at 8:19 each morning and again at 5:17 every evening. It was as familiar to her as her own bedroom, and maybe that's true for her killer too. Maybe he caught sight of her on that line, and stalked her on it, and finally followed her home from it."

He paused and frowned, as if he'd said more than he'd meant to. "Anyway, let's keep an open mind for the moment."

BREN DROPPED KATHY AT the north end of Blackfriars Bridge and continued across the river to the National Theatre, while she walked east down Queen Victoria Street. It didn't take her long to find the building in which Merritt Finance occupied floors five to eight. The Head Office Manager's suite was on the fifth.

"Mr. Ferry should be in any time now, Detective Sergeant," the secretary said. She seemed fascinated by Kathy, and kept glancing at her bag, as if it might contain some lethal arsenal. "Can I get you a cup of coffee? Or perhaps, if you told me what it was about, I might be able to help in some way."

"No coffee, thanks. But perhaps you could let me speak to someone called Rhona, a friend of Angela Hannaford. Do you know who that would be?"

"Rhona Clement. She works on the seventh floor with Angela. Whatever is it about?"

"You didn't notice in the paper this morning? I'm afraid Angela was murdered on Saturday night."

"No! Oh my . . ." The woman went pale and sank into a seat.

"Look, I'd like to speak to one or two people who would have known of Angela's movements on Saturday night, beginning with Rhona. Is there a room I could use?"

"Well . . . I suppose the boardroom. I don't think it's booked this morning."

"Thanks. Could you ring Rhona and ask her to come down here? You don't need to say what it's about. I'll tell her."

The woman nodded.

"When Mr. Ferry comes in you could explain to him that I'm here."

"Of course."

Incongruous within the featureless modern office building, the boardroom was panelled out in dark wood like a medieval manor house. It reminded Kathy of the hall in Angela Hannaford's home. Rhona Clement was obviously apprehensive about being summoned there. She too had not seen the brief report of Angela's death which had appeared in several of the morning papers, and was devastated when Kathy broke the news to her.

"Angela's boyfriend, Adrian, told us that he thought you were going with Angela to the theatre on Saturday night. Is that right?"

She nodded, wiping tears from her eyes and struggling with her sobs. "She'd managed to get two tickets for us to see *Macbeth* at the National. It's had such wonderful reviews . . ."

Rhona gulped and blew her nose before continuing in a rushed whisper. "She was really lucky to get them, and she was so excited about going. Anyway, on Thursday night Darren—that's my boyfriend—heard that his brother had had a bad accident on his motor-bike. He was in hospital, up in Manchester. Then on Friday afternoon Darren phoned me at work. His brother was worse, apparently, and Darren was ever so upset. He was going to drive up to Manchester that evening, and he wanted me to go with him."

Rhona's face crumpled again. "Darren's brother died on Saturday night too!" She gave a little howl of grief. She had a sweet face, framed in fluffy curls, which looked as if it had never had to come to terms with any bad news. Suddenly it was all being dumped on her at once.

When she recovered her voice, she gasped, "I came back on my own last night, on the train. Darren's still in Manchester, with his family. I'm going back up tomorrow for the funeral. I've never been to a funeral before, ever. Now there'll be two in one week!"

While she was immersed in another fit of sobbing, there was a knock and the secretary put her head around the door. She hesitated, seeing Rhona's state, then said, "Er, Mr. Ferry's here now, Sergeant. He says he'll see you as soon as you're free."

"Thanks. I'll be ten minutes or so. How about a cup of tea for Miss Clement?"

The woman nodded and left.

"Rhona, I'm so sorry about this. Do you think you could go on with telling me what happened? Are you saying that you didn't go to the theatre with Angela?"

"I'm sorry . . . Yes, that's right. It was all such a rush on Friday afternoon. I realized we probably wouldn't be back from Manchester in time to go out with her on the Saturday night. I can't afford to throw money away, and I tried to find someone else who would buy my ticket from me, only none of the other girls up here are into that sort of thing. It was almost the end of the day before I eventually managed to get rid of it."

"Who took it?"

"Mr. Gentle, the boss of our section—Sales and Marketing. He overheard me telling his secretary about it. I was really desperate and he suddenly said that he'd take it."

"I see. Is he a single man?"

"Oh no!" Rhona coloured slightly. "He said . . . he said that he was a great admirer of the play, and that he'd been wanting to get to see this production."

"Was Angela happy about it, when you told her who she was going with?"

"I never had the chance to tell her. She'd been working down here on the fifth floor all afternoon. I never saw her again!" The tears poured once more down Rhona's plump cheeks.

"I'm sorry." Kathy paused to let her recover. "Now, did Angela ever mention to you that she was being pestered by anyone? Followed home, perhaps, or getting phone calls?"

"No!" Rhona looked horrified. "Who told you that?"

Kathy shook her head. "No, I'm only considering the possibility. It's something we have to consider."

Rhona shook her head miserably.

"All right. Here's your tea, Rhona. I'll leave it at that for now. I'll give you my phone number in case you think of anything later."

Kathy followed the secretary out to her boss's office, where Clive Ferry rose cautiously to his feet to shake Kathy's hand. He was dressed stiffly in pinstripe suit, starched white shirt, and club tie, all as immaculate as the small, perfectly sculpted moustache on his lip, and this careful personal grooming seemed designed to imply total propriety. He hadn't seen the newspaper reports either, and he slipped quickly into expressions of regret, almost thankfully, Kathy thought, as if he'd been expecting something more immediately threatening from her visit.

"We'll co-operate in any way we can, Sergeant. A dreadful thing. I'll check later about Angela's entitlements from our staff insurance fund, and inform her parents, of course."

"At this stage we're trying to build up a picture of Angela's movements and the people she knew."

"Of course. You've been speaking to Rhona Clement, I believe."

"Yes. We thought that she went to the theatre with Angela on Saturday night, but it seems she sold her ticket to someone else. I'd like to speak to that person now if I can."

"Ah yes. And who was that?"

"A Mr. Gentle."

Ferry looked startled for a second, the moustache giving a little leap, as if it might be about to run for cover, and then his face went completely blank. "Really?"

"You're surprised?"

"Ah . . . a little. I wasn't aware that Mr. Gentle was interested in the theatre."

"But apart from that, was there anything else surprising to you about the arrangement?"

"I really don't know the circumstances. You'd better ask him."

Ferry hurriedly picked up his phone. He murmured into it, then looked at Kathy. "He's not in yet. His secretary is expecting him."

Kathy looked at her watch: 10:15.

"Well, perhaps in the meantime I could speak to some of the other people Angela worked with."

"Yes, of course. In the boardroom?"

"What about the seventh floor? I'd like to see her desk, make sure she didn't have a diary or anything like that. Is there a room where I could speak to people there?"

Kathy took the lift, and as she stepped out into an open-plan office area she was immediately aware that the news had preceded her, as a dozen pairs of eyes, bright with troubled curiosity, focused on her. She was shown to Angela's desk, where she found nothing of interest, and then to a small room separated from the main office by a smoked-glass partition. As she moved through the office, whispered conversations died in front of her and started up again behind. Alone in the small room, she spoke to each of the women who worked in the immediate vicinity of Angela's desk, getting little hard information from them, but gaining a distinct impression of wariness when she brought up Mr. Gentle's name. It might have been nervousness about discussing their immediate boss, she thought, but the reaction of one girl in particular bothered her. She wore more make-up than the others, and had a mischievous, knowing look about her. When Kathy mentioned that her boss appeared to have gone to the theatre with Angela, she sucked in her cheeks and rolled her eyes.

"What does that mean?" Kathy asked her.

The girl shrugged exaggeratedly. "What does what mean?"

"Did Angela have a problem with Mr. Gentle?"

The girl looked affronted. "Not as far as I know. I never suggested that."

"Well, what are you suggesting then?"

"Not a fing. I'm not suggesting anyfing, and you'd better not say I am."

Kathy followed her gaze out through the smoked-glass wall to the main office, where a man had appeared and was deep in conversation with one of the older women.

Tom Gentle gave the impression of being appropriately named. He was slight of build, medium height, neat, and middle-aged.

He came into the interview room, followed by the stares of the women who worked for him, with a look of immense distress. He sat opposite Kathy and spoke to her with a warm, soft voice, filled with concern. His most distinctive features, apart from his voice, were his large brown eyes, and Kathy suspected that he would be the sort of man that women might instinctively feel was in need of mothering.

"Now, I understand that you were at the National Theatre on Saturday night, Mr. Gentle, with Angela."

"No." He shook his head sadly. "No, I'm afraid I wasn't."

"Oh . . . Rhona Clement has just told me that she sold you her ticket late on Friday afternoon."

"Yes, that's quite right. Poor Rhona, she's had a terrible time of it. She was very agitated when I overheard her talking to my secretary about the ticket. She was on the point of leaving for Manchester, and hadn't been able to interest anyone. Well, on the spur of the moment I said that I'd take it. I thought at the time that my wife had arranged to have her bridge group round on Saturday night, and I was glad of an excuse to get out of the house. And of course I'd read a lot about how wonderful this production was. I didn't have time to check with my wife, though, and when I got home I discovered that her bridge night is actually next Saturday. Well, that made it difficult. Muriel—my wife—did say that I shouldn't waste the ticket and that I should go anyway, but I really didn't feel comfortable about going out without her."

"So, what did you do?"

"I stayed at home."

"What about the ticket?"

"Well, I'm afraid that was just wasted."

"You didn't phone the theatre to see if they could sell it for you?"

"No—I wouldn't have had time on Saturday to take it up to the theatre anyway."

Kathy stared at him, and he stared back, a mournful smile on his face. But there was something else in his smile, a suggestion of sly impishness which, even in the present circumstances, he couldn't quite suppress.

When she returned to the fifth floor, Kathy rang Bren at the National Theatre. The operator tracked him down eventually to the booking manager's office, where he was copying information on bookings for the Saturday night performance.

"The story is that the seat beside her was never taken up, Bren. The girl who was going to go with her, Rhona, had to back out, and sold her ticket to a man in their office, who says he decided not to go after all. It would be useful to know if that was true."

"Yes. Trouble is that the system here isn't set up to trace people in particular seats after the event. It's going to take time to put a name and address to the seats in that part of the theatre, but I'll concentrate on the ones close by. What about you?"

"I think I might as well get down to Orpington. I thought I'd follow Brock's suggestion and take the train."

"Yes, well, sometimes he starts off with some funny ideas, Kathy. Best to let him play with them for a while."

"Yes, I had the feeling I spoke too soon this morning."

"Don't worry, he doesn't talk unless he wants to."

Kathy caught the 11:50 from Blackfriars, and settled back to discover Angela's London. More familiar with the underground railway system north of the Thames, she studied the surface commuter train with a fresh eye. The carriage was open down its length, and anyone standing up could see over the tops of the seats from end to end. It would be difficult to harass someone unobserved unless there were very few passengers, as now. She wondered how full the 11:05 from Charing Cross had been last Saturday night.

From her window she watched the city roll past as they crossed the river and swung east through the congested South Bank, past

Southwark Cathedral and into London Bridge station. Soon after there was a view of Tower Bridge, an improbable confection in the bright noon sunlight, and then the train picked up speed through the inner boroughs of Southwark and Lewisham as it headed down towards New Cross. The line had long since been absorbed and accepted into the fabric of the city. It offered a voyeur's view of London, at first from the vantage point of the brick viaducts on which it crossed the older districts near the Thames, and later from the embankments and bridges on which it slipped through the dormitory suburbs beyond St. John's and Hither Green. Thousands of homes lined the route, at first the blackened Victorian terraces and post-war tower blocks of the inner city, and then the endless sea of semis beyond. All turned their public faces away from the railway and towards the streets on their other side, addressing themselves to the hundred people who might see them from that direction each day and stubbornly ignoring the hundred thousand who stared down into their back yards from the railway, following the daily progress of their washing, the bungled construction of the rabbit pen and the never-ending paint job on the Cortina.

Kathy stepped blinking into the hot sunlight at Orpington station and found a taxi to take her to the Divisional police station. There she was shown to a room where Ted Griffiths was interviewing Angela's boyfriend, Adrian. He was freshly scrubbed and neatly dressed for the occasion, helping Ted compile a list of all the people who had been at the stag party.

"They're not going to be able to tell you anything," he added morosely, as if he resented having his friends bothered, "but that's up to you, innit?"

"Adrian," Kathy asked, "did Angela ever mention being annoyed or pestered by a man—at work perhaps, or on her train journey?"

He shook his head. "She never mentioned anything like that to me."

"Did she ever mention the name 'Gentle' to you?"

" 'Gentle?' Nah. Who's he, then?"

"Doesn't matter."

Bren arrived in mid-afternoon, followed soon after by Brock, who was not happy. The preliminary results from the post-mortem were inconclusive, and added little to what they already knew. All would depend on the forensic evidence, which would take days. Bren too was frustrated. After hours on the phone, working through the lists he had compiled at the National Theatre, he had been able to speak to only two people who were seated within a few rows of Angela's place. Neither could recollect whether the seat beside her had been occupied.

The prospect of days of futile phone calls and interviews, the sense of being miles away from the truth, grew as the hot afternoon wore on, and was heightened by Ted, who would stop in mid-sentence whenever a phone rang, and glance surreptitiously at his watch every few minutes. Brock sent him home at 6:00. At 9:00 Bren and Kathy were still at the desks they'd been allocated in the Orpington station.

"I'd best get going," Bren said to her. "Want a lift back to town?"

They stopped for a hamburger on the road back, and Bren put his exasperation into words. "This is busy-work, Kathy. Filling in time." He stretched his back and yawned.

"You think so?"

He nodded. "The theatre is irrelevant. So is the boyfriend. He and his mates didn't do this, and neither did anyone within a mile of the National Theatre that night."

"Who did, then?"

"A madman. Some evil, crazy bastard, out cruising the suburbs in the night, looking for a woman on her own."

"The monster theory," Kathy said.

Bren looked sharply at her to see if she was being sarcastic, then saw she was serious. "Yes, a monster, if you like. Some lunatic who's sat watching a few too many sick videos at home on his own, and decides to go out and play Freddy Kruger for real. God knows, there's enough sick bastards out there."

"Why did he come to her street?"

"Why not? Any one would do. He has no connection with Angela Hannaford, or Petts Wood, or anything else that we're likely to come across. It was random. He just kept driving till he spotted someone who would do."

"How would he have known that her house was empty?"

"He didn't know that, not at first. That was a bonus, gave him more time. He could just as easily have done it in his car, or taken her to the woods."

"How will we catch him, then?"

"We won't. Not unless he's got a record and left some prints, which seems unlikely, or got stopped for speeding on the way home and the copper noticed something odd, which is even less likely, or someone reports some bugger washing bloodstained clothes down at the local laundrette . . ." He shook his head. "We won't catch him. Not until he does it again, if he makes a mistake, or the time after that . . ."

Bren's pessimism worried Kathy. She remembered him as a big, cheerful bear of a man, quietly infecting the others with his confidence, and remembered Brock's comment about him having too much on his plate.

"Why are we doing this, then?" she asked.

"Because we have to do something. Because the girl's parents have to believe we can do something."

"Yes. I thought I'd go and see them tomorrow. It was difficult to get much out of them yesterday. Maybe they'll feel more like talking now."

"I'm sure they will, Kathy. I'm sure they will. Good luck."

Bren took another bite out of his burger, then tossed it down in disgust.

"This is shit," he said, his jaw tight with anger.

FOUR

THE FOLLOWING MORNING KATHY decided to retrace Angela's journey home on the night she died. She took the tube to Charing Cross as she had the previous morning, but this time walked across the Thames on the footway on the Hungerford railway bridge, alongside the heavy rumble of the commuter trains bringing their loads up from the south. Once again it was a brilliant, sunny morning, promising a continuation of the heatwave, and the skyline of the City beyond the river to the east, of St. Paul's and the NatWest Tower and its lesser clones, was enveloped by haze. She took the steps at the far end of the bridge down to the quiet expanse of terrace in front of the Festival Hall, and walked along the river through the precinct of cultural concrete which separated it from the National Theatre beyond Waterloo Bridge.

It was difficult, on such a morning, to picture the crowd spilling out of the theatre on that warm Saturday night, to see the boardmarked concrete made magic by floodlighting and mysterious shadows, and to visualize one single woman among the milling, chattering crowd, carefully folding her programme into her bag, and then walking away to catch the last train home.

Kathy followed the route she thought Angela would have taken southward to Waterloo station, bought a single ticket for Petts

Wood, and then, as she turned to make for the barriers, found herself confronted by Angela's smiling face.

The picture had been enlarged from a snap her father had taken of her that spring, in the garden at number 32. Her fair hair was held back from her forehead by a simple band, and her smile was playfully scolding, as if she'd just looked up and realized her picture was being taken. She was wearing no make-up or jewellery. The wording on the poster read, "This woman caught the 11:08 p.m. train from Waterloo to Petts Wood on the evening of Saturday, 8 September. Did you catch that train? Did you see her? Contact the Metropolitan Police on these numbers."

On this second journey along the corridor of Angela's London, Kathy began to recognize features and landmarks from the previous day. The difference was that, although her own train was again almost deserted, the rest of the system was in convulsive action, the city-bound trains packed with rush-hour crowds crammed behind the windows of the carriages, and the station platforms dense with rushing figures. The suppressed violence of commuting struck her, of squeezing into a metal tube in one part of the city, of being crushed against sweaty strangers for a while and then abruptly ejected into a charging mob in another part.

She recognized the names of the stations—Hither Green, Grove Park, Elmstead Woods, and then through dark woodland and out on to the long straight to Petts Wood and Orpington.

There were more posters of Angela on the metal bridge across the station at Petts Wood. Kathy took the steps down the east side and walked around the Tudorbethan loop of Station Square, with the half-timbered bulk of the Daylight Inn at its centre, named in honour of the district's most famous citizen, William Willett, the inventor of daylight saving time, appropriately enough for a community regulated by the clockwork discipline of the railway timetable.

The lights of the taxi rank and the shop windows would have finished here, she thought, *and then it would have been the street lights, partly screened by the thick summer foliage of the trees. Would you notice someone following on rubber soles? Or a car gliding slowly past, stopping around the next corner, its lights extinguished? At what point would he make his approach, ask to use her phone to get help for a girlfriend in the car, perhaps, suffering an asthma attack? Was there anyone else at home, he might ask, who could help him lift her out of the car? No, no one. I'm all alone. Come inside. Use the phone.*

As she walked the deserted suburban streets, heavy with the aroma of roses and cyclamen, murmuring with the sound of bees and foliage stirring, the sense of unreality and suspended time returned to Kathy. *The crimes that happen here happen indoors, hidden from the public eye by lush, lovingly tended gardens. Private crimes. Family crimes. And the occasional thunderbolt from outside.*

Mrs. Hannaford looked as if she'd aged ten years in the previous forty-eight hours. Weeping and lack of sleep had drained the colour and the muscle tone from her face, which sagged around the despairing points of her eyes. Her husband's face, by contrast, had hardened in the interval. His big head was fixed in an expression of grim outrage. The contrast between them was heightened by the distance at which they sat apart, as if they were suffering in isolation, without reference to one another. Glenys sat in the same armchair as before, beside the fireplace, while Basil Hannaford took the settee against the wall farthest from it, leaving Kathy to take the other armchair, at the third point of a remote triangle.

"I'm so sorry to intrude again. You must have seen more than enough of us over the last couple of days," Kathy began, lamely trying to break the heavy silence. "I have a list here of men that Angela may have known socially or through her work. I wonder if you could help us by suggesting any more names for that list."

Kathy gave a copy each to the silent couple. Mrs. Hannaford lowered her head to the piece of paper in her lap, but Kathy wasn't sure that she was really focusing on it.

Basil Hannaford glared at his copy. "I've never heard of some of these people. Clive Ferry is the manager where she works, isn't he? What is the point of this?"

"We want to eliminate everyone who was known to Angela from our inquiries, if we can," Kathy answered gently.

"Why would you imagine that the man was known to her?" He was speaking through clenched teeth, with the air of someone who has been taken advantage of once and is determined not to let it happen again.

"We don't know that, of course. But he was able to get in without forcing an entry, apparently . . ."

"It's perfectly obvious what happened, surely!" His anger came bursting through his self-control. "He came up behind her as she was opening the front door to let herself in. He pushed his way in and she dropped her bag!"

Mrs. Hannaford gave an agonized sob.

"That's quite possible . . ."

"This is utterly useless!" He crumpled the paper in a sudden violent gesture. "You must have names, on your computers, of perverts, don't you? The sort of filth who could have done this?"

"Yes . . ."

"Well, are you rounding them up? Are you?"

"That is another of our lines of inquiry, Mr. Hannaford. However, we'll be better placed to do that when we have the results of the forensic tests in a few days. They should help to narrow . . ."

"A few days! And in the meantime he'll have gone to ground, covered his tracks! I find this utterly astounding."

"I can assure you . . ." Kathy tried again, but it was clear that Hannaford's anger was not going to be mollified.

"I would be obliged if you would ask your superior officer—what was his name?"

"Detective Chief Inspector Brock."

Hannaford grimly made a note on a small telephone pad at his elbow. ". . . If you would ask Detective Chief Inspector Brock to come here in person next time. We would like *him* to report to us on his progress, within twenty-four hours."

Kathy took a deep breath. "I'll tell him, sir. Mrs. Hannaford, there is one thing perhaps you can tell me. Did Angela ever speak of being annoyed or pestered by anyone, at work perhaps, or on the train?"

There was a moment's silence, then Glenys rocked her head from side to side. Her husband gave a grunt of exasperation and got to his feet.

When she reached the front door, Kathy turned to face him. "Mr. Hannaford, I do understand . . ."

"You have no idea whatsoever, young woman." There was a panel of yellow tinted glass in the oak front door, and the light from it glowed unpleasantly on Hannaford's angry face. "She belonged to me, and he took her."

Kathy was startled by his choice of words, and she stared at him, her throat tight. But the choice was deliberate, and he repeated it.

"She belonged to me!"

He reached past her shoulder abruptly and opened the front door.

KATHY HAD BEGUN TO walk back to the railway station when she stopped and retraced her steps. She passed the Hannafords' house and rang the bell of number 30, next door. Pamela Ratcliffe, the woman who had spoken to her when she had first arrived at the scene on Sunday, answered.

"Yes, I do remember you," she said. "Some of your other people came to take statements from us." She led Kathy briskly through to the rear of the house. It had originally been identical to the Hannafords', but the dark timber had been painted a pale grey, the floors polished, and with modern chrome and leather furniture it was unrecognizably light and airy where the other was dark and claustrophobic.

"Have you had a chance to talk to Mr. and Mrs. Hannaford at all, Mrs. Ratcliffe?"

The other woman made an uneasy grimace. "I tried. I called round yesterday, but . . . Glenys is under sedation, and Basil . . . I don't know. He's very bitter. It's completely understandable, of course. I'm doing their shopping for them, although, in a way, I wondered if it might be better if they got out and spoke to people. I suppose they will when they're ready."

"Have they had visitors, do you know?"

"I've seen the doctor's car there. And yesterday, when I was weeding in the garden, I saw their vicar call in. He didn't stay long."

There was a sudden burst of pop music from somewhere close by.

"Warwick's having his breakfast in the kitchen," Mrs. Ratcliffe said. "I let him sleep in later during the school holidays. Quite often he stays up late at night with his radio. It's his hobby."

"Listening to the radio?"

"No." Mrs. Ratcliffe smiled and pointed out into the garden through the new aluminium sliding doors. For the first time, Kathy noticed the spidery structure of aerials and masts that were threaded through the silver birch trees. "He gets messages from all around the world, and he transmits them as well. He built it all, with his dad's help."

Kathy had already noticed a portrait photograph of father and son grinning at the camera, both with the same shock of red hair and wearing similar large round glasses.

"They had a bit of trouble with the neighbours for a while." Mrs. Ratcliffe rolled her eyes, as if to say that boys will be boys. "They were causing interference with everybody's TVs. The Hannafords got particularly agitated at one point, so we introduced the eleven o'clock rule. He's not allowed to transmit before 11:00 p.m., when everyone's switched off for the night."

"I see. Well, one thing I wanted to check again with him was the time he arrived home on Saturday night. There's no chance it could have been later than 11:55, as he said?"

"Oh no. He'd have been right about that. That's the twelve o'clock rule. He must be home by midnight, unless it's something very special. He is only fifteen. And I think young people appreciate having firm rules to work within, don't you?"

Kathy smiled. "I'm sure you're right. I get the impression from my friends that it's the parents who get tired of the rules first. You know, having to monitor them, staying up to midnight to check the kids are back, that sort of thing."

Mrs. Ratcliffe nodded. "Yes, well, we don't actually do that. We're usually asleep long before then, I'm afraid. There has to be an element of trust. Anyway, have a talk to Warwick, by all means."

Kathy asked the boy if he would show her his room upstairs, so that she could see how much of the house and garden next door was visible. From the main window, in front of which stood a desk crowded with electronic equipment, the elaborate array of aerials in the garden of number 30 was clearly visible, although almost nothing of the adjoining garden could be seen. However, there was also a small side window facing directly across to the Hannafords' house, and through it Kathy could see a corresponding window in what must be Angela's room.

"You can see directly across to Angela's room from here, Warwick," she said.

"Yes. She always kept her curtains drawn on that window."

"But you don't?"

He shook his head, cautious, but feigning indifference.

"So you would have definitely been aware of it if her light had been on when you returned on Saturday night?"

"Suppose so."

"And it wasn't?"

"That's what I told the other bloke."

"Did you draw your curtains when you returned?"

"Yes."

"And you heard no sounds from next door?"

"No."

"No sound of a car starting up? No sound of anything being broken? A voice? A cry?"

Warwick shook his head and looked away. His hand strayed towards the dial on a silver metal box and began to fiddle with it.

"And you are quite certain about the time? 11:55?"

"That's what I told the man."

"I know, but you probably didn't realize then just how serious this all was, Warwick. Look at me, please. Did you realize then that Angela had been brutally murdered? Did you realize then just how important your statement would be? You were probably more concerned at that point about your parents' twelve o'clock rule, isn't that right?"

Warwick swallowed uncomfortably, his eyes darting back and forward from Kathy's steady gaze.

"You realize you may well have to give evidence about this in court, under oath, Warwick. And the other people at the party you were at on Saturday night may have to do the same, to confirm the time you left. Now, you see how serious this is? I can give you this one last chance to revise your earlier statement, if there are any inaccuracies in it, and there'll be no more said. All right?"

He nodded.

"Well?"

"It was later."

"Yes. How much later?"

"It was after one o'clock."

"How much after?"

"Probably about 1:45. I'm not sure exactly." He looked at Kathy in appeal. "I couldn't tell them the truth before, not with Mum and Dad there watching me. They go on and on about their stupid rules. I didn't think it mattered much anyway."

Kathy nodded. "Anything else you want to change?"

He shook his head. "No, honest. There were no lights, and I didn't hear anything. I came in through our back door, with the key they leave under the flower pot for me, and I'd have noticed if there'd have been any lights on next door at that time. Honest."

"WELL, THAT CLEARS UP that little difficulty," Brock said.

"Yes," Kathy nodded. "And Mr. Hannaford asked me to ask you if you would go in person and explain what we're doing."

Brock raised his eyebrow at her.

"He's very angry and wants to have a go at someone. He wondered why we hadn't rounded up all the perverts in London for questioning."

"Good idea. Book Wembley Stadium for me, will you, Kathy?" Brock gave a low growl and tilted back in his seat, scratching his beard. "No, he's right, of course. I'm damn sure this mongrel's done something before that we know about. Maybe he didn't go as far as murder, but it was so . . . elaborate, and ritualistic, as if he was working to a script he'd thought very carefully about and probably rehearsed. I can't believe this was his first time. He must have worked himself up to this, through a series of stages, most likely."

"Isn't it possible that it was all just fantasy up to this point?" Kathy suggested. "Maybe borrowed from books, or films? Trying to cut off her face, for instance. It seems to make no sense, unless he was copying something."

"Like what?"

"Well, that was in *The Silence of the Lambs*, wasn't it, and in *Gorky Park*? Especially *Gorky Park*. Cutting off the victim's face was a big thing."

"Was it?" Brock curled his lip in distaste. "I'm thankful I didn't see either of them. And where would that take us?"

"I don't know," Kathy shrugged. "That he saw himself as Hannibal Lecter, perhaps, or Lee Marvin."

Brock grunted, obviously unconvinced. "Well, at any rate, we've got to find the precedents, whatever they are, in the ocean of unsolved murders, assaults, rapes, and missing persons. The most promising so far is a murder/rape in a park about five miles from here, three months ago. Nothing quite like what we've got. But it wouldn't be the same, necessarily. It would be the step that led to this, and the step before that. A question of knowing what to look for . . . recognizing it when we see it."

"I'd like to help look."

"You want an indoor job for a while?" Brock glanced up at her from under his thick eyebrows.

Kathy shrugged and nodded. Her encounter with Hannaford had unsettled her; not his anger, which was understandable, but the unexpected sense of elation that his powerlessness had given her. He could do absolutely nothing to catch his daughter's killer, whereas she might. He was dependent on her, and he knew this and hated it, just as she relished it. Afterwards she had felt ashamed.

"Well, how about the Sexual Assault Index? You're familiar with that?"

Kathy nodded.

"You can access it from the computer here. You might want to go up to the Forensic Science Laboratory at Lambeth too. They may have additional stuff they haven't put on to the computer record. Have you been up to the MPFSL? Leon Desai will set it up for you."

Kathy eventually found herself a terminal, and settled down to spend the rest of the day working her way through the hundreds of rape cases analysed in the SAI. It was a grim task, the Index a dreary catalogue of male brutality and female misery, but the possibility that the next case might provide a clue to Angela's killer, or the next, drove her on.

"Fancy a drink?" She looked up to see Bren at her shoulder. She shook her head and looked back at the screen.

"Not tonight, Bren. See you tomorrow."

"Oh." He looked surprised. "You don't want a lift back to town?"

She shook her head again and he noticed the gleam in her eye.

"On to something?"

"No. Not a thing."

He shrugged, hesitated, then padded off.

Half an hour later, Brock put his head round the door. "Any luck?"

"Nothing yet."

"Need a lift?"

"I'll wait for a while longer. Get a train."

He saw the preoccupied look on her face, her eyes straying back to the screen, and nodded. "I went to see the Hannafords this afternoon," he said.

"Oh." Kathy looked back at him. "How did it go?"

Brock shook his head. "Not good. She's doped to the eyeballs, but what good will that do? Just postpone the agony of coming to terms with it, I'd have thought. And he's like a bomb, ready to go off, poor bastard. They need help, but they won't see anyone except the doctor and the vicar—and us. I mentioned the programme to put them in touch with people who've been through the same thing as them, but they're not ready for it yet. I've told Ted to follow it up. Where is Ted, by the way?"

"Er, I don't know, Brock. I haven't seen him since lunchtime."

"Oh. Well, see you tomorrow."

KATHY WAS STILL AT her screen an hour later when a call came through for her from Manchester. It was a man's voice, agitated, speaking quickly.

"Hello? You're the one spoke to Rhona Clement, aren't you, at Merritt Finance?"

"Yes, that's me. Who am I talking to?"

"I'm her boyfriend, Darren. Look, I'm not going to talk long, only Rhona wanted to tell you something about Angela."

"Fine. Do you want to put her on?"

"No. She wants to tell you off the record. She doesn't want to lose her job, see? So I said I'd speak to you, and you can't say she told you. She'll deny it if you do."

"Darren, I . . ."

"Look! My brother's being cremated tomorrow, so I don't want to argue about it!" He was speaking very fast, almost a gabble, and Kathy could sense the tears welling into his eyes. "The thing she wanted to say is that Angela told her a couple of times that someone at work was bothering her—trying to chat her up, following her home on the train, touching her, you know."

"Yes. Who was it, Darren?"

"Tom, his name is. Tom Gentle. He's their boss."

"Ah . . . good, Darren. Thank you. Now look, if you'll just tell me where Rhona's staying, I'll come up there and . . ."

But the line had gone dead.

FIVE

KATHY AND BREN WERE waiting for Clive Ferry in his office the following morning. Once again he was a model of impeccable managerial attire. He rested his hands lightly on the desk in front of him, two inches of brilliant white cuff visible at each wrist, and spoke to Bren.

"And is there any progress, would you say?"

"In a way," Kathy replied, the abruptness of her tone registering with him. His precisely sculpted moustache gave a little twitch and he turned his head towards her.

"When I was here the last time, Mr. Ferry, you reacted very clearly to something I said, then avoided explaining why. I'd like to give you a further opportunity to tell me what was in your mind. And I have to warn you that obstructing a murder investigation is an extremely serious matter."

"I beg your pardon?" Ferry looked at Kathy in surprise, then turned to Bren, who stared back at him impassively.

"I mentioned to you that Mr. Tom Gentle had bought a ticket to accompany Angela to the theatre on Saturday night, and you clearly were alarmed by that suggestion. Further information has now come to us which suggests why that may have been the case. Would you please now tell us what you know?"

Comprehension spread across Ferry's face at the mention of Gentle's name. "Ah," he said, and lowered his eyes to consider his shirt cuffs for a moment. "You must understand," he said at last, "that I did not see it as my place to plant unwarranted suspicions in your mind. But since you now ask me directly . . ."

"Yes."

"Tom is a married man . . ." He looked to Bren for understanding. "When you mentioned that he had arranged to go to the theatre with Angela . . . I thought it odd."

"Has he done this sort of thing before?"

"What sort of thing?" Ferry said cautiously.

"Asked women from the office to go out with him, had affairs . . ."

"No. As far as I know, he's never done that."

Kathy stared at him and he avoided her eye, glancing across at Bren, who had taken out his notebook.

"What then?" Kathy insisted.

"Nothing. That's it."

"Had he been making approaches to Angela?"

"Not that I'm aware of."

So carefully phrased, wanting neither to lie nor to tell the truth.

"Well," Kathy shrugged, "if you can't help us get to the bottom of this, Mr. Ferry, we'd better talk to the women again."

"The women?" He looked at her in alarm.

"On the seventh floor. Maybe they'll be more forthcoming this time."

Ferry cleared his throat. "There was . . ." He hesitated, then started again. "There have been one or two misunderstandings in the past between Tom and women employees of the company. I suppose that came to my mind when you mentioned . . ."

"Misunderstandings?"

"Some people felt that he . . ."—Ferry searched for the phrase— "took liberties, one might say."

"Come on, Mr. Ferry," Bren broke in, with a little grin of sympathy, "what exactly was he doing?"

"Oh look, it was harmless." Ferry turned to Bren with relief. "A typist made a complaint that he was following her home after work. There was a perfectly innocent explanation as it turned out—he was looking for a new house at that time, in her area. But then some of the other girls joined in and claimed that he had, at one time or another, been improper in his manner to them."

"In what ways?"

"Oh, touching, mainly. Remarks that might be misinterpreted. One said she had felt he was spying on her when she went to the ladies' room. Things like that. I'm sure most of it was based on a misunderstanding of his manner, that's all, with just a pinch of hysteria, I suspect. But we brought it out into the open. I discussed it fully with him, and he agreed to avoid putting himself in a situation where such misunderstandings could happen again."

"Is the woman who complained still here?" Kathy asked.

"No. She left soon afterwards."

"Seems the wrong way round," she replied. "Why not get rid of him if he was the cause of the trouble?"

"We didn't get rid of her. She left of her own accord. And there was no real substance to it, Sergeant, I'm sure of that. He is a very mild and caring person. Besides which, his wife, Muriel, is the daughter of our chairman, Sir Charles Merritt."

"Ah," Kathy nodded.

"Look, I've explained all this to you because I wanted you to hear a balanced account of what happened. But the point is, it's completely irrelevant to your investigation. For God's sake, you've met him—it's unthinkable! Tom Gentle is not a violent man. Whatever else he may be, it is impossible to believe that he is that."

"Where is he now?"

"He's at home. He's been complaining of a summer cold since

the weekend. Muriel phoned in this morning to say she was going to keep him at home for a day or two."

"Where is that?"

"I'll get you the address. It's in Chipstead, near Sevenoaks."

"Sevenoaks is beyond Orpington, isn't it? On the same commuter line that Angela used?"

"Yes." Ferry nodded reluctantly. "I believe it is."

"Please don't contact him in advance of us getting there."

On the way down in the lift, Bren said, "Don't look so worried, Kathy. We might be getting somewhere."

"Yes. But none of the women wanted to tell us about it. I asked Rhona straight out about whether Angela might have mentioned anything odd and she said nothing. It was only later she got her boyfriend to speak to me, and he made the point that she'd deny it if pressed. What worries me is that by the time we get the truth out of them, Gentle will have destroyed whatever hard evidence might still be remaining."

"Any ideas?"

"Yes. I want to hit him hard, now, before he gets wind we're onto him. Do you think Brock will go for a search warrant?"

"Hmm. Bit thin at this stage, isn't it?"

"Yes."

THEY WAITED FOR THE search warrant and another car of local CID officers at Orpington, then continued down the A21 to the Chipstead turn-off just beyond the M25. The Gentles' home had once been two farm cottages, joined together and given a loft extension. It nestled comfortably between a stand of beeches and an orchard of ancient apple trees. A cottage garden spilled around the driveway in drifts of blue and pink and white, studded with columns of purple foxgloves and delphiniums. Muriel Gentle came round the side of the house, attracted by the sound of their wheels on the gravel. She wore a gardening hat and gloves, and carried a basket full of cuttings. A basset-hound trotted along in her wake.

"Hello." Her cautious smile to Kathy turned to disquiet as the second car turned into the drive. She had an attractive, intelligent face, and Kathy found herself staring at her, wondering how well she really knew her husband.

"Mrs. Gentle, we're police officers, investigating the murder of Angela Hannaford. She worked in your husband's office. Did you know her at all?"

"I believe I did once meet her there. I don't recall her very clearly. Of course, I was very shocked to hear what had happened to her."

"We think your husband may be able to give us some more help."

"I see . . . He's not very well at the moment. I'd better . . ." She watched the four men get out of the second car. "There are an awful lot of you, aren't there?"

"We have a search warrant, Mrs. Gentle. I'm afraid we shall have to search your property. We shall be as quick and as careful as we can."

Her mouth dropped open, colour draining from her face. "No! That's not possible. There's been some mistake!"

She turned to face the front door, from which the figure of her husband, in dressing-gown and slippers, had just emerged.

"What's the matter, Muriel? What on earth is going on?"

She turned back to face Kathy. "I'm going to call our solicitor," she said, and ran past her husband and into the house.

They followed her in, Kathy informing Tom Gentle of what they were doing as Bren and the others spread out through the house. He led them into a living-room with the look of a man who has just been mugged. His nose was red with his cold, and his eyes even more mournful than before.

The furniture in the room was, like the house, old, comfortable, and worn. A couple of pieces were unusual, a chest and a sideboard of blackened oak, Elizabethan or even earlier. After a moment Muriel followed them in. She looked fiercely at Kathy. "I don't want you to ask him anything until Mr. Denholm gets here. Do you understand?"

"Very well, Mrs. Gentle. May I ask you one or two things while we wait?"

"Me? I told you, I hardly knew the girl."

Kathy nodded and went to the door, where she called for one of the other detectives. "Mr. Gentle, would you go with this officer, please?"

She closed the door after him.

"Mrs. Gentle, can you tell me where your husband was on the evening of Saturday last?"

"Saturday . . . Oh, I see!" Relief began to spread across her face. "The theatre! You think . . ."

"He went to the theatre?"

"No! But that's what you think, isn't it? That's why you're here! I knew there must be a mistake!"

"Go on."

"Oh . . ." She laughed, stroking her cheek with her hand. Kathy saw that the fingers were trembling. "Tom is such an ass. He told me on Saturday, about lunch time, that he'd bought a ticket at work for the theatre that night. He'd done it on impulse, because he thought I was having my bridge group round, and he thought he might as well be out of the way. Well, I told him that he'd got the night wrong, because my bridge isn't till next Saturday. At first he said he wanted to go anyway—said it would let down the others in the party if he didn't go. But I told him that he wasn't going on his own, without me. He doesn't even like the theatre, anyway!"

She smiled at Kathy. "You see? He didn't go. Why? Was the poor girl part of the group?"

"She *was* the group, Mrs. Gentle. Only her."

The woman's face froze, startled, but not as shocked as it might have been. "I see. Well, obviously I misunderstood."

"Did your husband ever speak about Angela to you?"

"No, why should he?"

"What about anyone else? Had anyone else mentioned her name to you?"

"Not that I can recall offhand. Why? What is the point of this?"

"So Mr. Gentle stayed at home with you all Saturday evening?"

"Yes . . . well, no. He went out to the local at around 9:30. He quite often does that on a Saturday night. He meets one or two friends for a pint."

She looked defiantly at Kathy, who nodded. "I'm sorry about this, Mrs. Gentle, I really am."

The solicitor's Jaguar swung into the drive after ten strained minutes in which Muriel Gentle winced with every thump and scrape of her furniture being moved in the rooms around them. He strode in, a tall, thin, white-haired man of around sixty, and went straight to Muriel, who rose with relief.

"I told them, Victor. I told them that they mustn't speak to Tom until you were present. But . . . I spoke to them."

"That's perfectly all right, my dear." He looked at Kathy. "Are you the officer in charge?"

Kathy showed him her gleaming new warrant card and the search warrant.

"Are you laying charges against Mr. Gentle?" he asked.

"No, sir, not at this time. We have reason to believe he may be holding evidence relevant to our inquiry into the murder of Angela Hannaford at her home in Petts Wood on the night of September 8."

"I find that very hard to believe, Sergeant," the solicitor said dryly, "but no doubt we shall see."

"Yes, sir. Shall we interview him now?"

He nodded. "Muriel, my dear, is there a neighbour you might have a cup of coffee with until this is over?"

"I couldn't leave Tom. I shall go outside and wait in the garden. I take it"—she spun on her heel and glared at Kathy—"that you don't intend to dig up my garden!"

"I sincerely hope not, Mrs. Gentle."

Kathy and the solicitor found Tom Gentle sitting in the kitchen, squeezing his nose in a handful of tissues. The crumpled face of the basset-hound regarded them gravely from between its master's legs. Gentle sniffed loudly and spoke. "Would you like something then, Sergeant, Victor? I'll make a pot of tea if you like."

Both shook their heads, surprised at how unconcerned he seemed. Kathy decided to get straight to the point. "Mr. Gentle, we've received reports that you made advances to Angela Hannaford, followed her in the train, and sexually harassed her."

"Have you indeed?" Gentle stared at Kathy calmly.

"Is it true?"

"Where on earth did you get hold of rubbish like that?" He sat back in his Windsor chair and regarded her with an air of disappointment. Taking the cue, the dog gave a snuffle of contempt and rolled over.

"You deny it?"

"Of course I do." He sneezed suddenly and loudly into the tissues. "I certainly travelled back and forward to town on the same train as Angela sometimes, and occasionally found myself in the same compartment, but I'd be very surprised if anyone who witnessed that would describe my conduct as improper in any way."

"What about your arrangement to go out to the theatre with her last Saturday?"

"I already explained that to you, Sergeant." He rolled his large eyes in exaggerated despair. "I arranged to buy a theatre ticket that was going spare; I did not arrange to go *out* with Angela."

"But you seem to have hidden from your wife the fact that you were going to meet Angela alone."

"Oh really! I can't remember the precise words I used to Muriel, and I don't suppose she can either. The fact is, I didn't go!"

"Sergeant," the solicitor broke in, "I take it that magistrates, even today, are not in the habit of serving search warrants on law-abiding citizens on the strength of office tittle-tattle and typists' gossip. I must ask you if you have some substantial piece of evidence concerning my client's conduct with the murdered woman. Something that can be corroborated?"

Kathy hesitated, and at that moment a detective put his head round the kitchen door and raised his eyebrow at her.

"Just a moment, please," she said to the two men, trying not to sound relieved, and made for the door.

She followed the detective upstairs and into a room on one side of a small landing. There were no windows in the space, which appeared to be set up as a photographic dark room. The lack of outlook and the sloping ceilings of the room beneath the roof pitch gave it a claustrophobic atmosphere.

"This filing cabinet over here," the detective pointed. "It was locked."

It was a three-drawer grey steel office type of cabinet. The detective slid open the top drawer and began to pull out piles of magazines.

"A few photographic mags," he said, "but mainly soft porn. Some not so soft."

Kathy thumbed through the pile. "Anything violent, sadistic?"

"Didn't spot anything. His tastes seem fairly straightforward." He pulled out a magazine with the title *King-Sized Knockers*.

"Mmm. Subtle." Kathy nodded. "You'd better make a list of the titles and make a note of anything remotely nasty, OK? Is that all?"

The detective closed the top drawer and opened the second. He began to pull papers from the file-hangers at the front.

"What's that?" Kathy asked. "Just looks like bills."

"Yeah. Mainly telephone bills."

"So what?"

"Have a look."

Kathy thumbed through them for a while. "Sorry. Don't see anything."

"The 0891 numbers. See?"

"So? He kept up with the cricket scores or the weather or something."

The CID man snorted derisively. "*Talk dirty to me.* You know. Listen to some bird telling you what she'd like you to do to her, for a quid a minute, or whatever it is. You know."

"No, I don't. I had no idea."

"You've led a sheltered life," he grinned.

"Obviously. Still, it's nice to know that the world we live in is so wonderfully rich that there're still things like this to discover. Would you classify it as a hobby, do you think?"

"A hobby?"

"Yes. He seems to have spent enough time and money on it. However"—she dropped the phone bills back in the cabinet with a sigh—"we're going to need more than this to nail the creep."

"Yes, Kathy." She could tell from his voice that they were coming to the really interesting bit. Kathy was aware of the smell of his sweat filling the stuffy room.

"I'm not sure I can face this," she said, her claustrophobic reactions to the room, the Sexual Assault Index, the Hannafords' house, the suffocating leafy suburbs, all suddenly pressing in upon her.

"Oh, I think you'll like what we've got here," he said, and drew out a plain manilla folder from half-way back in the drawer. Kathy opened it, saw the pictures of Angela inside, and became very still. "Oh yes," she whispered.

She was walking down the street, dressed for work, or sitting on a park bench on a day warm enough to need only a light summer frock. In a couple she was sitting reading by a window, and Kathy realized, from the rounded corners of the window and the heavy sliding door-lock by her knee, that she was in the compartment of a Southern Region electric commuter train. In none of them did she seem aware that she was being photographed.

"The back half of this drawer and the whole of the bottom drawer are full of files like this," the detective said. "Photographs of women, black and white 10×8s or 7×5s: he probably developed and printed them himself up here. Some have other things as well—restaurant bills, letters, hand-written notes about train times and addresses."

"She doesn't look as if she realized he was there," Kathy said.

"No. Most of them are like that. A few have the girl smiling at the camera. I haven't had time to take a thorough look. There're hundreds of pictures here."

Kathy returned downstairs to the kitchen, and saw Gentle's expression change as he recognized the file in her hand. But still he wasn't panicking. She sat down and placed the file, closed, on the table between them.

"We've found the filing cabinet in your darkroom, Mr. Gentle," she said flatly.

"It was locked," he said. "I hope you haven't damaged it."

"Sergeant, what . . ." The solicitor began to speak, then went silent as Kathy opened the file and he saw the pictures. He frowned. "Who is that?"

"The murdered woman, Angela Hannaford," Kathy replied. "Your client has been photographing her, it seems."

Mr. Denholm looked sharply at Gentle, who caught his look, shrugged, and sat back in his chair with a look of bland innocence. "So what? Yes, they're my photographs. It's my hobby."

"What is your hobby, Mr. Gentle?" Kathy said, quietly.

"Photography. I like to photograph people, ordinary people, going about their daily lives. That's my subject matter."

"Your subject matter seems to be exclusively female."

"Yes . . . well, Renoir spent his whole life painting pictures of nude women. I don't think anyone has suggested he was a pervert."

"They knew he was doing it, didn't they? Agreed to be his models?"

"Oh, come on! Cartier-Bresson made his name wandering about the streets of Paris taking impromptu photos of people in cafés, on the streets. That's all I'm doing."

"How did you do it? What equipment did you use?" Kathy turned one of the pictures towards him, of Angela walking down a leafy street.

"From my car. I have a camera with a telephoto lens."

"So you waited in your car for Angela? Where?"

"That one was in the suburb where she lives."

"Taken when?"

He shrugged. "A month or two ago. She was on her way back from work."

"So how did you take it? You must have known her route home from the station. You must have known where she lived. You must have got there ahead of her, knowing which train she'd come back on, then waited for her, in her street. In Birchgrove Avenue."

Gentle shrugged off-handedly.

"That means yes? What about this one, in the railway carriage?"

"Ah yes, I'm rather proud of those. I have a miniature camera, a Minolta. I've developed this technique where I aim the camera from behind a newspaper. I can do it without anyone noticing, even in a quite crowded compartment."

Kathy reached forward and closed the file. "I'd like you to get dressed, Mr. Gentle."

"What for?"

"So that you can come back to Orpington police station with us and make a statement. We shall want you to identify the women in all of the files you have upstairs."

"All?" the solicitor queried.

"Yes, there are dozens, just like this."

"But that's pointless," Gentle protested. "I don't know the names of half of them."

"Maybe your wife does. We could show them to her."

"Now look . . ." Gentle began to splutter until he was cut off by Mr. Denholm. "I am sure, Sergeant, that, despite his condition, Mr. Gentle will be happy to comply with your request to go to Orpington. I don't think we need cause Mrs. Gentle any further unnecessary distress."

Although he wasn't looking at Gentle when he said this, Kathy sensed that it was aimed firmly at him.

Gentle's bottom lip curled in a sulk. "There's no law against taking photographs," he said.

"That's what you call it," Kathy replied. "The word we use is stalking. Your hobby is stalking women, Mr. Gentle. Let's go and find out how many of your *subjects* are no longer alive."

It proved to be a bigger task than she expected. Of the seventy-three women photographed in Gentle's files, he was able, or willing, to provide the full names of only eighteen, and first names of a further dozen. Of the more than five hundred photographs, he gave a location for the picture in about two-thirds of the cases, and an approximate date for rather more than that. Throughout he appeared genuinely to be trying to co-operate, sniffing and sucking throat pastilles. He spent most of Wednesday at Orpington, and returned voluntarily the next day. By Thursday afternoon he had become part of the background, chaffing with the typists at the coffee machine, sharing a sly joke with the lads from Traffic in the next office, and occasionally catching Kathy's eye with a rueful, impish grin.

A scan of photographs of nationwide missing persons took until the end of the week, and yielded only one, doubtful, correspondence with a picture of an unnamed woman in Gentle's collection. The Sexual Assault Index didn't include photographs of victims, and none of Gentle's eighteen names appeared on it.

"He's not likely to name anyone he's raped or bumped off, is he, Kathy?" Bren commented. "But the locations are interesting, aren't they? Maybe there's something in Brock's theory after all. The more recent files, since 1987, are all women who live somewhere along the Orpington–Sevenoaks line. Before that they come from the south-western suburbs—Hinchley Wood, Surbiton, Berrylands—all places on the Esher line, which is where he and his missus used to live."

"Even the ones we do track down don't want to talk to us," Kathy said. "I spoke to a couple of women this morning who claimed they knew nothing about him, and were obviously desperate for me not to call on them to talk about it. I finally got one to agree to meet me tomorrow morning while she's doing the Saturday shopping."

"Gently, gently, catchee monkey." Bren grinned encouragingly, then changed tack. "Did I do something wrong the other evening, Kathy?"

"When?"

"Couple of nights ago, I offered you a lift back up to town and a drink. You seemed put out."

"Did I? Sorry, I was probably preoccupied."

"It wasn't me, then?"

"No, no. You're looking more cheerful these days, Bren. I thought you were a bit down early on in the week."

Bren looked away. "Not me, Kathy. If there's one thing I can't stand it's moody people. So"—still not looking at her—"it's hot as buggery, isn't it? And muggy too. How about a nice cool drink on the way back tonight?"

"Oh . . . well, fine, OK."

At that point Brock put his head round the door. "Anyone seen Ted Griffiths?"

Kathy shook her head. "I think he left, Brock. More than an hour ago."

He frowned, then shrugged. "Well, anyone fancy a cold drink? No doubt you'll be anxious to return to the bosom of your family, Bren, but you might consider postponing that pleasure for the sake of your unmarried colleagues here. Help Kathy and me fill a few minutes of our empty lives between shifts."

"God save us," Bren muttered under his breath.

IT RAINED DURING THE night, and when the Saturday shoppers left home the next morning they found that the world had changed. New smells filled the suburbs, of damp earth and vegetation. It was still warm, but the sky was dark with clouds that spasmodically soaked the world below with showers of heavy raindrops. The certainty of endless sunny days was shaken, replaced with a sense of the inevitability of autumn. Kathy found the coffee shop in Bromley High Street, and went inside, half-expecting the woman not to be there. But she was, wearing, as she had arranged, a straw summer hat, incongruous now with the change in the weather, and reading a copy of the *Guardian*, headlining the drought crisis.

"Mrs. Oakley? I'm Kathy Kolla."

The woman shook her hand reluctantly, as if she still hadn't quite made up her mind to go through with this.

"I don't live here any more," she said. "It's funny coming back. I hope I don't meet anyone I used to know."

"Thanks for agreeing to speak to me."

"I almost didn't come. I don't know anyone called Tom Gentle, you see, so you're probably wasting your time."

But you did come, because you didn't want me showing up at your home, Kathy thought, and smiled. "Well, I appreciate your help, anyway. This is the man I was talking about." She showed the woman a picture of Gentle they'd taken at Orpington.

"Ah." It was clear that she recognized him. Kathy waited while she hesitated, and then finally nodded. "Yes. This is Bryan Jordan. That's Bryan with a 'Y.' "

"Tell me about him."

Mrs. Oakley sighed, removed the straw hat from her head, and ran her fingers through her hair. She had the weary, embattled look of someone who has just fought their way out of a very crowded supermarket.

"Once both boys were at secondary school, I decided to go back to work. I managed to get a job with an insurance company in the City. Well, after I'd been going up and down to Blackfriars for a few months I began to recognize some of the regulars on the train, the way you do. Bryan was one of them. One day we were crammed together in the evening rush hour, and we got talking. I said I'd only recently returned to full-time working, and he said he'd only recently moved to Bromley, so we were both newcomers, in a way. He was nice to talk to, very quiet, considerate, a little bit sad. When we got to Elmstead Woods it was raining. He said he'd got his car at the station, and could he give me a lift. Well, the thing is, living in Bromley I was really on the Victoria line, but I worked in the City, so Elmstead Woods was the closest station, and it was always a pest getting home from there. So anyway, I said yes."

She took a sip of the coffee the waitress had brought them and tugged at her hair again.

"We began to see each other quite often on the train after that, and Bryan would give me a lift home. He told me a bit about himself, about his invalid wife and everything. I began to look forward to seeing him. There was something about him not belonging to either home or work, but being something in between, a friend just for the journey. Then one evening, after the clocks changed and the evenings were getting dark, he stopped on the way home and, well, he gave me a cuddle." She shrugged, embarrassed. "It never got beyond that."

She saw the look that passed briefly across Kathy's face and she said, "No, really. We had the opportunity, but he never took it any further. I did wonder if it was me. Anyway, he told me, a month or two after, that he felt he must stop seeing me on account of how he could never leave his wife, who depends on him for everything, and in a way I was secretly relieved. I have seen him sometimes since then on the station at Blackfriars, but we never speak, and I've noticed he doesn't get off at Elmstead Woods any more."

Kathy hesitated.

"Is that any help to you?" Mrs. Oakley said. "Obviously, I don't want my husband to know about it. You do understand that, don't you?"

"Of course. Thank you for being so frank with me. The only thing I'm really interested in is if he was ever violent, or tried to make you do anything against your will."

"Oh no!" Mrs. Oakley looked shocked. "He was never like that. That's what I liked about him really. He was so gentle, and sort of sad. You couldn't help wanting to cheer him up. It was on account of his wife, of course."

Then a small doubt crossed her face. "His wife does have a handicap, doesn't she?"

"Oh yes, Mrs. Oakley," Kathy nodded, "she has a handicap all right."

THAT EVENING KATHY WAS surprised by a phone call from her cousin Di in Canada. Since their contact was usually restricted to Christmas and birthday cards, Kathy assumed there was a new crisis in her life.

"No, no. I just wanted to wish you luck with your new job,

Kathy. Have you started yet? I wasn't sure if you were back in your flat."

Kathy blinked in surprise. It was hard to imagine that Di would have known about her movements, let alone cared.

"Are you sure nothing's wrong? Are Tom and Mary all right?"

Di gave her warm mid-Atlantic chuckle. "Can't stop being a suspicious detective, can you, Kath? Mom and Pop are fine, I guess. You haven't spoken to them recently?"

"Not for a month or so. How's everything with you?"

Strangely, Di didn't seem to have much to say about the things that usually filled her conversation, the boys, her new husband, their vacation. After a few more minutes they ran out of things to say. When she hung up Kathy still had no idea what the call had really been about.

SIX

IT WAS SUNNY AGAIN the next morning, Sunday, just one week since Kathy had started working on the Hannaford case. She opened the Sunday paper over her coffee and toast, and discovered the twelve-letter-word answer to the previous weekend's word quiz—*melodramatic*. Of course. She didn't look at the new puzzle in case it became a habit. The thought of measuring her future Sundays in word-puzzles made her heart sink. Instead she dug out her swimming costume and a towel and took the tube into town.

She went first to the offices at Queen Anne's Gate, for which she now had a key. As she made her way through the building she could hear the sounds of other people, but there was no one from Brock's team in the basement, nor any messages to indicate new developments. She thought of Gentle's puppy-dog smile and of all those unnamed women's faces in his files, and she felt restless. She sat down at a computer and called up, once again, the Sexual Assault Index, this time concentrating on cases within the Metropolitan Police Number Five Area, covering south-west London and the Esher suburban rail line, and Number Three Area, for the Sevenoaks line. Eventually she fixed on seven cases which might, she thought, from the bare details given, conceivably correspond with pictures of women from the relevant areas. She then faxed the photographs to the case officers cited for each assault, in the hope that someone might recognize them, using the photocopied set of Gentle's pictures which she'd brought with her from Orpington.

She switched off the machine and headed back upstairs to the street. She'd been told of a pool nearby in Pimlico which people from Headquarters used, and she walked briskly south, trying to get Bren's prediction out of her mind, that they were wasting their time.

After the first couple of lengths, the rhythm of the crawl took over, gradually easing the tension which the keyboard had built up across her shoulders and neck. Twenty minutes later, she pulled herself out and sat dripping on the edge of the pool. Despite the warm day, there were only a couple of other people there. One of them, a dark-haired man with goggles who had been trolling steadily up and down the pool since she arrived, completed a fast length to her end and got out. She took no notice until she became aware of his dark-skinned legs at her side, and then of him sitting down beside her.

"Hi."

She was surprised to see Leon Desai.

"Oh, hello. I didn't recognize you without your clothes on," she said.

He looked coolly at her without smiling for a moment, and then, just as irritation began to tighten her mouth, the corners of his eyes creased, just a fraction. What really irritated her was the fact that she felt uncomfortably self-conscious in her swimming-costume.

"How are you finding Brock's team?" His voice was quiet, measured.

"OK. How are you finding it?"

This time his smile almost reached his mouth.

"I'd say it's going through a difficult patch. Brock's under a lot of pressure with the current reorganization of Specialist Operations, and I don't think he's getting much help from the rest of the team. He seems to have a lot of faith in you, though."

Kathy looked at him in surprise. "What do you mean, he's not getting much help?"

Desai shrugged and turned away to watch two boys climbing the high diving-board at the far end. "I think you should come and have a look at what we've got so far at Lambeth."

"Oh?" She didn't feel inclined to sound too enthusiastic. "Have you made progress?"

"We've been having our own difficulties—technical rather than personal." This time there really was a smile, sardonic, which Kathy interpreted to mean that only lesser mortals had the personal kind.

"Come down tomorrow morning if you like—9:30. Know where it is?"

"Yes. But Brock's called a conference at 10:00."

"Oh yes—8:30, then? I'll tell Morris." And then he was on his feet.

She watched him stride off towards the male changing-rooms, trying not to stare unduly at his sexy bum.

TOWARDS FOUR O'CLOCK THAT afternoon the doorbell of Kathy's flat rang. She was startled to find her Aunt Mary standing on the threshold, her small round figure enveloped in a thick yellow winter coat, her silver hair capped by one of the many hats she owned, this one a furry brown helmet trimmed with a gold ribbon. The whole effect was like a plump teddy bear. As she came into the flat, Kathy saw that she had a small suitcase in tow, strapped to a folding aluminium frame with little wheels.

It had been some years since Kathy had spent much time with her aunt, the uncertainty of that gap making their embrace more awkward than either intended.

"Are you on your own?" Kathy beamed, trying to sound as if it was the most natural thing to have her aunt call on a Sunday afternoon, when in reality the sight of the familiar figure here in her flat, outside of her native Sheffield, seemed as bizarre and exotic as if an Amazonian Indian in full ceremonial dress had dropped in.

"Yes, dear." Aunt Mary seemed abnormally short of conversation, just as her daughter Di had been on the phone. There was something odd about the way she looked too—dazed, not quite registering her surroundings, avoiding eye contact with her niece.

"No Uncle Tom?"

"No, dear." Then, after a long pause, "I thought I'd get away on my own. To London."

"That's a good idea." Kathy tried not to sound alarmed.

"Do you mind, Kathy?" Aunt Mary said heavily, looking hard at Kathy for the first time. "Do you mind if I stay here for a day or two?"

"Of course not. Mrs. P next door has got a folding bed I can borrow. Here, take your coat off. You must be sweltering. What train did you catch?"

"Mid morning, it was."

"Really? And what did you do when you got to London?"

"I got the underground, dear. To find you."

Kathy stared at her. She must have been down in the tube for two or three hours, trying to find Finchley Central. It was a miracle she'd made it.

"You could probably do with a cup of tea."

DESAI COLLECTED KATHY AT the reception desk of the Forensic Science Laboratory the following morning, and took her with barely a word to a room on the third floor. A balding man with thick glasses straightened up from a cluttered laboratory bench in the centre of the room and came over to shake her hand.

"Morris Munns is our best scene photographer." The man beamed at Desai's compliment. "He's with our Serious Crimes Unit. Up with all the latest laser stuff."

"Even so"—Morris shook his head—"we've been 'aving an 'ell of a time with this one, Kathy. It's been a real challenge."

She thought them an odd couple, the young Desai tall, long-skulled, and cool, the elderly Munns short, broad cockney, bustling around enthusiastically. Yet they obviously got on well together: Desai's admiration for the older man's work was clearly genuine, and seemed to be reciprocated.

"How come, Morris?"

"Plenty of latent marks, but very few legible ones. No fingerprints we could visualize, so we concentrated on the possibility of footprints. I think we were 'aving a go at that with the portable laser when you looked in, Kathy. Masses of marks on the carpet, but not one clear enough to visualize on that thick pile, see? The only decent marks we found were on the 'earth."

Desai selected a photograph from a pile on the bench and showed it to Kathy. "They sealed up the fireplace when they put in central heating, but they left the tiled hearth in front of it. That's the only part of the floor of the room that isn't carpeted."

"There were two small partial shoe prints on the corner tile, Kathy," Morris went on, showing her another photograph. To Kathy's eye the traces were indecipherable.

"Yes, not a lot," Morris agreed. "But clearly two different patterns, the lower one in blood, probably a partial 'eel mark, then partly obscured by the larger upper one."

"That's what made us think for a while that there could have been two men involved," Desai added.

"But you don't think so now?"

Desai gave his sardonic smile. "The second one belongs to one of the police officers who was first on the scene. That's why I'm paranoid, you see."

Kathy nodded. "But . . . there's almost nothing of the lower shoe print."

"We photographed it *in situ* under different lights, then tried to get more detail with gelatine lifting and treatment with tetra-aminobiphenyl," Morris said sadly.

"No good?"

He shook his head.

"Well . . ." Kathy looked at him doubtfully, then saw the gleam in his eye as he turned to Desai.

"OK." Desai became businesslike, taking charge. "The post-mortem examination revealed a large bruise on Hannaford's back, about the size of a foot, as if she'd been stamped on."

You cold bastard. Everyone else calls her "Angela."

"The section of her blouse corresponding to that position showed no significant marks on the outside surface. But we know that, when a body is run over by a vehicle, for example, the tyre marks are sometimes printed on the *inside* surface of their clothing, by absorbing material from the skin. So we tested the inside surface of Hannaford's blouse."

Morris Munns pulled a sheaf of photographs from an envelope and selected one for Kathy. Like the previous one of the shoe prints on the hearth tiles, it had a scale rule across the bottom. Apart from that it was an undifferentiated grey.

"That's it under ordinary white light. Nothing much."

He pulled a second print from the sheaf. "Under an argon-ion laser. Getting better."

The ghostly, distorted outline of a foot was emerging from the gloom.

"Then we treated it with DFO, which reacts with amino acids to fluoresce under laser light."

A third photo, brighter still. There was something unsettling about seeing this image of a grossly violent act teased into visibility from the fabric of a dead girl's blouse.

"Then ninhydrin, which reacts with both amino acids and proteins. The marks are visible under white light."

Kathy stared at the fourth and final photograph, quite clear now. "Why is it so distorted?"

Desai replied. "The material of the blouse is loose, crumpled. He brings his foot down and the material is pressed against her flesh, soft, contoured, resilient. In some places the material stretches, in others it bunches up. You end with an image distorted in all sorts of unpredictable ways. That's why the print on the tile is important. It gives us a basic fragment of true scale to work from."

"To undo the distortions."

"Right. We're not there yet, but we've got a pretty good idea."

Desai reached over for a fat A4 folder and turned the pages to one marked with a slip of paper. Kathy realized that they had probably laid out all their exhibits here specially for her to see this morning. She felt rather gratified. She also wondered what was in the carrier bag sitting on the end of the bench.

"Do you know the Footwear Index?"

"I've heard of it."

"It has over ten thousand sole patterns. We reckon this is the one."

Kathy looked at a pair of shoe prints reproduced on a file sheet. The information boxes at the top identified them as Doc Martens.

"Several manufacturers have copied the classic Doc sole pattern, but we think this is a genuine one."

"Size?"

"That's the tricky bit. We're still working on that. At the moment our best guess is a ten."

Now Morris reached for the carrier bag and produced from

inside it, with something of a flourish, a pair of black, shiny Doc Martens, size ten.

"Used to be only bovver boys and coppers wore 'em. Now everyone does, from pre-teen girls to grandpas. It's the best we can do."

"Thank you, Morris," Kathy said. "I'm impressed. And if you can be any more certain about the size, we'd be really grateful."

She was thinking about Tom Gentle's dapper frame and neat little feet.

DESAI WAS MORE RELAXED with her now, driving back across the river, as if she'd passed some kind of initiation test. He even cracked a joke of sorts, about using one photographer to catch another, and Kathy, trying to encourage this faint thaw, asked what Morris did for a hobby, arrange car loans? He actually laughed, a short bark, head tipped briefly back, and she admitted to herself, reluctantly, that he had a certain style.

The mood in the Bride of Denmark was more troubled. Bren looked tense and short of sleep, Brock preoccupied. Only Ted Griffiths seemed relaxed, giving them a little wave as they sat down.

"Bren," Brock started abruptly.

Bren cleared his throat and straightened in his seat. "We held the re-enactment on Saturday night. A WPC dressed much like Angela joined the crowds leaving the National Theatre at 10:30 and made her way to Waterloo suburban station, where she caught the 11:08 to Petts Wood, then walked to Birchgrove Avenue. It hasn't produced anything new so far. We have managed to find a couple of people who were in the audience for *Macbeth* on the eighth near Angela, and can remember seeing her, sitting alone, the seat beside her empty. We've also had people come forward who were on the train that night, but nobody who recalls Angela on the journey, or at Petts Wood."

He paused and took a deep breath. "We do have a taxi driver who recalls seeing a pale grey BMW parked near the taxi rank at the foot of the station steps at Petts Wood one night about a week ago, but he can't swear it was the Saturday. Tom Gentle has a pale grey BMW. One of the barmaids in the Daylight Inn thinks she recognizes Gentle's picture, but can't be any more precise than that. No one at Gentle's local can vouch for him being there that evening."

There was another pause. "I can tell you all the other things we've done, Brock, but so far, these are the only results."

Brock nodded. "So, the hypothesis is that Gentle went out at about 9:30, telling his wife he was going to the local. Instead he drove to Petts Wood, where he waited for Angela to return from the play, maybe had a drink in the pub there while he waited. Probably he knew that her parents were away, and saw this as a chance he couldn't let slip. She was surprised to see him, but accepted a lift. When they got to her home he asked to use her loo, or the phone or whatever, she let him in, then resisted when he made advances. He lost control, killed her, and went home."

Bren nodded. "That's about it."

"Kathy?"

"I haven't got much that's solid, Brock. I've been unable to get any positive matches between the faces in Gentle's files and either Missing Persons or the Sexual Assault Index. We've got addresses for eight women so far. I've spoken to five on the phone, and one in person. They all knew Gentle, but not necessarily under that name, and none realized he'd been photographing them. The most damning was the typist who made the complaint against him at Merritt Finance, and whose picture was in his collection. The words she used were creepy, sleazy, and devious. The others were more generous; they saw him as charming, persuasive, a bit sad.

They would make very reluctant, embarrassed witnesses, and they never saw a violent side to his nature."

"That's because they all went along with him," Bren retorted. "We've got to find the ones who slapped his face and told him to fuck off, like Angela did."

"Yes, but why show your face in the local pub, or park your car in front of the taxi rank, if you were up to something?"

"Because he planned to poke her, not murder her!" Bren was irritated, his voice tight.

"He doesn't seem to have . . . to have had sex with any of the women I contacted, actually, although I gathered that at least two of them would have agreed to it. But he must have anticipated enough to be carrying the knife, and whatever he tied her thumbs with. And what about the mess his clothes would have been in?" Kathy hesitated. She hadn't meant to get into an argument over this. "Anyway, Leon's got something that has a bearing." She was aware of Bren turning and staring at her as she said this.

"Ah," Brock said. "Something at last, Leon?"

Desai gave a summary of what he and Morris had told Kathy at the Laboratory, his voice sounding calm and reasonable after Bren's. Kathy, eyes lowered, noticed Bren's large, grubby shoe tapping with impatience whenever the other man used the technical names of chemicals and processes.

When he had finished, Desai produced the pair of shoes from his bag, and passed them round.

"So what's the difficulty, Kathy?" Brock said.

"I think Gentle has small feet."

"How sure are you about the size, Leon?"

"We're working on that. It's only a probability at present."

Brock nodded and turned to Ted Griffiths. "How are things going in Orpington?"

"Steady, Chief. No great developments. I think we've pretty well eliminated the boyfriend and his buddies at the stag do."

"How did you manage that?" There was a note of scepticism in Brock's voice.

"Well, they all support each other's accounts. It would have been next to impossible for any one of them to have spent time alone at Angela's house before 2:00 a.m., and the post-mortem seems to rule out a later time."

"We don't know it was one man alone. What if it was a group of them?" Brock's voice was hard now.

"Well . . . seems a bit far-fetched."

"Does it?"

His irritation with Griffiths' apparent complacency was palpable. After a moment he spoke again, quietly. "What about the Hannafords? How are they coping?"

"I suppose they're all right. We haven't heard from them."

"I asked you to go and see them last Wednesday, Ted. I told you to keep in close touch with them."

Griffiths coloured slightly. "Oh . . . I didn't get time, Brock. I reckoned, let sleeping dogs lie."

"You reckoned."

Kathy hadn't ever seen that look in Brock's eye before, and she was very glad it wasn't directed at her.

"I'll do it this morning," Griffiths said hurriedly.

"Yes." Brock's monosyllable hung in the air. "I think we have to bring Gentle in, Bren. You agree?"

Bren nodded.

"We'll make it formal. Grill him on his movements that Saturday evening. Kathy, why don't you go down to his home again? Check his shoe size and have another word with his wife. Also, these searches for precedents, have you circulated the county forces around the Met area?"

"Yes, Brock. Especially south of the river. I've followed up with phone calls too."

"If we're talking about commuters," Leon Desai came in, "we

could look further afield. People commute into London from Brighton, Bristol, Barnsley, even. Boulogne too, pretty soon, I suppose."

"True enough," Brock grunted. "Better send out another request, Kathy; make it nationwide. Emphasize the peculiar features of the assault."

He pushed his papers back into their file. "All right, let's get on with it. Ted, I'd like a word in my office, in ten minutes. Kathy, hang on here, will you?"

The meeting broke up, Kathy and Brock remaining silent in their seats. When the others had gone, Brock said to her, "What was all that about, between you and Bren?"

Kathy frowned. "I . . . I don't think there was anything, Brock."

"You sure? You haven't been having disagreements about the case?"

"No, no, not at all."

He met her eyes for a moment, not doubting exactly, but searching for something. "It's important that you two can work together, Kathy. You understand, don't you? The importance of the team."

"Of course I understand, Brock." It wasn't like Brock to be stating the obvious. She wondered what he was worried about.

He nodded and picked up his file as if to go. "Bren's wife's father died last week. After a fairly grim illness. It put a lot of strain on the family."

"Ah. I'm sorry. He didn't say anything—to me, anyway."

Brock shrugged and got to his feet. "You sounded there as if you were having doubts about this Gentle character, Kathy."

"No, I think he's the one all right. I've just been trying not to jump too soon to conclusions. They kept telling us that at Bramshill."

Brock smiled. "Very commendable."

"But since we found his photographs, and after talking to the women, I've begun to get a very bad feeling about him, to be honest. His whole behaviour seems to be like a mask, hiding what he wants, what he feels—what he really *is*. He hasn't shown the least concern since we started paying attention to him. I've never seen a murder suspect so unconcerned."

"I'll look forward to meeting him, then," Brock grunted, and led the way out of the room.

On her way up to the entrance, Kathy passed Ted Griffiths' desk, its top carefully composed with framed photographs—the wife, the wife and the baby, the baby, Ted and the baby. She found it vaguely embarrassing.

MURIEL GENTLE'S INITIAL PANIC had been replaced by a cold fury at the disaster which had burst into her tranquil life. She seethed at the injustice of the police treatment of her husband, the heedless obstinacy of their suspicions. Kathy's second visit gave her the opportunity to express some of this. She harried Kathy with every step as she went through the house, checking Gentle's shoes. They were all size seven: Hush Puppies, trainers, slippers, wellington boots—nothing remotely like Doc Martens.

"You have simply no *idea*, do you?" she stormed at Kathy's back. "You demolish our whole existence on the flimsiest of pretexts, turning innocent people's lives into a nightmare on the basis of some second-hand rumour, because you simply have no *idea* what you're doing. You don't know where to look for that girl's murderer, so you go around kicking innocent bystanders to the ground. You're stupid! Stupid! Stupid!"

After five minutes of this, Kathy led her back to the living-room and asked her to sit down. She did so, abruptly silent, chest heaving with the exertion of her invective. She stared at the mantelpiece and its framed photographs of herself and her husband, the two of them together, and another with an elderly couple, parents presumably. No children. Then, in a low, furious voice, she began again.

"Do you *imagine* that I could be married for twenty years to a sex monster, a *thrill-killer* as the papers put it, and not have the faintest idea? Do you? Don't you think I would know?"

"Did you know about the photographs, Mrs. Gentle?"

"Oh, that's ridiculous! Tom is a photographer. That's his hobby. He's always done that. He has his darkroom upstairs. Of course I knew."

"I mean, following women, and taking photographs of them secretly."

"There you go, you see! Turning him into a monster. It wasn't like that! He's told me all about it. He likes his sitters to be natural, unposed."

Her use of the word struck Kathy. She thought of Angela's body on the bed, rigidly posed.

"Angela believed that your husband was following her and harassing her. Other women in his office have made the same complaint before."

Mrs. Gentle heard the calm voice, the professional dealing with a case, not her life but a *case*, and she decided to make one more effort to break through the detective's stubbornness, to make her understand. "Look, my husband has a hobby, he's an enthusiastic photographer, a girl notices him looking at her and she misinterprets it. That's all. The thing with the girl in the office happened years ago, when Tom was under a lot of stress at work. He snapped at her over something, and she took offence. Some spiteful gossips blew it up out of all proportion, and then people started saying 'no smoke without fire.' My God, that's a long, long way from murdering Angela Hannaford, isn't it?"

Kathy nodded. It was a good try. But she thought of the filing cabinet, the bureaucratically neat files of photographs of unsuspecting women, and tried to imagine the efforts of a wife to rationalize that.

"The point is," Muriel Gentle's voice became low, pleading, "when you've finally eliminated Tom from your inquiries, and you've discovered who did actually do it, will we be able to put our life back together again? Will Tom be able to face the people at his work again? Will I be able to go to the shops? Or will we always hear people whispering behind our backs, because you once pointed a finger at an innocent man? Please, I beg you, please be careful!"

LATER THAT AFTERNOON KATHY caught up with Bren, and asked him how their interrogation of Gentle had gone.

"Brock finally got him to admit that he drove to Petts Wood that night. He said he had felt awkward about not turning up at the theatre, and wanted to explain to Angela how it had happened, so there'd be no misunderstanding. He said he didn't want her discovering at the office on Monday that he had bought the other ticket, and maybe jumping to the sort of conclusions that had started the misunderstandings at the office the last time."

"Very considerate. So what happened?"

"He says he had a couple of beers at the Daylight Inn, then sat in his car in Station Square, waiting for her."

"That's great! We've got him then."

Bren shrugged non-committally. "He claims she never appeared. He says he waited till after midnight, then gave up and drove home."

"But he admits he was there! That's the crucial thing. God, he's surely not expecting us to believe that Angela had *two* stalkers on her trail that night!"

"Every step along the way, he's only admitted as much as he

thinks we already know. But this time, I'd say he was scared, for the first time, probably. We've taken his car for forensics."

"What about him?"

"He's free, for the moment. How did you go with the wife?"

"She believes, like all the other women I've spoken to, that he's incapable of violence."

"Yeah, that's what Dr. Crippen's wife thought too."

"And he takes size seven shoes."

"Well, to be honest, Kathy, I wouldn't place too much weight on all that crap Desai's been feeding you."

"How do you mean?"

"He gets a bit carried away with those lab blokes. The way he drools over the technical terms, like he's got argon ions flowing where the rest of us have blood. Brock calls it 'physics-envy.' I call it ambition. He sees that as his way up—interpreting the boffins to all the dumb buggers like us."

"Still, that doesn't mean they can't come up with a shoe size from Angela's shirt. I thought it was pretty impressive, what they'd done."

"The make I grant you, but not the size." Bren regarded her, stony-faced. "How sure can they be? How safe? A couple of millimetres and you've got completely the wrong answer. Remember, they're under pressure just like the rest of us. So far they've come up with sweet F.A., and they don't like that, any more than we do."

FOR A MOMENT, WHEN she opened the front door of her flat, Kathy thought she'd been robbed, the lights all on, table and sideboard bare. Then, just as the small figure bustled out of the kitchen, she remembered her aunt. It looked as if she'd spent the whole day finishing the job of cleaning the flat that Kathy had begun over a week before.

"You shouldn't have done that," Kathy said, trying to keep the irritation out of her voice. It wasn't just the fact that her aunt had taken over the place with her cleaning. The intrusion was of a deeper kind, the familiar face and voice and lily of the valley perfume inadvertently sparking intense traces of things which Kathy thought she had safely cordoned off in the past. "You're supposed to be on holiday. Didn't you go out?"

"I was quite happy," the old lady said vaguely.

"I'm really sorry I couldn't take the day off to take you up to town. We should sit down and work out things for you to see, and how to get there. At the weekend we can go somewhere together." *If you're still here, that is.*

"I'm perfectly happy, Kathy."

"Have you phoned home? Let Uncle Tom know you arrived safely?"

"Mmm."

"Well . . ." Kathy said, "perhaps we could go out and see a film tonight." She tried to imagine Aunt Mary grappling with Peter Greenaway.

"Thank you, dear, but I'll just have an early night, if you don't mind."

"You are feeling all right, are you?"

"It's all been more of a strain than I imagined."

Later, when Aunt Mary had closed the bedroom door, Kathy noticed her battered old school atlas lying on the corner table. A sliver of paper marked the page for Canada.

TOWARDS THE END OF the following afternoon, Brock suddenly called them together again in the small conference room they had the use of at Orpington police station. He looked puzzled.

"I've just had a call from the Gentles' solicitor, Victor Denholm. He was complaining about his clients being harassed."

"Oh, come on!" Bren groaned, disgusted. "Denholm was with him all the time we questioned him yesterday, and we haven't been near him since."

"Not harassed by us. By Angela Hannaford's father, Basil Hannaford."

"What?" They all sat up.

"Basil Hannaford phoned Tom Gentle at home last night—three times, threatening and abusing him, until he took the phone off the hook. This morning Hannaford was on to Mrs. Gentle's father, Sir Charles Merritt, the chairman of Merritt Finance, asking if he was aware that his son-in-law was the pervert who had tortured and murdered his daughter."

"Jesus!"

"But how?" Kathy said. "How could he know that?"

"Exactly. He told Merritt that he, Hannaford, knew that *we* know that Gentle did it, but we haven't been able to prove it yet. He wants to force Gentle to confess."

Muriel Gentle's appeal for them to be careful suddenly flashed back into Kathy's mind.

"So," Brock went on, "who told him?" He looked at Kathy and saw the consternation on her face. "Kathy?"

"No . . . no, I was just thinking of Muriel Gentle. She was frightened that something like this was going to happen. I . . ." She was desperately trying to cast her mind back. "I'm sure I never mentioned Gentle's name to the Hannafords. I did ask someone—the boyfriend, I think—if Gentle's name meant anything to him. But I didn't say who he was, and he obviously didn't recognize it."

"Bren? Ted?"

"No way." Ted spoke first. "I saw Basil Hannaford yesterday like you said, Brock. But I never mentioned Gentle, I kept it all pretty vague."

"Bren?"

"I've never even met Hannaford, Brock."

"Well, someone's been talking to him. Maybe he knows someone who works here, with Orpington police. Try to find out, will you, Ted?"

"Do we talk to Hannaford?" Bren said.

"If we can find him. I've been trying the number, but there's no reply."

NEXT MORNING KATHY WAS roused from Mrs. P's folding bed by a call from the duty office at New Scotland Yard, telling her to get in to Queen Anne's Gate immediately. There was no explanation, but when she reached the news kiosk at the tube station she saw it for herself. The banner headline read STALKER ON THE 8:19. It framed a familiar photograph of Angela Hannaford sitting reading in the window seat of a commuter train.

"They don't name him." Brock was crouched over the paper on his desk, face dark with anger. "But they do everything but. 'The Stalker is believed to be a work colleague of the murdered woman, who has made a habit of following and photographing hundreds of unsuspecting women on the commuter rail lines around London, using a hidden spy camera.' Good grief!" Brock shook his head.

" 'The man is believed to be the main suspect in the police hunt for Angela Hannaford's killer, but so far police have been unable to gather sufficient evidence to lay charges against him.' Then there's the editorial, have you seen that? Pious drivel about the rights of ordinary people to privacy. That's pretty rich coming from this rag. They're outraged because Gentle's been doing what they do every day of the week."

He threw the paper down and glared at Bren and Kathy. "The point is, how did they get hold of it? If Hannaford fed it to them, how did *he* get hold of it?"

Kathy pulled the set of photocopies out of her bag and began to compare them to the picture in the paper.

"It's this one, see?" she said after a moment. "They've used the central section of Gentle's photograph. It's quite a good reproduction too."

"Meaning?"

"Well, it doesn't look as if they've worked from a photocopy."

"And the original set is at Orpington," Brock growled. "Where the hell is Ted?"

He lifted a phone and snarled into it for a while, then slammed it down.

"Look," he said, "we can't wait. I'm going to have to stay here to fend off the wolves. I want you two to get down to Orpington and find out what the hell's happened down there. And track down Hannaford. We've got to get him to understand that his playing the lone vigilante is going to screw up our investigation and maybe end up letting Gentle walk away scot free."

AN HOUR LATER BREN and Kathy were sitting in Orpington police station with the CID Sergeant with whom Ted Griffiths had been liaising.

"Yeah," he said, "Ted got on to me last night about a possible leak to Hannaford, but I don't see it, frankly. I've talked this morning to all the people involved, and nobody's heard of anyone having contact with him. I mean, I suppose it's possible that the Hannafords know someone in another department, who's been talking to them, but what would they know? And as for this . . ." He stared at the paper and shook his head.

"Ted went to see the Hannafords on Monday, didn't he?" Bren said.

"Yes, Monday. I went too. There was nothing said about Gentle. We didn't mention his name and neither did Hannaford."

"Did you take the photographs with you then?"

"No, course not. What would be the point?"

"And Hannaford hasn't been in here since then? Or been in touch?"

The sergeant shook his head. "Nah. The only one's been in was the boyfriend, Avery. He came in late Monday to pick up his clothes that Forensic had finished with. I saw him, over there, talking to Ted, at his desk."

"Where are the photographs kept?" Kathy asked.

The sergeant hesitated, then nodded his head towards the desk. "Ted keeps the prints. The negatives were sent down to the evidence store."

They got up and walked over to Ted Griffiths' desk. Another, smaller, gallery of family portraits decorated its top. The rest of the material on it was more chaotically stacked—paper trays, printouts, notepads, and on one side, the buff manila files of Gentle's photographs.

"Just like that?" Bren said. "Left out for anybody to pick up?"

Angela's file was on top. Inside, the picture published in the newspaper was missing.

THERE WAS A GREEN Escort parked outside the Avery house.

"Isn't that Ted's?" Kathy said.

"He's probably worked it out for himself on the way here," Bren replied.

Mrs. Avery answered the front door so quickly that she must have been standing directly on the other side of it. She looked worried. "Oh. More of you!"

"Where are they, Mrs. Avery?"

"Upstairs, in Adrian's room. The other gentleman went straight up . . ."

They could hear the muffled sound of Ted yelling even as they reached the foot of the stairs. They followed the noise to a bedroom door. Inside Ted Griffiths had Angela's boyfriend by the hair, steadily banging his head against the far wall. The lad was stark naked.

Ted looked angrily back over his shoulder, glaring at Kathy and Bren. "Come in. I'm just about to tear this little bastard's balls off."

"Put him down, Ted," Bren said calmly, as if he was always coming across this sort of thing. "What's the story?"

"He admits he pinched the photograph from my desk when I turned away to use someone else's bloody phone. He gave it to Hannaford. Go and wait for me downstairs, Bren."

"No, Ted," Bren said, in the same matter-of-fact voice. "You go downstairs with Kathy, while I have a quiet word with our friend here."

Kathy didn't think Ted would do it. He turned away from them, his grip on Adrian's greasy hair tightening. Then, with an abrupt final bang of the man's head against the wall, he let go and stormed out.

Bren joined them outside in the car five minutes later. His face was sombre, and he sat for a moment saying nothing, staring through the front windscreen.

"Well?" Ted demanded. "He didn't try to deny it, did he?"

Bren shook his head. "No." He twisted round to face the other detective in the back. "He says you started telling him about this bloke who'd been secretly taking photos of Angela and other women. He says you told him the man's name was Gentle, and that we were dead certain he was responsible for Angela's death, but we couldn't prove it."

"No! Look, it's bloody obvious that we need more on how Gentle was harassing Angela, and the only place to look is among those people who were close to her. For Christ's sake, if Gentle was giving her a hard time, she must have said something to her boyfriend. It stands to reason."

Kathy shook her head. She didn't think so.

"When that little creep came in for his clothes on Monday,"

Ted went on, "I grabbed him and started trying to prod his memory a bit. I mentioned Gentle's name—I didn't know you'd already done that, Kathy. It obviously meant nothing to him. Then I told him about the photographs—showed them to him."

"Why, for God's sake, Ted?"

"Because if Angela had realized that Gentle was snapping her, she might have threatened to tell on him, which would have been an extra motive for him to kill her. If she'd mentioned something to Avery, then we'd know that she knew about it. Look! The point was that Avery didn't know who Gentle was. I never told him that he worked with Angela."

"No, but Hannaford knew that," Bren said. "It was Hannaford who put Avery up to coming to see you on Monday, Ted. Hannaford thinks we've been jerking him around, so he told Avery to try to find out what we're doing. He told him to tell you that he would love to help if you could just prod his memory a bit—point him in the right direction. Is that right? Did he say that to you?"

"Christ." Ted looked away, out of the window.

"Before he retired," Bren went on, "Hannaford used to catch the same train up to town as Sir Charles Merritt. They got to know each other, and when Angela got her A-levels, Hannaford asked Merritt what she should do, and his advice was, forget about university, waste of time for women, do something useful like typing, and he'd fix her up with a job in his firm. Hannaford has met Gentle, for all we know he may have heard the office gossip about him, and when young Avery went round on Monday night with the photograph he'd pinched from you, and the information you'd given him about Gentle, Hannaford went berserk."

Bren paused. "All this is what Avery just told me. Does it make sense, Ted?"

Ted Griffiths gave a little nod, his face pale. "Makes me look pretty stupid, doesn't it? What do we do now? Find Hannaford, I suppose."

"Bang his head against the wall?" Bren shook his head. "I think Brock's going to have to do that."

"Yeah." Ted sat for a moment, then opened the car door.

"Where are you going?" Bren asked.

"To see Brock," Ted replied.

They watched him drive off, then Bren started up the car and they returned to Orpington. Later that morning he took a call from Brock. It went on for some time, but at the end of it he didn't have much to tell Kathy.

"They still can't trace Basil Hannaford," he said. "Oh, and just to make our day, the boffins have decided that the shoe print on Angela's back was a ten for sure. Definitely not less than a nine." He shook his head and walked away.

At 8:00 that evening he reappeared. "Brock's been on the blower again, Kathy. Big conference down here tomorrow morning to review the case. He'd like to talk to us about it now."

"OK, I'm coming." She closed down the computer and stood up, suddenly aware of the tension across her shoulders again. *I need another swim*, she thought, and then immediately pictured Desai's trim bum in his black briefs. She hoped this wasn't going to become some kind of reflex.

DRIVING UP TO CENTRAL London, Bren suddenly said, "So, what do you get up to on your time off, Kathy?"

The question took her by surprise. She replied, "Oh, it's amazing how many things there are to do."

"Yeah." His voice held an unfamiliar tone of resentment. "Yeah, I'll bet there are. I envy you, Kathy."

"Really? I thought you had things pretty well sewn up. You've got little kids, haven't you? Don't tell me they're beating you up already?"

"Don't ask, Kathy," he said quietly. "Just don't ask."

Kathy didn't ask.

They passed Ted Griffiths' desk on the way to Brock's office, and Kathy noticed with a shock that the rampart of family portraits had gone: the desktop was completely clear. She pointed it out to Bren, who didn't look surprised.

Brock was brusque in his acknowledgement of them, his own desk heaped with documents. He waved them to seats, then pulled a bottle of Scotch out of a desk drawer, and three small glasses, which he filled and passed to them without a word.

They sipped in silence, then Brock growled, "There are people, and sometimes I am one of them, who think that I'm getting too old for this. There are also people who, for reasons of their own, would like to see changes in the way we work. Their favourite phrases are *operational autonomy*, which is accountant-speak for giving less resources to operational units like us, and *operational accountability*, which means greater control from above. I find myself increasingly unable to be civil with these people, which probably proves that I am senile.

"Anyway," he sighed, and topped up their glasses, "the point is that we can't afford any more mistakes. Do you see? Ted has agreed that he'd be more comfortable in another place, and he's now out of it. Which may put more on your shoulders. I'm sorry."

Kathy saw that he was looking at Bren as he said this.

"I want you to go home, have a bath, a few drinks, and awake refreshed on the morrow, ready for a complete review of the case. Unfortunately we'll have some observers. That's operational accountability. Their time will be billed to our budget—that's operational autonomy."

KATHY WAS SURPRISED TO find her aunt still up when she got back.

"I'll make you a nice cup of tea," the old lady said. "You look quite worn out."

"Thanks, I am." Kathy sank into a chair. "How did you get on today?"

"Oh, grand. I went out."

"Did you? That's good. Where did you go?"

She had been to the Imperial War Museum.

"The *what*? I thought . . . well, we talked about Madame Tussaud's, or the Tower . . ." Kathy took a deep breath. "Well . . . what was it like, the Imperial War Museum?"

"Oh, grand. Very nice, love," Aunt Mary replied vaguely, and wandered out to the kitchenette.

Grand? Very nice? It was at this point that Kathy began to consider that her aunt might be suffering from dementia. She wondered how she could find out for sure.

PART TWO

THE VERB TO CORPSE

SEVEN

THE ROOM AT ORPINGTON was crowded, and for the first time Kathy was made aware of how many people were involved in the hunt for Angela's killer. Among them, over to one side and unintroduced, were the two observers.

Brock sketched a summary of the case so far, of the frustrating absence of the murder weapon and the shortage of forensic or any other kind of leads. He discussed the possibility of Gentle's guilt, especially in the light of a psychological profile of Angela Hannaford's attacker which had now been prepared by a consultant psychologist. This profile was so much at variance with what they knew of Gentle that he was forced to conclude that, regrettably, it didn't seem plausible to inflate him from sleaze to murderer. This was the first time that Kathy had heard Brock's opinion of Gentle after he had interviewed him for himself, and his verdict, the opposite of her own advice to him, gave her a jolt of disappointment. She wanted to ask just how much reliance could be put on the psychologist's report, but decided to keep her mouth shut.

Brock then returned to the savagery and apparent randomness of the crime. It was this that, for him, lay at the heart of the matter.

Was it conceivable that such an act could just burst upon the world without warning or precedent? He was convinced not. So where were the earlier steps which had led to 32 Birchgrove Avenue? He asked Bren to take over.

"There are no current serial sexual murder investigations that Angela's death can be readily connected to," he began. He didn't look as if a night's sleep had done him much good. "In other words, if this is part of a series, it's one that hasn't been identified previously. It's possible that it is the first murder in what has previously been a series of rapes, but again, although there are quite a few of those on the books, the extreme violence in this case, and the absence of DNA evidence, makes it difficult to establish any connection to a known rape series."

Bren cleared his throat. "That takes us to past unsolved murders that were assumed to be isolated, and the possibility that one or more may have been the work of our man. We've identified four within the past twelve months or so that we think are worth reopening. I'll go through them backward . . . in time . . ."

Bren stopped fumbling with the words and took a drink from a glass of water on the lectern at the front. ". . . In reverse chronological order. The most recent, three months ago, and not much more than five miles away as the crow flies from either Petts Wood or Orpington stations, seems the most likely. You'll remember it, I'm sure. On the evening of Saturday June 9 last, a seventeen-year-old, Carole Weeks from Croydon, was raped and strangled in Spring Park, West Wickham. At least that's where she was found the next morning."

Bren paused and pinned a photograph of a young woman, blonde hair, happy smile, on the board behind him. "There were some odd features of the case. Carole was found with her tights removed, rolled up in a ball and stuffed into her mouth. Her handbag was by her side, but her shoes were missing. That same Saturday night another girl was attacked near another park,

Langley Park, a mile to the north. She managed to get away from her attacker, and a search was made of the area, without result. She gave a description of a bearded man with an odd smell, which was never identified. Carole's attacker used a condom, and left insufficient material for either a blood group or a DNA profile to be established, although the make of condom was established from the lubricant traces. Quite a lot was made of that in the press, if you remember. We've now established that it was the same make used in the Angela Hannaford murder. The cord used to strangle Carole Weeks wasn't recovered."

Bren took a deep breath. "So, that's Carole from Croydon. A sexual murder, like Angela. Same type of condom. Something odd about the way her mouth was left stuffed open. Not far from here, and very recent."

"A Saturday night too," someone called out. Someone else followed with, "And she was a blonde."

"Yes, right, a fair-haired woman on a Saturday night. On the other hand, a very different weapon and setting, and nothing like the mutilation of the body. Still, much the most likely connection, we think.

"Now, working backward, the next is a missing person, Zoë Bagnall, who disappeared last January." A second photograph went up, brunette, older than the first.

"She was a divorced lady, forty-two, living alone in a flat near Shortlands station in Bromley, again very close to here. The reason for our interest in her is that we initially thought she was one of the women in Gentle's portrait gallery. However, when we showed the picture to her old mum, who lives in Barnet, she said it definitely wasn't Zoë, and I suppose she should know. The other reason for doubting that it is the same woman is that, although she lived close to Gentle's route, she worked in Pimlico and commuted on the Victoria line, not the Charing Cross–Blackfriars line that he uses, so it's unlikely he would have come across her.

"Zoë from Shortlands, then. A longer shot, especially since we don't know she's dead."

"What day of the week did she disappear?" the voice called out.

Bren consulted his notes. "Not sure. Last seen at a party on Saturday the twentieth, but not reported until Wednesday, January 24.

"Next is also a long shot. Kirstie McFadden, last August, murdered in Edinburgh."

There was a murmur of surprise at the geographical leap four hundred miles to the north. The photograph showed a peroxide blonde with heavy eye make-up.

"The connection here is a footprint at the murder scene, a size nine Doc Martens, and the only correlation we've been able to make from DS Desai's discovery. We haven't been able to establish that it's the same shoe, only that it's the same pattern and a similar size to what Angela's attacker is thought to have worn. The other interesting feature is the brutality of the attack. Kirstie was killed by repeated stabbing blows to her eyes, probably with a screwdriver, which has never been found."

Bren studied his notes again and added, looking in the direction of the voice from his audience, "This one was a Friday, August 25."

He paused and pinned up a fourth portrait. "The previous month, but back in South London again, we have the unsolved murder of Janice Pearce at her flat near Blackheath, some time between the evening of Tuesday July 4 and Wednesday July 5. This is the only unsolved murder of a woman commuter on Gentle's line, in her case from St. John's station up to London Bridge. On the other hand, she doesn't figure among Gentle's photos, there was no sexual assault involved, and no mutilation. She was strangled, probably with a pair of her own tights."

Bren looked across at Brock, who nodded and got back on his feet.

"We'll concentrate on the murder of Carole Weeks. Assume that both she and Angela Hannaford were killed by the same man. We're looking for connections between the two cases, things that contrast, things that seem the same. We're working on the basis that the pattern of a series can tell us things that each individual case cannot. Unfortunately, a series of two is not a very strong one, but still, we must be alert for connections.

"It would be nice to find connections also with the other three cases, but they seem much less likely. Nevertheless, we'll reopen them all, have a fresh look."

In the following discussion, most people seemed interested in pursuing the case of Kirstie McFadden in Edinburgh, for reasons which didn't seem to have much to do with detection, but had more, Kathy guessed, to do with the chance of getting away from home. She herself was disappointed to be allotted the missing Zoë Bagnall, which seemed to Kathy the least likely of the lot.

THE REST OF THE morning didn't make her feel any happier. She had phoned the number they had for Zoë Bagnall's mother in Barnet, and spoken to a woman who sounded as elderly and vague as Aunt Mary. Of course, the woman had said, come over whenever you like, I'll stay in and wait for you.

Only she hadn't. When Kathy found the house, soon after 11:30, there was no reply to her knock. After several minutes of knocking, a woman's face appeared over the hedge which formed the boundary with the garden of the other half of the semi-detached house.

"She's out, ducks. Can I help?"

"Are you sure? I phoned her an hour ago and she said she'd wait in for me."

"Well, I saw her leave ten minutes back with the little boy."

Kathy swore under her breath. "I don't suppose she said where she was going, did she?"

"I didn't speak to her. But she was pushing her shopping-basket."

"Are they far away, the shops?"

"Depends which ones she went to, ducks."

"Oh, well . . . She'll probably not be long. I'll wait in the car. Thanks."

An hour later, Kathy was wondering what to do. Barnet was on the far side of London from Orpington, and she was reluctant to write off the time it had taken to get there. At 1:00 she decided to have a drive around the local shopping areas. Towards 2:00 she bought herself a sandwich, having seen no sign of an elderly lady with a shopping-basket and a small boy. She returned to the house, and again got no response to her knock. At 2:30 she was drumming the steering-wheel with impatience, about to leave, when she spotted them in the wing mirror, ambling towards her at a snail's pace. The contraption the woman was pushing—a walking-stick handle on a wicker basket mounted on a pair of wheels—reminded Kathy of her aunt, as did the vague look in the woman's eyes when she turned at the garden gate in response to Kathy's call.

"Oh!" Confusion filled the old lady's face. "I'm so sorry. It quite escaped my mind. We had to go to the shops, you see, to meet Big Dog."

"Big Dog," said the little boy, kicking the wheel of the shopping-basket in disgust, "was just a man dressed up. Anybody could see that."

They went inside, put on the kettle, sat the boy in front of the TV and retired to the front lounge, where Zoë's mother kept her collection of photographs. Then they had to get up again and go back through the other rooms, searching for her glasses. When they were finally settled, Kathy gave her the photograph she had brought with her, from Gentle's collection.

"Yes, this is the picture the other officer showed me. It's definitely not our Zoë. See, this one's fair."

"We got a better copy made," Kathy said. "Just to be sure."

"Well, it's not her. Look, here she is on her wedding day, June 6, 1979. Isn't she just lovely?"

A plump brunette beamed at the camera. Kathy nodded. There was little similarity to the blonde in Gentle's picture. It was only the eyes that had deceived someone, making the comparison. The same almost feline character to the eyes. But Zoë's nose was too big, everything about her was too big.

"Do you have anything more recent?"

Her mother's collection of pictures came to an end with the birth of the little boy. After that, it seemed, there had been no one around with a camera.

"That was six years ago," she said. It was the same bride, a little plumper if anything, clutching the baby, his pink eyes lurid from the flash.

"Well, thank you very much. I can see we've made a mistake. We'll let you know if anything else comes up."

Kathy decided to head out to the M25 and take the orbital motorway clockwise. It was a mistake. It was almost 5:00 when she crossed the river into Kent, having inched her way through one huge jam on the M11 approaches, and another at the Dartford Tunnel. Her skin crawled with irritation at the wasted time. In a kind of desperation to justify the day, she turned off at the A20 and headed, not to Orpington, but to Shortlands, where Zoë Bagnall had been living when she disappeared.

The flats were three-storey walk-ups, developed fifteen years before in what had been an old orchard, conveniently located near the station. Kathy started knocking on doors, and at the fourth attempt found a woman in her thirties who had known Zoë.

"You still looking for her, are you?" she said.

"We try to follow up missing-person cases to check they haven't turned up without us being told."

"Not Zoë. Not as far as I know. They took all her stuff back to her mother's. She lives in Barnet. I've got the address somewhere."

"That's all right," Kathy said. "We're checking photographs at the moment, getting our records up to date. This isn't Zoë, is it?"

Kathy showed her Gentle's picture, ready for the negative answer.

"Yes," the woman said brightly, "that's her."

"It is? Are you sure?"

"Oh yes. No doubt about it. Look, there's the corner of our flats in the background. She must have been walking home from the station. Who took it?"

"Er, look, can I come in and talk to you about Zoë?"

The woman shrugged. "All right."

The front door opened straight into a compact sitting-room with a view out to the rear yard, largely taken up with car parking for the residents of the flats. In the far corner of the garden a solitary gnarled apple tree had somehow survived from the original orchard.

"The thing is, I showed this picture to Zoë's mother this afternoon, and she said it wasn't her. She showed me pictures of her that didn't look at all like this."

The woman laughed, a throaty, smoker's laugh. "Oh, Zoë changed a lot after her divorce. She turned blonde, had her hair cut short, and lost at least two stone, maybe three. And she had her nose done. She said that was the best thing she ever screwed out of her ex. I don't think her mum liked the new Zoë. I think she preferred to think it wasn't happening. Leastwise, that was my impression."

"I see. Do you know how Zoë came to be living here in the first place?" Kathy said.

"It was when she and her husband split up. She knew someone who was living down here, and when a flat came free she took it. That would have been about three years ago, I reckon."

"What did she do with her little boy, when she was at work?"

"Yeah, well, he went to live with his gran, didn't he? I mean, tenants here aren't supposed to have kiddies, and she was out at work all day, so she asked her mum to look after him. It was meant to be temporary, but you know . . ." The woman shrugged.

Like other cities that have grown suburbs in all directions, the development of London resembles a series of concentric rings, the age of buildings within each ring being roughly the same, right around the circle. It occurred to Kathy that Zoë had chosen to live in the same ring as her mother, but on the opposite side, as far distant as she could be.

"She just got caught up in things here. She didn't have much time to look after the little one."

"Is there much to do around here, then?"

"Oh, you'd be surprised. She had a great social life. She was completely caught up in the theatre."

"The theatre? That's interesting. I don't remember it being in her file."

"Yeah. Amateur theatre. She was mad about it. She was an actress. That's all she cared about, really. The next play—and the next leading man." She smirked.

"Did she go up to town to see plays, do you know?"

The woman thought. "Yeah, I think so."

"About the time she disappeared? The National Theatre, say, something like that?"

"Oh, I don't know. I wouldn't have thought so, 'cos she was in the middle of one of her productions, and she never had time for anything else when they were on. That's why I didn't realize she was missing at the time, 'cos when she was in a play you wouldn't see her from one week to the next. I can't remember the dates now, but it would be in my original statements to the detectives."

Kathy nodded. "Right. Do you remember her ever mentioning a trip to the National Theatre?"

"Sorry, not that I can recall."

"That's OK."

"I suppose her acting friends would know. She was in at least two different amateur groups, I think, but I wouldn't know their names or anything. I remember the play she was doing at the time was supposed to be on board a train, 'cos I went to see her in it." She wrinkled her nose, thinking. "Only I can't think what it was called. They put it on at the Shortland Rep, just round the corner. Her boyfriend would know more about it. He was in the same play—they were starring together."

"I don't remember a boyfriend being mentioned on the file, either," Kathy said, puzzled. Zoë had been last seen at a party in Bromley.

"Probably not. He's married, see. Probably wanted to keep his head down."

"Do you remember his name?"

"Sorry, we were never introduced. Zoë kept her love life pretty private."

Kathy showed her the photograph of Gentle. "Ever seen him before?"

"No, sorry. Don't recognize him at all."

KATHY FOLLOWED THE WOMAN'S directions to the Shortland Repertory Theatre, tucked a couple of blocks away on a side street. The 1950s red-brick façade looked too utilitarian for a place dedicated to illusion and fantasy, but the curling posters crowded inside the notice cases on each side of the heavy timber doors all advertised theatrical productions. She went up the steps and tried the doors, which proved to be locked.

Kathy looked at her watch and decided to leave it for that evening. Her encounter with Zoë's mother had made her uneasy about the long periods that she was leaving Aunt Mary on her own.

She was relieved to find the old lady safely busy in the kitchen when she got home, making macaroni cheese for their dinner.

"You said you liked Italian food, dear," Aunt Mary said.

"Oh . . . right. It smells lovely. Did you get out at all today?" Kathy crossed her fingers behind her back.

"No dear, not today. Maybe tomorrow."

Kathy sighed. She wondered if she'd ever get used to Mrs. P's folding bed, and the sound of Aunt Mary's dry cough coming softly through the bedroom door all through the night.

EIGHT

THE NEXT MORNING KATHY returned to the theatre in Shortlands. The solid timber doors had been folded back to expose an inner pair of glass doors, locked, but revealing the glow of a light over to one side of the dim interior. Kathy tapped her keys on the glass.

After a moment a woman's face appeared on the other side. There was a clicking of metal, and then one door swung open.

"We are closed." She raised her eyebrows at the warrant card that Kathy showed her. "What's it about?"

"I need some information from you. It shouldn't take long. I'm wanting to contact an amateur acting group that put on a production here in this theatre last January."

The woman nodded. "Come in then." She locked the door again behind Kathy and led the way across a dim foyer to the ticket office window from which the light was glowing. "Wait here," she said, and disappeared through a side door. The whole place was deathly quiet, with the air of suspended life that civic buildings have when the public has gone. There was a distinctive smell too, of polish and old musty fabric. After a moment the woman reappeared on the other side of the ticket-office window carrying a large ledger.

"What date was it?"

"Around January the twentieth."

"That was the last night of a production by SADOS. Would that be it?"

"Could be. What was the name again?"

"Shortland Amateur Dramatic and Operatic Society—SADOS. I've got a telephone contact number here if you want it."

"Thanks, that would be great. Do you know them yourself?"

"Not really. I haven't been doing this long. The number is for the club's secretary, Ruth Sparkes."

Kathy wrote down the details. "Thanks."

"*The Lady Vanishes,*" the woman said.

"What did you say?" Kathy looked at her in surprise.

"That was the play they put on, *The Lady Vanishes*. That's what it says here, anyway." She saw the expression on Kathy's face. "What's the matter? Is something wrong?"

KATHY DROVE BACK TO Orpington and walked into the incident room. She was surprised to find it crowded with people.

"What's going on?" she asked one of the local detectives.

"Something on the Carole Weeks case. Bren's called a briefing."

Bren had been assigned the case of the girl murdered in Spring Park, and given the biggest team. The door to one of the side offices opened, and he came out, followed by Desai, Munns, and finally Brock, who hung back and perched on the corner of a table. He gazed around the room, his expression benign.

"Right." Bren looked as if he'd been given an energy boost. "We seem to be getting somewhere. Most of you know that we spent quite a bit of time yesterday with the girl who was attacked in Langley Park on the same night that Carole Weeks was murdered in Spring Park, a mile to the south. We made progress with her over the computer enhancement of the picture of her attacker's face."

Bren pointed to a colour print taped to the wall behind him, of a black-haired, bearded man, glaring at his audience beneath bushy eyebrows.

"There are copies here, and details of a revised physical description." Bren nodded, as if to himself. This all seemed to be merely a preliminary, the big story held back.

"After interviewing her here, we took her up to Lambeth, to MPFSL, for a detailed physical examination. You'll remember in her statement that she described a man jumping out of the bushes on the edge of the park and rushing her, knocking her to the ground and stamping on her left upper arm when she tried to push herself upright. He then started dragging her back towards the bushes, when a car came round the corner from Ravenswood Chase towards them, and slowed down. That's when the girl managed to break free and run out into the street.

"At the time of her physical examination after the attack, the doctor noted a large bruise covering her left upper arm as a result of the man stamping on her, as you might expect. That was about as much as anybody could say at that stage. However, Morris Munns has performed his usual miracle, and he has something very interesting for us. Morris."

Bren turned and waved to the photographer, who blushed, bobbed his head, and shuffled forward. His obvious shyness at having to address the group was engaging in someone who was probably the most senior man in the room, apart from Brock, and it provoked a number of remarks, generally intended to be encouraging.

"Well, what 'appens," he began, adjusting his thick glasses and scratching his nose, "when a body 'eals itself after an injury, there are a number of biochemical compounds introduced into the flesh as part of the natural 'ealing process, see."

"Oooh." Mock amazement registered around the room. Morris flushed, adjusted his specs, and waded gamely on. "These compounds affect the amount of ultraviolet light that's absorbed or reflected, like, by the flesh at that point. And if you photograph the injury site under UV light, you can record these variations."

"But Morris," someone objected, "this happened three months ago."

"The effect can last for six months," Morris replied. "There might be no sign of any bruising left on the skin at all, but underneath there's this invisible chemical record of the thing that caused the injury."

They were impressed, and silent now.

"It's important, like, to photograph the victim in exactly the same position as she was in when the injury 'appened, if at all possible."

"Show them, Morris," Bren prompted, and the photographer gave his shy smile and produced an enlarged photograph from his file. It was a perfect image of a large red heel print on a pink background.

"Doc Martens," Morris said. "Size nine."

A cheer broke out from the gathering as he shuffled back to the rear of the group, head bowed in bashful pleasure.

Kathy was interested to notice that Bren, grinning, now nodded to Desai to step forward, without any sign of his previous animosity. It seemed that team spirit was breaking out all over.

"Just to add," Desai said, "that the image is so good that we can definitely identify it as belonging to the same right heel that kicked Angela Hannaford in the back. There are at least three distinguishing detailed features of damage and wear common to both, the most distinctive being this nick in the second of the parallel strips that run across the centre part of the heel print. There is also the strong possibility that this new image can be matched to the Edinburgh footprints, at least from what we can make out on the copies they've sent down."

"Exactly," Bren said. "So Leon and Morris are going to fly up there today to check on that. This means we now know what our man looks like, what he wears on his feet, and we have three—possibly four—sites where he has operated. All that remains is to pick him up."

"What about the smell the girl noticed?" someone asked.

"Yes. Who was following that up?"

"Me, Sarge." A young detective got to his feet. "I spoke to Bromley CID about it. They set up tests to cover everything they could think of at the time. They tried every kind of soap and perfume and deodorant. They tried washpowders, hair oils, industrial solvents. They had the lady sniffing at assortments of sweaty T-shirts and jock straps from the gym."

A ripple of appreciative laughter went round the room.

"But it was no good. The best she could say was that it seemed a bit like some kind of cough linctus, mixed up with something else."

Bren nodded. "Well, let's concentrate on what we do know." He began to outline tasks relating to the search for the source of the shoes and for publicizing the killer's appearance, concentrating on an area within a five-mile radius of Hayes station, which lay roughly at the centre of the triangle of the three South London sites. "There's going to be a lot of publicity with this now. A serial killer active in the suburbs. DCI Brock will be holding a press conference later this morning. Do you want to add anything, sir?"

Brock shook his head.

"Questions? All right, let's go."

As the meeting broke up, Kathy struggled across the crowded room towards Brock, who, head bowed, was listening to something from Bren.

"Sir!" she called as he turned to leave.

He looked back. "Kathy, we wondered where you were. Come through, will you?"

She followed him, Desai, and Bren into a small, cluttered office.

"Well done." Kathy beamed at Desai. "That was brilliant."

He shrugged off her praise. "Morris's work entirely."

"Kathy," Brock said, as they sat round the small table. "We've decided that we can drop the Bagnall and Pearce inquiries now. They seem to be dead-ends. We need to put everything into this link with the Carole Weeks murder and, if Morris and Leon confirm it, the Edinburgh case. I'd like you to do as you did with Angela Hannaford, get to know all about Carole's background, her personality, and so on."

"Brock . . ." Kathy hesitated. The solidity of the evidence that Morris Munns had produced made her own discovery seem painfully tenuous by comparison. "I think I may have found a link between Zoë Bagnall and Angela Hannaford."

"Have you now? What kind of link?"

"Well, first, she *is* the girl in Gentle's photograph. That's been confirmed by a friend of hers in the flats where she lived, in Shortlands. She'd changed her appearance since she divorced and moved to South London, and her mother seems to have been confused."

"Two possible murdered women among Gentle's collection of seventy-three," Bren muttered. "I wonder what the odds are on that? It would be a lot stronger, of course, if we knew for sure that Zoë Bagnall is actually dead, and isn't just living on a Greek island with some guy who owns a bar."

"Yes," Kathy had to agree.

"Go on," Brock said. "You've got more for us, Kathy?"

"Well, Zoë was a blonde at the time of her disappearance, which means that all five of the women we've considered were fair— if that's significant. Also, it seems that Zoë was interested in the theatre. In fact, like Angela, she probably had been at the theatre on the night she disappeared."

Brock looked up sharply. "Really? That is interesting. The National Theatre?"

"Well, no. I haven't been able to get all the information yet, but she was probably acting in an amateur show at a theatre in Shortlands that night, just near where she lived."

"Mmm . . ." Brock looked up at the ceiling, tugging his beard as he tended to do when he was thinking, rather as if he was absent-mindedly stroking a pet dog. "So, you're wondering if our killer is a theatre buff, and went to a local show that night, rather than up to town. Saw Zoë on stage and decided to have her."

Kathy nodded.

"Anything else?"

Kathy wondered whether to mention the name of the play that Zoë had been in. She was aware of Leon Desai and Morris Munns glancing at their watches, working out their timing to the airport, and Bren wanting to get on with his team.

"Not really."

"No chance that Carole Weeks or the Edinburgh victim might be among Gentle's photographs?"

"No," Bren answered. "We've been through them all again. I don't think there's any possibility of a second mistaken identity."

"Well, it's intriguing," Brock said. "But I think you're wrong, Kathy."

"Why?"

"What bothers me is that the primary link between Angela and Zoë—the thing that led you to this theatre connection—is Gentle and his photographs. But, as I said just now, the more we learn about the killer, the less likely does Gentle seem as a suspect. He doesn't remotely fit the profile—wrong age, wrong interests, wrong socioeconomic group, wrong family history. Frankly, I simply can't see him as the murderer of either of those two women. Then there's the shoe size, and the physical description—even granted the unreliability of eyewitness descriptions. But for me the clincher is the brutality in each case, the sheer violent indulgence, stamping on them, raping them, hacking Angela's face off . . . I simply can't see Gentle doing that. He's a creep, not a savage.

"Now, if he isn't the killer, then his photograph collection, and all the leads that flow from it, are just so many red herrings. Isn't that right?"

"I . . . I suppose so," Kathy conceded.

"I have to go." Brock got to his feet. "I'll leave it to you, Kathy. If you feel strongly enough about it, stick with it for a day or two more. It's not as if Bren's going to be short of manpower. But I honestly think you'd be better sticking to the main game."

Kathy nodded, and he left the room. When he was gone, Bren said quietly, "He's right, Kathy. Come in with us. We're going to nail the bastard, soon. I'd like you to be a part of it."

"Thanks, Bren." She hesitated. "It just seemed too good to ignore, that coincidence with the theatre. But I suppose he's right."

"Look, tell you what. I'd really appreciate your assessment of the character of the girl in the park, Carole Weeks," Bren urged her. "Why don't you have a look at the file, maybe go out and talk to her mum in Croydon, friends at school. You never know—she might have been a theatre-goer too."

Kathy nodded. "Yes, OK, I'll do that."

"Good. Now, we've all got to get going."

For a while Kathy stayed in her seat reading the file on Carole Weeks, aware of the sounds diminishing around her, until the whole building was silent. There was no hint from the reports that the girl had had any interest in the theatre. Kathy rang and made an appointment to see her mother, then dialled the number she'd been given for the secretary of SADOS, Mrs. Ruth Sparkes.

She sounded an intelligent woman, retired, as she explained, and hence at home during the day. Kathy explained that she was following up Zoë's disappearance, and wanted to get more information on her movements in the weeks before her disappearance.

"Did she visit any other theatres, do you know? In central London, for example?"

"Not that I know of, Sergeant."

"Not the National Theatre?"

"No, I really don't think so. We do sometimes book a group outing to the National or the Old Vic, but I'm pretty sure there was nothing at the beginning of this year. I could check, if you like."

"Please, I'd appreciate that. Also, I wanted to speak to her boyfriend."

"Boyfriend?" The voice was suddenly cautious.

"Yes. I understand she was having an affair with one of the other men in the cast of the play they were doing."

Silence.

"Hello?"

"Yes . . . I wonder where you heard that?"

"Isn't it true? I understand the man was married at the time."

"Ah . . . Oh dear, there's someone at the front door. Could I get back to you, Sergeant? If you'll give me your number . . ."

Reluctantly Kathy let her go, then left to keep her appointment with Carole Weeks' mother. Carole had been still at school, an athletic girl, keen on swimming and tennis. The woman assured Kathy that her daughter hadn't been anywhere near a theatre during the year before she was killed. The headmistress and the drama teachers at her school confirmed the same thing, as did her closest school friends. None of them recognized Tom Gentle's face.

LATER THAT AFTERNOON KATHY took a call from someone called Edward Quinn. "Ruth Sparkes got in touch with me," he said. "Suggested I ring you."

The line was bad, the sound of an engine revving in the background.

"You knew Zoë Bagnall, Mr. Quinn?"

"That's right. We were both in the cast of *The Lady Vanishes*. Ruth said . . ."

His voice was drowned out by a roaring noise.

"I'd like to meet you, Mr. Quinn."

"I'm half-way up the M6 at present. At a service station."

"Will you be at home tonight?"

"No! No . . . Look, I'll be at rehearsals tonight. We could meet there if you like. We hire an upstairs room at the Three Crowns, on the Beckenham Road."

"Yes, all right, I can meet you there. What time?"

"I'll wait for you downstairs in the saloon bar at 7:00."

"OK. What do you look like?"

"Pretty nondescript really. How about you?"

"Five six, short fair hair."

"Fine. See you then."

Kathy wrote some notes for Bren on what she had done in connection with Carole Weeks, then phoned her flat to check on Aunt Mary. There was some confusion until her aunt understood that it was Kathy on the line, not someone else trying to contact her.

"I'm sorry, I'm going to be late home again, Aunt Mary. Will you be all right on your own?"

"Of course, dear," the voice came vaguely back. "I'll keep your dinner till you get home."

"No, don't bother, please. I'll get something in the canteen here."

"But it's something special, dear. A surprise."

"Oh . . . well, that's lovely. I'll get back as soon as I can, but it may be nine."

NINE

KATHY SPOTTED HIM STRAIGHT away, nondescript as he had claimed, sitting alone at a corner table in the saloon bar reading a well-thumbed paperback. She went first to the bar and bought herself a lime soda, watching him while she waited to be served. He was frowning at the book as if he was struggling with it, and it was several minutes before he looked up and noticed her. He gave a tentative little wave and she smiled at him, pocketed her change, and went over to his table.

"Mr. Quinn? I'm DS Kathy Kolla."

"Hello. Sit down, please." Mid-forties, bit overweight, tired from a day on the road.

"Ruth Sparkes got in touch with you, then," Kathy began.

"Yes. She said you wanted to speak to me about Zoë." He looked at his watch. "I've got about fifteen minutes before I'm needed upstairs. Stafford, our producer, is not happy with people who are late for his rehearsals." He gave an apologetic little smile.

Kathy nodded at the paperback. "Is that the play you're doing?"

"*The Father*, yes. Know it?"

Kathy shook her head.

"Not exactly a bundle of laughs," he said.

"Have you got a big part?"

He nodded. "With lots of lines, unfortunately, which I should have learned ages ago. Anyway, what about Zoë? Have you discovered something? Is there any news?"

"No, I'm afraid not. We're reviewing a number of cases at present. She's one of them."

"Why come to me?"

"We've only just learned that you were lovers."

He frowned at his book but said nothing.

"I couldn't help wondering why that didn't come out at the time."

"We weren't any more, not at that stage. It was over." He sounded weary.

"Tell me about it."

"Oh . . ." He sighed. "Look, it isn't relevant, believe me."

He caught the look on her face and shrugged. "All right. But I'll need another one of these." He pointed at his glass. "How about you?"

Kathy shook her head and waited while he took the empty half-pint glass up to the bar and returned with a full pint one. While he was away she turned over the opening pages of his book and began to read the introduction.

The Father, A Tragedy in Three Acts, 1887.

Strindberg wrote this play at the time when his marriage with Siri von Essen was finally breaking up. Much of the torment of those unhappy years has gone into it; though, as always, a great deal of the suffering was bred out of Strindberg's own dark imaginings.

"We started rehearsals for *The Lady Vanishes* late October or early November last year," Quinn said, settling back into his place. "Do you remember the Hitchcock film?"

"I'm not sure. Who was in it?"

"Margaret Lockwood and Michael Redgrave—those were the

parts Zoë and I played. It's about an old lady who mysteriously disappears on a train journey across Europe in the late thirties. Anyway, that doesn't matter, except that Zoë and I were in it, and we were having an affair at the time we started rehearsing. We reckoned it would give us opportunities to see more of each other, of course. But as the weeks went by it turned into one of those messy situations."

"In what way?"

"Well . . . I think, in point of fact, that the thing had run its course by the time we started on *The Lady*, only we didn't realize it at the time. Zoë was getting impatient with the precautions I had to go through to avoid my wife finding out about us, and I was beginning to wonder if it was all worth the trouble. Then, towards Christmas, my wife did finally discover what was going on." He winced. "Which was ironic really, because Zoë had just let me know that she was now interested in someone else."

"Who?"

"I've no idea. She didn't elaborate. Anyway, we were left in the impossible position of having to continue rehearsing and finally performing on stage together, even though we now found it embarrassing to be together, and family dramas were raging all around us. It was the Christmas holidays, I mean . . . can you imagine?"

"Your wife let you go on with the play?"

"Sergeant, you obviously haven't met Stafford Nesbit, our producer. He would never let some trivial domestic life-and-death problem get in the way of one of his productions. By that stage, if I dropped out, the whole thing would fold—we don't have understudies, and it was too late for someone else to learn the part. So he persuaded her that it would be best to let me continue. God knows how he did it, but she agreed, and we decided to patch things up."

Edward Quinn gave a grim little smile. "It was pretty gruesome.

We had six performances in the theatre—technical dress rehearsal, dress rehearsal, and four public performances from Wednesday through to Saturday, and my wife came to every one. Every moment I was on stage with Zoë I was conscious of Rosemary out there in the audience, watching. It was a great relief when we got to the end of that week, believe me. We went to the party after the final show, but it was just for the sake of Rosemary putting on a front. We didn't stay long. That would have been the last time I saw Zoë, although I didn't say a word to her there, not with Rosemary at my side every inch of the way."

"Was Zoë with anyone at the party?"

"No, it was just a general celebratory booze-up for the cast and their partners. I think you lot established that she didn't stay long either—got a lift home with a couple who were leaving early."

"Yes, they were the last people we were able to find who had seen her."

"But it took the best part of a week to discover that, didn't it? It was only when the people at her work started ringing her mother . . ."

"You say you found it embarrassing to be in Zoë's company. Was it more than that? Did you come to hate her, perhaps, going off with someone else?"

Quinn shook his head wearily. "No, no. Nothing like that. I suppose she was my mid-life crisis. When I first fell for her she seemed exciting, glamorous. But we were completely wrong for each other. She needed someone to give her a good time, and to be honest, I just didn't have the stamina. Not any more. I was relieved when she said she'd got someone else, dead relieved."

"What was your reaction, when it seemed she'd disappeared?"

Quinn hesitated, taking a sip of beer. "I'll tell you what I thought. I thought that that was exactly what Zoë would do. She decides to run off with some bloke, so instead of telling people in the normal way, she says nothing, goes through her performances in *The Lady*

Vanishes, and then promptly vanishes herself. Melodramatic, see? That was her. It was her way of making a big exit."

"Is that likely? What about the man, did you ever meet him?"

"No. I was curious—we all were. But I don't think she showed him off to any of us in the society."

"Did you have any ideas about him?"

"Married, if she stuck to form. Rich, if she thought him worth running away with. Someone who didn't want her kid tagging along."

"You think she would have abandoned her little boy?"

"Well, she probably didn't think past a month or two. Probably told herself she'd come back for him when the time was ripe. Her mum could cope."

"And you're sure you never saw her with anyone? Wouldn't he have come to see her in the play?"

He shrugged. "If he did, she never let on."

Kathy reached in her bag for Gentle's picture. "Ever seen this man before?"

Quinn peered at it. Kathy wondered if he needed glasses and wasn't doing anything about it.

"No. Don't know him. Is he Zoë's boyfriend?"

Kathy shook her head. "It's just someone we're checking on. There's probably no connection. You're sure you wouldn't have seen this man in the audience for your play?"

"I was in the cast—you don't see the audience. They're just a terrifying presence out there in the darkness. You'd be better to ask someone doing front-of-house, you know, tickets or refreshments. Ruth perhaps. She's upstairs with the others. Why don't you come up and ask her?"

"Right."

"One thing." Quinn paused as they were getting to their feet. "The thing between me and Zoë . . . my wife's still pretty prickly about it. You're not going to have to resurrect it, are you?"

He looked at her sheepishly. Kathy wondered what sort of actor he was on the stage. He didn't seem to be much good in real life.

He led the way to the door of the saloon bar and up a flight of carpeted stairs. At the top he pushed through a pair of doors into a large function room and was welcomed by a loud cry of "At bloody last!"

The room had a bare timber floor and was almost unfurnished, apart from a number of old bentwood chairs and one small table behind which the man with the voice was standing. Two women were poised alone in the centre of the room, and half a dozen other people sat around the perimeter, watching.

"Sorry, Stafford. Have you reached me, then?"

"We have indeed, Edward. While you were downstairs in the bar, doing whatever you were doing"—he looked pointedly at Kathy—"we reached you."

Stafford Nesbit seemed to Kathy exactly what a theatrical producer should be, tall, gaunt, expressively featured with hollow cheeks and temples, and punctuating each phrase with flourishes of his extended claw-like fingers. The long locks of hair which swept back from his skull and the thin beard clinging to his chin were grey, an elderly lion's head on a stork's body.

"This is a detective sergeant from Scotland Yard, Stafford. She's following up Zoë's case."

The producer froze, staring at Kathy with surprise. In the instant that their eyes met, Kathy felt almost as if he recognized her, or had been expecting her.

"DS Kathy Kolla, sir," she said, and he replied, after a dramatic pause, "Well, yes. Kathy Kolla." Then he roused himself and gave her a little stiff bow. "And I am Stafford Nesbit. Do you wish to address us? Do you have news of Zoë?"

"No, I'm afraid not, sir. I would like to have a word with your secretary, Ruth Sparkes, if she's here."

"She is presently in the ladies'. Please take a seat, she won't be long, I'm sure. Is it all right for us to continue, then? Good. We are at the bottom of page forty-nine, Edward, your scene with the nurse."

"Right, Stafford." Quinn hurried round the edge of the room turning the pages of his book, slipped off his jacket and threw it on to a chair, ran his fingers through his hair, took a deep breath, and then stepped forward into the centre of the space.

"*Are you still up?*" he said to the older of the two women. The other, a stocky girl with short blonde hair, walked away and sat down, eyeing Kathy with a frown. Kathy thought there was something familiar about her, but couldn't place it.

"*Go to bed.*"

"Two things, Edward." Stafford Nesbit stopped him with a tone of exaggerated forbearance. "Where has the Captain just come from, might one inquire?"

"He's been out all evening with his orderly, Stafford."

"Exactly. Then one does rather tend to wonder how he managed to enter the sitting-room from stage left, which is the door from the other rooms of the house, instead of downstage right, which is the door from the outside hall."

Edward seemed untroubled by the producer's sarcasm. "Oh yes. Sorry. Wasn't thinking. The other thing?"

"What is that"—he pointed his long forefinger—"in your hand?"

"The book, Stafford."

"But we were supposed to get rid of our books two weeks ago, weren't we?"

Quinn shrugged. "I'm nearly there. I'm still a bit weak on act two."

Nesbit sighed theatrically, and turned as the doors opened and a woman came into the room. "Ruth. This is Detective Sergeant Kathy Kolla, and she wants to speak to you."

"Ah yes, of course." The woman flashed a smile at Kathy.

"You knew?" Nesbit snapped, with exaggerated pique. "You knew she was coming? What *is* going on here? Am I the only one who wasn't informed?"

"Of course not, Stafford," she replied briskly, clearly used to his tantrums. "Sergeant Kolla phoned me this afternoon . . ."

Her words were cut off by Nesbit, who swept his arm in a wide curve. "No matter! Let's get on for pity's sake. We're going to be here all night at this rate."

The woman smiled at Kathy and sat down beside her. "Hello," she whispered, while Edward Quinn started his scene again. "Did you get what you wanted from Edward?" Her eyes sparkled bright and inquisitive through her wire-rimmed glasses.

"I'm not sure, Mrs. Sparkes."

"Ruth, please."

"Ruth. Were you at the party they had to celebrate the last performance of *The Lady Vanishes*, last January?"

"Yes, of course." She glanced up at Nesbit, who was glaring at them pointedly. "Look, let's go over to the corner. We can talk more easily there."

They moved out of earshot of the others, and Ruth gave Kathy her version of what had happened during the final rehearsals and the performances of *The Lady*, which corresponded well enough with Quinn's account.

"It must have been pretty painful," Kathy said. "Especially for Edward's wife."

"I'm afraid it isn't an uncommon feature of amateur theatre," Ruth said, with some relish. "There is a sense of . . . bonding, I suppose, with fellow-actors in the excitement of it all, perhaps of normal rules suspended . . . which leads to accidents. Remember poor Simone Signoret in *Room at the Top* . . . And sometimes they aren't accidents."

"How do you mean?"

"Well, some people are attracted to the theatre for this very reason. Perhaps Zoë was. And then again, some producers have been known to select their cast with an eye to throwing certain people into each other's arms, so to speak."

"Why?"

"For the sake of the electricity, the excitement it generates."

"Stafford Nesbit?"

Ruth looked across the room at him, gesticulating like a conductor in time to the phrases of the pair rehearsing in front of him. "Oh, I never said that, did I?"

"Is he doing it with this one?"

Ruth laughed. "Well, to tell you the truth, this one could really do with a bit of spicing up. I mean, *The Lady* was fun, but this . . ." She shook her head. "Why Stafford chose this play is beyond me. We were going to do *Blithe Spirit*, which he would have done splendidly, and we'd certainly have got reasonable audiences. But then he decided we should get our teeth into a tragedy, and came up with this. Goodness knows how we'll fill the theatre. I ask you, who in their right mind would put themselves through an evening of gloomy, misogynous rubbish like this?"

Kathy smiled. "You're involved in ticket sales, are you, Ruth?"

"Yes. I'm in charge of all that."

"Would you have a list of the people who bought tickets for *The Lady Vanishes?*"

"Oh dear me no. A few people would have written directly to me for tickets, and I suppose I might still have a record of them, but the great majority of tickets were sold by the cast, or through the theatre box office and at the door on the night."

"I see."

"You look disappointed. Were you after something in particular?"

"Edward mentioned that Zoë had a new boyfriend, and

obviously I'd like to speak to him. I thought he might have come to see her in the play."

"Ah!" Ruth Sparkes nodded. "Yes, no one seemed to know who he was. But I doubt if my records could tell you."

Once more Kathy brought out Gentle's photograph, again without success. "He looks a nice man," Ruth said, a little wistfully. "Rather sad."

"What about the name 'Gentle,' or 'Jordan?' They mean anything to you?"

"Not offhand. Do you want me to check my books when I get home?"

"Yes. I'd appreciate that."

The secretary made a note in her diary. There was another bellow from Stafford Nesbit as she replaced it in her handbag, and she rolled her eyes, turning to watch the players. Quinn, the Captain, was speaking to his old nurse.

"Margret, who was the father of your child?"

"Oh, I've told you time and time again: it was that scamp Johansson."

"Are you sure it was he?"

"You're talking like a child! Of course I'm sure, seeing he was the only one."

"But was he sure he was the only one? No, he couldn't be, even though you were sure. That's the difference, you see."

Stafford Nesbit brought his hand crashing down on to his table. The actors stopped and looked at him.

"Edward, my dear chap, it may come as a shock to learn that Strindberg was not thinking of James Dean when he created the character of the Captain. You are a soldier, a scientist of original opinions, and you are in the process of being driven to the brink of despair and madness by the women who surround you, especially your wife. You can relate to that, can't you?" There was the faintest snigger from some part of the room. "When I asked for *angst*, I

didn't mean the moodiness of a sulky teenager, for God's sake."
Nesbit's voice rose to a roar. "I want *anguish of the soul*!"

Quinn nodded, unfazed.

"Strindberg didn't like women?" Kathy whispered to Ruth.

"In the space of three acts, spanning only twenty-four hours,"
Ruth muttered dryly, "this admirable Captain is reduced from
apparent normality to a gibbering wreck by the fiendish
machinations of the wicked women in his household, and in particular his wife, who encourages his doubts over his paternity of
their daughter. I mean, it isn't just implausible, blatantly sexist
and thoroughly depressing, it's also bad theatre. The whole play
takes place in this one setting, and most of it is in the form of
static dialogues between pairs of characters."

"Oh, I thought it was a classic."

"That too," Ruth sighed. "We're doomed."

"I suppose it'll come right on the night."

"Oh no, this one is going to be a disaster, I know it. Because we'd
agreed to do *Blithe Spirit* this time, we lent all our nineteenth-
century costumes to another group, and now we haven't got a thing,
and the first performance is in two and a half weeks. We're going to
have to hire the men's costumes, but the budget simply won't run to
the women's costumes as well. We're going to have to do those
ourselves, somehow. I don't suppose you know a dressmaker, do you,
Sergeant? I'm absolutely desperate, I really am."

"Sorry." Kathy shook her head. "Anyway, I'd better leave you to
it. Good luck."

Kathy got to her feet. At the door she turned and saw Edward
Quinn give her a little nod. She also noticed the young blonde
woman, who had been rehearsing when they arrived, glare at her,
then look pointedly away. With a jolt Kathy realized where she
had seen her face. She reached into her shoulder bag and pulled
out the sheaf of photocopied pictures of Gentle's women and

thumbed rapidly through them until she found her, subject number sixty-two.

She went over to the girl and asked her to step outside with her. There was another, smaller function room on the other side of the landing, deserted, and Kathy switched on the lights and asked the girl to take a seat at the long banquet table set out down the centre of the room.

"What's your name?" she asked her.

"Bettina," she replied, a bit sullen, "Bettina Elliott. What's this all about, then?"

"I just need a few details, Bettina, then I'll explain. How old are you?"

"Twenty-two."

"Address?"

She gave Kathy an address in Shortlands.

"Do you work in town?"

"No. I work for Bromley Council."

"In Bromley? You don't take a train to work?"

"No, I take the bus. What is all this, anyway?"

Kathy showed her the photocopy of Gentle's picture. "That's you, isn't it?"

Bettina frowned at it, curling her lip. Her skin wasn't very good, Kathy saw, her blonde hair crudely cut and in need of a wash.

"Could be. Where was it taken?"

"I don't know. Can you take a guess? It seems to be through a window, do you see? There's a bit of the frame."

"Ye-es. S'pose so."

"Could it be where you live?"

She shrugged. "It's hard to say, isn't it? I mean, there's not much there."

"No, that's true. Have you ever been aware of anyone following you home? Or anywhere else come to that."

BARRY MAITLAND 144

"Well . . . not recently. Once, when I was at school . . . but that was years ago."

"No, this would be more recent."

Bettina shook her head.

"What about this man? Do you recognize him at all?"

Bettina looked closely at Gentle's picture, then shook her head again.

"Do you know anyone called 'Jordan,' or 'Gentle?' "

"No. Gentle's a funny name, isn't it? Is he a murderer or something?"

"No, no. We just have a list of people that we need to eliminate from our inquiries, you know."

"Oh yeah? But where did you get the picture of me from? Did he have it, this Jordan, or Gentle?"

"Look, this probably isn't significant at all. But just to be on the safe side, Bettina, it'd be a good idea if you took a few extra precautions. Don't open your door to strangers after dark, and try to make sure there's always someone else with you when you go out at night, things like that. Do you live with someone?"

"No."

"Do you have a boyfriend?"

She shook her head. "That's why I joined this lot, isn't it. Only they're all too old." She curled her lip disdainfully.

"Well, as I say, it's probably nothing, but best to be careful."

"You going to give me police protection?" She was being sarcastic, but the thought seemed to appeal to her.

Kathy smiled. "I don't think you're in that much danger. But if you think of anything, or notice anyone following you or paying you particular attention, get on to me straight away, OK? I'll give you my phone number." She wrote on the back of a card and handed it to the girl, who shrugged. "OK. Ta."

The car park of the pub was deserted when Kathy got downstairs, but when she drove her car to the entrance, and waited to turn out into the traffic, she was startled to find a car right behind her. It made her realize how jumpy it had made her, seeing another of Gentle's women.

AS SOON AS SHE opened the door of her flat, Kathy was hit by the smell. Liver. Liver and onions. And other things. Aunt Mary's special.

"You remember, do you, dear?"

"Yes, I remember. I haven't had that since . . . for years."

"It was your favourite."

"Was it?"

That wasn't Kathy's recollection. The small terrace in Atter-cliffe used to reek of it. That and Uncle Tom's foul pipe-tobacco smoke.

"You went out today, then. To the shops."

"Yes, pet. I think I'm beginning to get the hang of them tubes."

"Oh, you used the tube?"

"Aye. To Soho."

"*Soho?* Are you sure?"

"Of course, dear. I know where I went."

"But . . ." *Why?* For a moment Kathy had a bizarre vision of Uncle Tom sending his elderly wife down to comb the sex-shops of London for some exotic thing they couldn't find in Sheffield.

"What on earth made you go there?"

"I was interested."

Interested.

"And what did you think of it?"

"Oh, grand, love. Very nice."

She's a public menace, Kathy thought guiltily. *She probably risks a major traffic accident every time she crosses the street. I've been worrying about the likes of Bettina Elliott when I should have been spending time doing something about this.*

AS THEY SAT AT the table eating their breakfast toast and marmalade the following morning, Kathy said, "I'm sorry I've neglected you since you arrived, Mary." This was the first time she'd ever addressed the older lady without the title "Aunt." It seemed an important small preliminary to getting things straight. Her aunt seemed not to notice, sipping absently at her cup of PG Tips. She had become calmer during her stay, perhaps more withdrawn.

"I've only been in this job two weeks, you see, and I just couldn't take a day off before now, but I've told them I'm not working this weekend, so we can spend time together. Is there anything special you'd like to do? What about the big stores? Shall we go shopping? Mary?"

"Oh . . ." Mary looked out of the window. "Of course, pet, if that's what you'd like to do."

"What about you?"

"Oh, not on my account. There's nothing I want to buy."

It occurred to Kathy that her aunt might be short of money.

"Well, what about the sights, the places we talked about, the Tower . . ."

"It seems too nice a day to be indoors."

Kathy sighed, trying to remain calm.

"If you want to go out," Mary said suddenly, "why don't you pick somewhere you'd really like to go to? I don't have anywhere."

They would have to go *some*where, since the idea of staying at home together, trying to make conversation like this, didn't bear thinking about. For some reason, Kathy thought of the pagoda at Kew, and said they might take a picnic to the Botanical Gardens. "And on the way," she added, "I want to call in at my doctor's."

"Aren't you well, dear?"

"My annual check-up," Kathy lied. "I've made an appointment for us both. She might as well look you over while you're there. See about that cough."

"Oh, not me!" Mary looked affronted. "I have my own doctor at home. Dr. Skinner. I've been going to him for nigh on thirty years."

"When did you last see him?"

"Two weeks ago, as it happens. Kathy, I am not going to see your doctor." She glared at her niece defiantly.

"What did you see Dr. Skinner about?"

"A personal matter," the old lady snapped.

"Sorry." Kathy had only given the idea a fifty-fifty chance. "You're right, it is too nice a day. I'll cancel the appointment and go another time."

The conversation had got Mary more agitated than Kathy had seen her. She began to wonder if her aunt did have something seriously wrong with her health, something she didn't want to discuss. Perhaps this was the reason for the mystery visit.

They bought a roasted chicken and some bread and drinks from the deli round the corner, took the tube down to Embankment, then changed to the District line west to Kew Gardens. There had been no further rain after the previous Saturday, the summer firmly taking hold again in hot, hazy days, refusing to let autumn sneak in. They wandered silently for a while through banks of dense foliage, until they found a seat deep in cool shade in the Berberis Dell.

"This is grand," Mary said softly, and gave a deep sigh. "It always feels so peaceful in a proper garden."

"Yes, it is lovely. I can't think why I've never come here before."

"Oh, but you have, pet. You've been here before. Don't you remember?"

"Sorry?"

The old lady gave another big sigh and closed her eyes. "You used to love going to the Botanical Gardens. We'd take the bus

along Eccleshall Road to the bottom entrance, and walk right up
to the aquarium and budgie house at the top. Your favourite is the
springtime, with the crocuses and daffodils, and I like the summer.
Especially dahlia time. They do a wonderful display of dahlias. And
chrysanths."

Kathy's heart sank. So that was it. Mary didn't even know where
she was. She was thinking they were back in Sheffield together, in
the Botanical Gardens, Kathy a girl of twelve or thirteen. A wave
of sadness overcame her. She wanted to reach out to the small
figure at her side, but couldn't bring herself to do it. She knew the
gesture would feel empty and futile. All those bleak years cooped
up in that grim little house in Attercliffe with that miserable old
sod of a husband, and now her mind had gone. What could Kathy
say?

She began to think of practical things. *I'll have to get her home
straight away, this afternoon. The train, or car up the M1? And
who'll look after her when we get there? Perhaps Tom's mind's gone
the same way. Will the Social Services be open on a Saturday? Dear
God, I can't take time to sort it out now, I've only been in the job ten
minutes. Di knew! That's what her phone call was about, of course.
She must have realized from talking to her mother on the phone.
She'll have to come over from Canada and sort it out. How long will
that take? There's a neighbour, Effie, the big West Indian woman.
They probably have no idea where Mary is! They've probably had
the police combing the moors, and I didn't even think to phone them
and let them know she was safe.*

"It is strange, though," Aunt Mary said suddenly.

"What is, Mary?"

"You not remembering that you've been here before."

"Oh . . . yes, I do remember the Botanical Gardens on Eccleshall
Road. I remember us going there very well."

Mary turned and looked at her oddly. "No, pet. I'm talking
about here. Kew Gardens. You wrote to me about it when you

were a little girl—seven or eight. 'Dear Aunty Mary. Today Mummy and I went to China.'" Mary smiled at the memory. "Don't you remember?"

"China?"

"The tall red pagoda, you see. Your mum explained in her letter. You thought this was China. She said I'd love the gardens at Kew. It's funny to think it's taken me so long to come."

Kathy looked at her, stunned. "Oh," she said at last. "I see."

"Is something funny, pet? Are you all right?"

Kathy realized she was grinning with relief. "No, nothing. For a minute there I thought . . . I thought you didn't know where we were."

"What?" Mary looked intensely affronted. "I'm not bloomin' gaga, Kathy. Not yet, anyway."

"Why did you never come down when we lived here?" Kathy said, hastily changing the subject. "I don't ever remember you coming to stay."

"Tom would never allow it. Not after he quarrelled with your dad. But I did come to London the once, before we were married. We all came—Tom and me, and your mum and dad."

"Really? When was that?"

"Fifty years ago, love. That sounds such a long time. Doesn't really feel like it, though. Your dad was stationed down south with the army, and he'd heard he was going to be sent overseas, so he asked your mum to come down to London quickly. They were only just courting at that stage, and our mum said Christine could only go if I went too, as chaperone. Tom came as well, and we had a grand weekend, the four of us. We stayed at a little hotel in Wardour Street."

In Soho, Kathy realized with surprise.

"Was Dad sent abroad?"

"Yes. He was away for three years after that."

"And Uncle Tom?"

"No. He was in the steel mill, you see. He had to stay. It was what they called a reserved occupation during the war."

"Is that something to do with why you went to the Imperial War Museum?"

Mary didn't answer immediately. Her eyes were following the progress of a thrush, pecking its way across the grass in front of them.

"I first met Tom a year before we made our visit down here. I was on my way home from work one night when the sirens started. There'd been a week of heavy raids, and I went straight to the nearest shelter. Tom had just finished at the mill too. They'd been blowing the furnaces, and he was covered all over with red dust. I remember it very clearly, him stepping into the shelter, red from head to toe. He sat next to me, and asked my name. I said Maryanne, and he said that was too fancy. He'd just call me Mary."

"I had no idea that your name wasn't really Mary."

"I've been Mary ever since. I suppose I should have realized when he said that." She shrugged. "The travel agent told me about the museum. They have a thing called the Blitz Experience. You go into what's supposed to be a shelter, about a dozen of you, and then you hear the bombs, and dust comes down from the ceiling, as if there's been a near miss. Then the all-clear sounds, and you go out into the street that's just been bombed. Some houses have been knocked down, and you can hear people shouting. In the middle of the street is a pram, upside down, with the wheel still turning."

"So you were retracing your steps," Kathy said. "Did it work?"

The old lady shook her head. "It wasn't the same," she said. "I found the place where we stayed in Wardour Street, but it isn't a hotel any more. This lad was standing at the door, trying to get the men that passed to go inside. When he saw me staring he asked if I wanted a job there. He was trying to be funny. The Blitz Experience wasn't the same, either, not really. It was quite exciting, especially when I realized that all the other folk in the shelter with me were German people. I was worried what they would think, but they seemed to enjoy it too. Only, it just wasn't the same. It wasn't real."

"What did you mean just now, when you said about your name, that you should have realized something?"

"I should have realized what he was like, that's all." She lowered her eyes, and added in a voice so low that Kathy had to lean forward to hear, "I've left him, Kathy. After all these years, I've left your Uncle Tom."

"Oh . . ." For a moment Kathy was speechless.

"Do you think . . . do you think that's very shameful?"

The old lady seemed to have shrunk with the effort of confession. She sat, hunched, her hands clasped tightly on her lap, and tears welled into her eyes.

"Oh, Aunt Mary." Kathy moved to her side, wrapped her arm around her, and pulled her close.

At that moment a family of Japanese tourists rounded a dense bank of purple *Berberis thunbergii*, chattering happily. They halted at the sight of the tableau on the bench, the young blonde woman cradling the tiny silver-haired lady, and backtracked deferentially.

"I think," Kathy said slowly when they had gone, "that you should have left the old bugger years ago."

Aunt Mary made a noise that was half-way between a sob and a giggle, bobbed her head a couple of times, and began groping for a hanky.

Kathy waited. When her aunt had recovered somewhat she said, "Do you want to tell me how it happened?"

Mary sniffed. "He loved a glass of whisky, I expect you remember."

"Yes." Kathy could picture very clearly her uncle seated in his armchair beside the fireplace, glass of whisky in one hand and pipe in the other.

"It always put him in a very . . . aggressive frame of mind."

"Was he hurting you?"

"Only with his tongue, dear. He could hurt well enough with that."

"Yes. I remember how he was with Mum."

Mary nodded and bowed her head. "I know I should have stopped it then, the way he spoke to her. Only I was afraid he would turn you both out into the street if I came back at him. That was the important thing, to give you and Christine a home after your dad died, until you were on your feet again."

"He felt vindicated, didn't he, by what had happened to us? He couldn't help gloating, making Mum suffer."

"I told myself it was a matter of his principles, his political principles, his socialism, that turned him so hard against your father. But it wasn't that at all. He was just filled with envy. He hated Ray because he had done so well down south, while Tom had stayed where he was, on the furnace floor, and gone nowhere. And he also hated him because he had wanted Christine, not me, and Christine chose Ray instead. I was the other sister, you see. The plain one."

"Oh, Mary," Kathy groaned. "That's just so . . . It's like a bad melodrama."

"I know. But it's the truth all the same, love. Even a bad melodrama can be true."

"So, after all this time, what changed? Why did you decide to leave him now?"

"A week ago last Thursday he said something to me, after he'd been into his whisky for a while. I can't even remember exactly what it was. Something about me. How useless I was. And it was as if all those things I'd never said and should have, all boiled up inside me, and I saw that nothing had been settled. I realized that I had forgotten nothing, and I had forgiven nothing, and if I didn't do something there and then, I never would."

"So you told him all the things you should have said before?"

"No, I couldn't. I didn't know how to begin. I just said that he must choose between the whisky and me. I told him that he couldn't have both. That's all I said. Then I went upstairs to the spare room, the one you and your mother had, and I stayed there the night. The next day neither of us said anything more about it until it came to evening, when he would have his drink. He sat down very deliberately in his chair, took the glass and the bottle from the shelf beside him, and filled the glass with whisky almost to the very top. He took a drink—a big drink—and then he said, 'I'll have my supper now.' So I went upstairs without a word, and packed my bag, and left. I stayed the night at Effie's, and the next morning I caught the train to London."

"Just like that?"

Aunt Mary nodded.

"Well, I think that's great. Have you contacted him since?"

Mary shook her head. "He's so stubborn, Kathy. He's probably still sat in that chair, determined not to move until I get back and apologize."

"But you're not going to, are you?"

"No." Looking down on the old lady as she shook her head, Kathy noticed the bald area in the silver hair. "I couldn't. Not now. But I'm worried that he won't be able to cope."

"He should have thought of that, shouldn't he?"

"You're the strong one, Kathy. I need that now. That's why I didn't go to Di. She's soft, like me."

It had taken Mary three hours to reach Finchley Central from St. Pancras. Kathy wouldn't have given much for her chances of finding her way to her daughter in Calgary, Alberta.

"Not like you, Mary. She's on to her third husband already."

"Aye." The old lady nodded, her bottom lip quivering as if she might burst into tears, but instead she gave a little whimper of a giggle, and when Kathy smiled they both began to laugh.

"I always wondered why you and Mum chose such bastards," Kathy said after a bit. "I thought it must be something to do with the way Grandpa had treated you both. I don't really remember him. Do you think that could be it?"

"Oh, Kathy, you mustn't call them that."

"But it's true. They were both hard, self-centred bastards, and you and Mum made doormats of yourselves."

Kathy took a deep breath and stopped herself going on. They sat in silence for a while, and then Kathy said, "Do you suppose it's possible that it wasn't an accident, me choosing to come here?"

"Do you think about your mum very often, pet?"

"Not often. At Christmas, and on her birthday. And my birthday too, I suppose."

"And your dad?"

"No," she said firmly, "I *never* think of him."

Aunt Mary said nothing for a long while, then murmured, "That's very sad, love."

Kathy began to unpack their lunch. "Maybe I was retracing steps, like you," she said. "You landing up on my doorstep is like the replay of Mum and me coming up to you in Sheffield, isn't it? Maybe it has made me go back. The funny thing is that I found this just a few days before you arrived."

Kathy dug in her bag for the scrap of blue writing-paper she had found in her flat on the day that Brock had rung to tell her about Angela Hannaford's murder.

"I recognize his handwriting," Mary said.

"That was the note he left when he went out that day. Imagine . . ." Kathy could hear the hardness creeping into her own voice but somehow couldn't prevent it. "*I'll be back soon.* Talk about famous last words! What a bloody stupid thing to say . . ."

"Perhaps he wasn't sure, when he left the house . . ."

"He knew exactly what he was going to do," Kathy said bitterly. "I remember a letter that Mum got from someone he worked with, saying what a wonderful communicator he had been. I remember I looked the word up in the dictionary to be sure I'd got it right—I was twelve, wasn't I, or thirteen? The thing was that I couldn't remember him ever communicating with me at all. Not once. And as it turned out, he hadn't communicated with his wife either, not about anything that counted."

"You have to remember, dear, that he was quite old when Christine had you. He must have been almost forty. He'd been away in the war all those years, then came back and took your mother to London, and then it was another ten years or more before you came along. By that stage he was so involved in his work . . . He wasn't really interested, I suppose."

Terrific. Kathy sighed, letting the bile in her throat die away. They stared morosely at the berberis for a while, and then she said, "Crap," and repeated, "crap, crap, crap." She turned to her aunt. "You'll have to learn to say that to yourself, Mary, to stop yourself making excuses."

Aunt Mary shook her head. "I don't think I could, dear. But we'll both have to learn to forgive them, eventually."

THAT EVENING MARY ASKED Kathy if she had a needle and thread, so that she might mend the tear which the tenant had made in the bedroom curtain. As the old lady worked, Kathy remembered Ruth Sparkes's plea. She watched the nimble fingers, unaffected by arthritis, and remembered the sewing-machine in the Attercliffe house, rattling away furiously whenever things got tense. She said, "Do you want something to do while you're down here, Mary? How would you fancy an unpaid job, dressmaking?"

TEN

MARY WAS SURPRISINGLY RECEPTIVE to the idea, and when they phoned Ruth Sparkes she was so overjoyed, and established such an immediate rapport with the old lady, that Kathy found herself being persuaded to take her down to Bromley to make a start the next morning, even though it was Sunday.

It was clear, when they set out, that Aunt Mary had gone to some trouble over her appearance, her blouse crisply ironed and a touch of lipstick and powder on her face, just as if she was presenting herself for a new job. Kathy took a route straight through the deserted City and across Tower Bridge for her benefit, and throughout the journey she was as bright and chirpy as the sparrows flitting through the sunlit gardens they passed. They found Ruth Sparkes's flat in Bromley South without difficulty, and were immediately welcomed inside.

"And you're Mary," Ruth said.

"My real name is Maryanne," Aunt Mary said diffidently, "but everyone calls me Mary."

"What a shame! I prefer Maryanne. Would you mind if I called you that?"

Ruth was brisk, businesslike, and decisive. A retired schoolteacher, she had said. *Perhaps she'll clap her hands if our attention strays.*

Aunt Mary beamed. "I wouldn't mind that at all, Ruth. Not at all."

"Well, now, are you stopping, Kathy?" Ruth went on. "There's plenty to do."

"No, I'm going on down to Orpington police station to do a bit of work there. Mary's got my number in case you need me. I'll come back and pick her up at lunchtime, shall I?"

"Oh, but it's already 10:30. Couldn't you leave it a little longer? Say till 3:00, or 4:00? If Maryanne doesn't mind, that is. I'll give her lunch."

"Oh yes, I think that would be best, Kathy. Give me a chance to see what's what," the old lady interjected. Kathy knew when she was beaten, and left them to it.

She found Bren in the incident centre at Orpington, working through a pile of reports.

"Not having a day off?" she asked.

He shook his head. "Got to keep pushing at this one, Kath."

He looked pasty and tired.

"Anything new?"

"Forensic have a theory about the knife used in Angela's murder. They think it may have been a military weapon, a bayonet, a stabbing rather than a cutting weapon. We're out checking army surplus shops, getting the owners in to go through their books."

"That's interesting."

Bren nodded, looking more weary than interested. "Could be. How about you? What are you doing here? Couldn't keep away?"

"Something like that."

"How's your theatre connection coming along? I saw your note about Carole Weeks. Nothing there, eh?"

"No. I did track down a boyfriend of Zoë Bagnall, and spoke to some of the theatre people she acted with, but they couldn't tell me anything more."

"But?"

"What?"

"Come on, Kathy. You're holding something back. It's written all over your face." Bren gave a sigh and rubbed his own face with both hands, as if trying to wipe away any hidden messages it might contain.

"Is it? Yes, there are things that bother me . . . bother me a lot. But I can't see at the moment where they're leading."

"Come on, Kathy! If you've got some ideas, you owe it to all of us to share them, put them out on the table, discuss them, let us help develop them. This isn't some kind of competition, a private game . . ."

"No, of course not!" Kathy shot back, angry at being pressured this way.

"Well then, let's have it. If you're in the team, you've got to be in it a hundred per cent. We share our ideas openly."

"I don't mind sharing ideas, Bren, but this isn't ready yet. It's half-baked. I haven't worked it through."

"You're being precious, Kathy."

"Precious!" She glared at him, and he glared right back. She noticed the red veins in the whites of his eyes, and the dark circles beneath, and felt ashamed. She'd had eight hours' sleep last night.

"All right," she sighed. "The problem I have is what Brock said about Gentle. I can see the sense in what he says, but I think he's wrong, and I need to have something solid before I can come back on it.

"I think Gentle is the one, because if he isn't, his stalking of Angela Hannaford and Zoë Bagnall are just the most amazing coincidences of all time. What's more, I discovered another woman last night, in the same theatre group as Zoë, whom Gentle had photographed. Now, Angela and Zoë and this other woman were linked by their interest in the theatre, and that must be part of Gentle's thing. Maybe the circumstances of Kirstie McFadden's death had a theatrical connection, one that we haven't established yet. At any rate, there's the common footprint and the similarly violent MO. I thought I'd try to find out where Tom Gentle was on the night of August 25 last year—the night Kirstie McFadden was killed. He may be able to fudge an alibi with his wife for an hour or two on a Saturday night, but a trip to Scotland would be more difficult. If there's no possibility he was in Scotland that night, well, I'll accept that Brock was right. That's what I thought I'd check on today."

"So, what is Gentle's *thing*, Kathy? What makes him tick?"

"He has a need to prove himself continually with women. He is also a secret photographer, a voyeur. Maybe the theatre is a part of that—sitting in the darkness watching some unattainable woman on the stage, and afterwards, hunting them down, or someone who looks like them, or was there in the audience too, and possessing them, absolutely, finally, without pity."

Kathy frowned, picking fiercely at the laminate of the table top as she tried to organize her thoughts coherently. "Brock says he isn't the type, and of anyone, he has the experience to be able to say that. But I just wonder whether you *can* say that. I don't think any of us can see into the mind of someone who would do what that man did to Angela. And I don't think, if we met him in the street, that we would have the faintest idea that those things were going on inside his head. When they catch people like this, they don't turn out to be deformed monsters at all. You read the reports of their trials—John Duffy, Michael Ryan, all the rest—and everybody is saying how surprised they were that it was him, because he's so ordinary, so insignificant, just a quiet sort of bloke working away at the next desk. Bit of a wimp, really. Just like Gentle.

"I think Gentle is devious, secretive, and driven by all kinds of dangerous fantasies about women. I think he's had lots of practice at disguising his real self, at being the charmer, the little boy who never grew up, the basset-hound. And I think he could do that equally well with his physical characteristics too. I think it would be perfectly within his nature to put on a pair of shoes two sizes too big for him, and bulk up his clothing, and put on a false beard, and wash the body carefully afterwards, if he wanted to do something *really* naughty, and didn't want to get caught."

"A false beard?" Bren raised his eyebrows dubiously.

"Yes," Kathy sighed, "that was another of my half-baked theories. That the smell that girl told us about was the smell of the glue they use in the theatre to stick beards on with. All right, I know that sounds like I'm getting obsessed with the theatre thing."

Bren stared down at the papers on the table in front of him for so long that Kathy thought he was dozing off from exhaustion. But then he looked up at her and said, "Leon Desai faxed down a report from Edinburgh last night. I've just been reading it. They're certain that the footprints at the scene of McFadden's murder match ours. He also said that he'd picked up something from the files on her murder that he wanted me to pass on to you."

"What's that?" *The name of a good swimsuit shop?*

"The week she was murdered, the Edinburgh Festival was on. There were probably more actors and theatre buffs within a mile of Kirstie McFadden that night than anywhere else on earth. Every theatre, hall, and club room in the city would have been bulging with them. They would have come from every corner of the globe."

"My God!" Kathy sank on to a chair.

"Yeah. Give me ten minutes, then I'll come with you to see Gentle. If that's all right?"

SHE DROVE, BREN BESIDE her, jacket off, shirt sleeves rolled up, and arm resting on the open window sill. "Great day," he said. "Needed to get out."

"You look all in, Bren."

"No, no," he said, "coping fine," and promptly fell asleep.

Kathy had spoken to Muriel Gentle on the phone, and been told that they would be shortly going out for lunch with friends. They were appropriately dressed for a summer picnic on the lawn, making Bren in his dark, crumpled suit look sweaty and out of place.

"We won't take more than ten minutes," Kathy said. "It's just a matter of cross-referencing, eliminating names from lists." She found it hard to meet Gentle's eyes, her mind unable to suppress the picture of him taking a blunt bayonet to Angela Hannaford's face, a screwdriver to the eyes of Kirstie McFadden. His presence seemed like an obscenity, and no matter how hard she told herself that this wasn't going to help, she felt such an intense animosity every time he did anything with his hands, blowing his nose or stroking the dog's neck, that she felt physically sick. He said nothing, letting his wife arrange things and speak for him. He appeared entirely untroubled.

"You keep a diary, I recall, Mrs. Gentle. Would you have last year's handy?"

"Yes. It's in my bureau. Shall I fetch it?"

"Please."

They waited in silence while she did this, Gentle clucking to the dog as it rolled on to its back to have its stomach tickled.

"Here it is." Muriel Gentle hung on firmly to the book in her hand.

"Would you have a look at last August, please? Friday the twenty-fifth. I just wanted to establish that you were both in the London area that night."

The frown which gathered between Mrs. Gentle's eyebrows as she turned the pages abruptly cleared as she came to the place. "No!" She smiled in triumph at Kathy. "We weren't! We weren't anywhere near London, as it happens. All right, Sergeant?"

"Ah," Kathy held her breath, keeping her voice neutral. "You're absolutely certain?"

"Absolutely! We were hundreds of miles away."

"Where were you?"

"We were on holiday, all that week, and all the following week as well. We were together all that time. A touring holiday. In the Dordogne."

"Where?"

"The Dordogne, in France. On that Friday we visited Rocamadour and the Padirac Chasm, then drove down to Cahors, where we spent the night. I have the name of the hotel here, the Hotel Roaldès."

She passed the diary over to Kathy, who took it and stared at the tiny, neat handwriting without taking it in.

"Does that satisfy you? Sergeant?"

"Yes, that's fine, Mrs. Gentle." Bren had spoken. "Couple of other dates, while we're at it. The previous month, July, Tuesday the fourth. Were you at home then?"

"Let me see . . ." Mrs. Gentle took the book back from Kathy and turned to the entry. "Well, yes, we were at home. I have nothing special marked for that day."

"Do you remember it at all? What you did that evening, for a meal, or afterwards?"

"No . . . no, of course not. How could I, over a year ago? What are you asking this for?"

"Bear with us, please. I know this must be tiresome. Just one more, this year, January 20."

Muriel Gentle pursed her lips, then relented and went back to her antique desk in the corner of the room and returned with her current diary.

"A Saturday," she said when she'd found the place. "No, nothing special. It was an ordinary Saturday."

"How about you, Mr. Gentle?"

Tom Gentle made a face, rolled his eyes, and shook his head.

"Well . . . anything else, Kathy?" Bren looked at her.

Kathy looked at Gentle and suddenly said, "Tell us about Bettina, Mr. Gentle, Bettina Elliott."

Gentle looked at her in surprise.

"Who is she?" his wife demanded.

"One of the women your husband photographed, Mrs. Gentle. Only he didn't identify her for us. She knew Zoë Bagnall, who disappeared."

"Sergeant, I don't like your threatening manner. I am going to call Mr. Denholm." Mrs. Gentle turned to the phone.

"It's all right, Mrs. Gentle," Bren broke in quickly. "We're finished now. What about Mr. Hannaford, by the way? Has he been causing you any more difficulties?"

"No, thank God. He seems to have decided to leave us alone."

"Right. Well, sorry to have troubled you, Mrs. Gentle. Enjoy your Sunday lunch."

"SLOW DOWN, KATH. WE don't need to give the bastard the satisfaction of reading our obituaries in the paper."

Kathy had said nothing since leaving the Gentles'. She gritted her teeth and eased back their speed in the narrow lane.

"Hang on . . ." Bren was looking out of the side window. "That'll do. Pull in over there."

"Where?"

"That pub. I'll buy you lunch."

"I don't feel like lunch."

"Well I do. I haven't eaten since last night. You can have a drink. Cool you down."

Kathy parked the car and they ducked through a low doorway

in the side of the cottage inn, into an interior dark after the bright day outside. The bar was crowded with jocular locals having a pint before Sunday lunch.

Brock brought a couple of cool lagers over to the corner table Kathy had found. They sipped in silence, and then she said, "I'm sorry, Bren. I was so certain about him. Brock was right after all."

"It was your pet theory, Kath. We never like to have them proved wrong. Who's Bettina Elliott, anyway?"

"She's the woman in Zoë Bagnall's acting group that I recognized the other night from Gentle's photographs. That really worries me, Bren. He knew who I was talking about, when I mentioned her name. I saw it in his eyes. He knew her, and he hadn't told us. I think she might be in danger."

"Hang on, Kath. I thought we'd just agreed that Gentle's in the clear? We can check the Dordogne story, but it sounded pretty convincing to me."

"Yes . . . yes." Kathy shook her head. "She was telling the truth. Gentle couldn't have killed anyone in Edinburgh that night."

"Look, I know it's sometimes hard to admit you've made a mistake about someone. But still, better sooner than later, eh?" He paused, then added heavily, "Sometimes you only discover you've made a big mistake years down the track."

The way he said this made Kathy look up. Bren didn't seem to be talking about Tom Gentle any more. She thought with misgiving of her aunt, and the same tone of voice, working up to a confession.

"Things haven't been going right for you," she said neutrally. There seemed no point in pretending not to have noticed.

"Oh . . ." He shook his head and rubbed his eyes. "I'm bushed. Too tired to bother."

"I remember when we worked together, at Jerusalem Lane. I envied your self-confidence. You seemed so calm, well-balanced."

"You notice a difference, this time, do you?"

She nodded. "You seem to be under a lot of stress."

"Yeah, well, it's not work." He took a gulp of beer. "There's nothing as boring as somebody else's domestic troubles, is there?"

"Brock told me your wife lost her father recently. They were very close, were they?"

Bren nodded. "Yeah. Foundation of her life, it seems."

"And he was ill for a while?"

"Yeah, yeah. That broke her up. But . . . oh, there's other things as well."

"If there's anything I can do . . ."

Bren gave a little snort, as if this was funny.

Not understanding what that was supposed to mean, Kathy said, "I just thought, I lost my father too. Mind you, I don't think that qualifies me for anything."

"The thing that gets me, Kathy," Bren said with sudden ferocity, "is the way she sticks by him—Gentle's wife. Hell, she must turn over inside with every new bit of slime we come up with on that creep, but she doesn't show us a thing. She sticks by him every inch of the bloody way. You've got to admire loyalty like that, haven't you?"

He said it very bitterly.

"No, I don't admire it, Bren. Not really. I feel sorry for her."

They fell silent, Bren biting his lip.

Then he said, "Do you think you could kill him, if you were her, his wife? If you knew he'd killed those women?"

"Probably not."

"I think I could kill June, my mother-in-law. Really, I mean that quite literally. I imagine driving home one night, turning the corner into our street and seeing her there, coming out of our house after spending the day poisoning Deanne and the kids, and crossing the road, and I really do think, in the moment I have to decide, that I might hit the accelerator rather than the brake."

"No you wouldn't."

He smiled at her. "Pretty sick, eh? The grieving widow, newly bereaved, my wife's dear mother, and I get pleasure from thinking about bumping her off."

He lifted his glass. "Here's to you, Kath. I look at you, and I remember that life doesn't have to be like this."

She was conscious of him staring thoughtfully at her.

"What?"

"Oh . . . nothing." He sipped from the glass. "Oh, here, there is something. I meant to say this before. I only discovered a couple of months ago that I owe you."

"You do?"

"Yes. Do you remember, at Jerusalem Lane, how I got into trouble over making a search without a warrant? The office of that hairdressing salon, you remember?"

Kathy nodded. She did remember, and she began to feel apprehensive about what was coming next.

"Well, I met the solicitor again recently, the one who swore he was going to nail me for that. Martin Connell. Remember him?"

Kathy concentrated on the glass in front of her, avoiding his eyes. "Yes, I believe I do."

"Well, he made it clear to me that the only reason he didn't pursue the matter with me was because he owed you a favour, and you asked him to lay off. I meant to say thanks before. I had no idea you'd done that, Kathy, no idea at all. That's what impressed me most, that you'd quietly do something like that for a mate, and not say a word."

Kathy met his eyes and thought she caught sight of something warm and yearning there that she wasn't sure she wanted to see or to encourage.

"Is that the way he put it? That he owed me a favour?"

Bren nodded. "Didn't say what it was."

"We'd been lovers," Kathy said, keeping her voice cold. "He'd gone back to his wife, but he hadn't been open with her about me. I told him that if he didn't leave you alone, I'd speak to her."

Bren's mouth dropped open, then closed again. "Hell. Sorry, Kath. I had no idea." He looked stunned.

"What of it?"

"Well, it's just . . ."

"Go on."

"Well, I didn't think he was a very nice guy. I mean . . . I reckon you deserve better."

Deserve? "He was a shit, Bren. But that didn't stop me falling in love with him. I made a bad choice. He was a terrific fuck." Kathy said it deliberately, and watched Bren's face redden. "He taught me two things, anyway."

Bren gave a little cough. "What's that?"

"Avoid married men, and avoid men that I have to deal with in the course of my work."

"Ah." Bren's colour deepened. He fumbled for his handkerchief and wiped his brow. "Uh, maybe we should get going then."

AFTER THE DRAMAS OF confessions and failed theories, Kathy determined that life was going to be simpler in the following week. She was relieved to see Bren on Monday, suit and shirt freshly laundered by someone, looking in considerably better shape than on the previous day. After being briefed about Leon Desai's fax from Edinburgh, and Kathy and Bren's interview with Gentle, Brock gave a grim smile. "Looks like we score one each, Kathy," he said. "You may well be right about our man being a theatregoer, and I may be right about him not being Tom Gentle. Agreed?"

She nodded.

"OK," he said. "So now we come to the tedious bit. Gathering the names of everyone who was at the Edinburgh Festival on the twenty-fifth of August last year, the Shortland Repertory Theatre on the twentieth of January this year, and the National Theatre on the eighth of September. Are we aware of any connections at all between these three events, apart from the murders?"

Bren shook his head. "Leon sent down a list of the theatre companies performing at the Edinburgh Festival last year, and there's no match with either of the other two performances. Trying to track down the audiences is going to be a mammoth job. And probably pointless. If I were a serial killer finding my victims at theatres, I'd make damn sure I bought my ticket in a way that didn't reveal my identity."

"Maybe. Let's hope he wasn't thinking as clearly as that. Any other ideas?"

"Well," Bren said, "two obvious things. If he does use the theatre to find his victims, and he's done it at opposite ends of the country, we should ask forces nationwide to review all unsolved murders in their areas to see if there could be a connection to a theatre or stage performance in the vicinity at the time. The other thing is to remember that one of his attacks, the Carole Weeks case, seems to have had no relation to the theatre at all, so we can't necessarily count on the connection."

Brock nodded agreement. "Anything else?"

Something else had occurred to Kathy, but she decided to say nothing.

Later that day she called into the public library, down the High Street, and spoke to the woman at the desk. "I wondered if you would have a copy of a play, *The Lady Vanishes*?"

"That was a film, wasn't it?" the woman replied. "I don't remember a play, but I can soon check."

She rattled the keyboard of her computer for a while, then shook her head. "No, sorry, we don't have it. I could order it for you."

"Yes, all right. What about *Macbeth*?"

"Should have that . . . Yes, here we are, the four Shakespeare tragedies, *Macbeth*, *King Lear*, *Hamlet*, and *Othello* . . . Should

be on the shelves, over there. I'll write down the number for
you."

"Thanks. Also, I wondered if you could help me to find a play I
don't know the name of."

"Do you have the author's name?"

"No. All I know is that there's a scene where one of the
characters has their eyes stabbed or put out."

"Mmm . . ." The woman thought for a moment. "Well, what
about *Oedipus Rex*? Sophocles. You know, Oedipus murders his
father and marries his mother, as the oracle had foretold, and
when he discovers what's happened, he puts out his own eyes."

"That could be it. Do you have it here?"

"Expect so. Let's see . . . Yes." She wrote another number down.
"Or there's *King Lear*. Gloucester has his eyes put out, I think.
You'll find that in the book with *Macbeth*."

"That's a great help, thank you."

"Doing a project, are you?"

"Sort of. Look, I don't have a library ticket, and I don't live in
your area. But I need the books for a few days for reference."
Kathy showed the woman her warrant card.

"Oh, that sounds interesting. No problem, I'll get you to fill out
a form."

Kathy put the books in her bag, and didn't mention them to
anyone when she got back to Orpington police station. Before she
left for home she dialled the number she had for Aunt Mary's
neighbour in Sheffield. After a moment Effie's broad Yorkshire
accent boomed down the line.

"Hello, Kathy! How's the runaway, then?"

"You knew she was down here then, Effie?"

"She told me she were going to stay with you, love. Is she all
right?"

"Pretty good. How about Tom?"

Uncle Tom was not doing so well, it seemed. He had behaved almost exactly as Mary had predicted, sticking to his armchair, uncommunicative and uncooperative.

"Meals-on-Wheels calls most days, and I look in and give him his tea, like, and do his shopping. But he's a stubborn old bugger. Hardly touches his food. Do you think she might come home soon?"

"She's not giving any signs of it."

"You don't think you could persuade her?"

"I don't know that I want to. I think he deserves it."

"Aye, but what good will it do now, love? Bit late to teach an old dog like him new tricks."

WHEN SHE GOT HOME that night, Kathy found an Aunt Mary transformed from the lost soul of the week before. Her work with Ruth seemed to have revitalized her. The task of creating period costumes for the three female characters of *The Father* was apparently going to be formidable, but not as formidable as the combined determination of Mary and Ruth.

"I can't believe they've got themselves in this pickle, pet," she said, eyes bright. "But Ruth says she's got more hope of us being ready on time than the actors. There's only two weeks left now to dress rehearsal, and they're in a right shemozzle. Stafford's going mad, and some of them are losing their nerve, Ruth says. She's never seen things in such a state. It's so *exciting*, love. It's really grand."

Kathy smiled, unpacked the take-away she'd bought on the way home, and said nothing about her call to Effie.

Later, after Mary had gone to bed, Kathy got out her library books. She started on *Macbeth*, sitting at the dining-table with a cup of coffee and a notepad in which she wrote from time to time as she went through the text. When she reached the end she looked back over the lines she'd written down, starting with

> *Is this a dagger which I see before me?*

and then going on,

> *I see thee still,*
> *And on thy blade and dudgeon gouts of blood . . .*

followed by

> *Go, get some water,*
> *And wash this filthy witness from your hand.*
> *Why did you bring these daggers from the place?*
> *They must lie there: go, carry them, and smear*
> *The sleepy grooms with blood.*

The play was scattered with references to daggers and stabbing. Kathy saw in her mind the punctured torso of Angela Hannaford, her body posed, mouth open, as if declaiming her lines, face unmasked.

THE FOLLOWING MORNING MARY established the new pattern of her working day, waking Kathy on her folding bed in the living-room with a cup of tea, hurrying her through breakfast, and then joining her on the trip south across the river. At Bromley Kathy dropped her aunt off for the day with Ruth and her fabrics and sewing-machine, and went on to work in Orpington. The first thing she did there was to send a fax to their contact with the Edinburgh police, asking him to check whether any of the theatre companies on his list had performed either *King Lear* or *Oedipus Rex* at the previous year's Festival. Towards lunchtime she got the negative reply.

Bren came by a little later. "Got something here should cheer you up," he said. He reached into the bag he was carrying and produced a tiny bottle which he handed to Kathy. It was full of an amber fluid, like liquid honey.

"What is it?"

"Read the label."

Kathy looked. "Leichner New Formula Spirit Gum No 165. The adhesive for beards and moustaches. Apply with brush and allow to become tacky before applying the crêpe hair. 25 cc. Leichner, London, England."

"We gave the girl a sniff. She thinks it's very like the smell she remembers from the man who attacked her. Leon's getting his lads to go back over the fibre traces from Angela's bedroom and Carole Weeks's clothing, make sure there weren't any black crêpe fibres we missed, or gum residues."

ON THURSDAY, AUNT MARY said they were going to have a preliminary costume fitting for some of the cast before the evening rehearsal, and Kathy agreed to pick her up at the Three Crowns at seven. When she got there, however, the cast were just arriving.

"I'm sorry, Kathy," Aunt Mary said. "I got it mixed up. We have to do the fittings during the rehearsal. Do you mind waiting till we're done, pet?" Her arms were full of bundles of cloth, a tape measure round her neck, eyes alight with anticipation.

"Aren't you tired, Mary? You've been at it all day."

"Oh, you don't get tired when you're busy, pet."

"What about food? Aren't you hungry?"

"We had something at Ruth's. But what about you? You'll be starving, I dare say."

"That's all right. I'll get something downstairs."

There was one exhausted sausage roll under a plastic cover on the bar, and Kathy returned with this and a half of lager to the rehearsal room upstairs. She tried to slip unobtrusively into a corner seat, but Stafford Nesbit spotted her and she suddenly found him dragging a chair to her side. "Sergeant Kolla. How very nice to see you again." His angular elbows and knees stuck out like the limbs of a tree, trapping her in the corner. "We missed you on Monday night."

"Monday?"

"Yes, your colleagues paid us a visit. They questioned us extensively for the names of people who bought tickets for *The Lady Vanishes*. Caused quite a stir."

"Oh yes, of course."

"Some people have had follow-up visits at home too, I understand. So very thorough, but about six months too late, one would have thought. One wonders indeed what has caused all this latter-day activity. Could there be new evidence? Or is one to detect the hand of a new investigating officer behind all this, one more thorough and more determined than her predecessors?"

He raised one eyebrow conspiratorially, leaning forward unnervingly close. When Kathy didn't reply, he went on, "Your aunt has confessed all to me, Kathy. She has told me that you have recently been recruited to the top murder investigation unit in Scotland Yard—indeed, are practically running it! So you see, there is no need to hide your light under a bushel where I am concerned. Tell me the truth, what are you seeking tonight? Let me assist you."

Kathy shook her head, exasperated, by her aunt and by this rather pathetic old ham. She was aware of the others looking in their direction, waiting for the producer to start the rehearsal. "There's nothing new, Mr. Nesbit. I just came to take my aunt home after she's finished the costume fittings."

"Ah, now, she's been an absolute godsend. Really, a gift from the gods. We are indebted."

"She's enjoying herself."

"Salt of the earth, your Maryanne. And she worships you, Kathy, understandably enough."

He seemed almost to be flirting with her. Kathy squirmed and managed a thin smile.

"Oh my God!" He suddenly drew back and made a little gesture of horror with one bony hand.

"What's the matter?"

"You are surely not going to eat that?" He pointed at the pathetic sausage roll.

"Yes, that's my dinner, Mr. Nesbit."

"*Stafford*, Kathy, please. If this is not an official visit, we can't go on addressing each other like aliens. Now there is a perfectly ordinary but no doubt sanitary Indian takeaway not three minutes from here. With your approval, I shall send Svärd the Orderly on a mission of mercy for some samosa, rogan josh, and rice. What do you say?"

"No, really . . ."

"And in return, to pay for your supper, I should like to beg something of you."

"What's that?"

"Our prompter's taken to her bed, and we are desperate. While you're sitting here, waiting for your aunt to finish her work, would you consider prompting for us?"

"Oh . . . I don't think so. What does that involve, exactly?"

"It's simplicity itself. You follow the text in the book, and when someone dries—forgets their lines—or misses bits out . . ."—he glared pointedly across the room at Edward Quinn—". . . you speak out. Very simple."

Kathy wondered what he was playing at. It was as if he were trying to draw her into something. She shrugged. "All right."

"Excellent! And there really is no new development in Zoë's case, then? No breakthroughs, no flashes of insight?"

" 'Fraid not."

"Well, that is a shame. But your aunt has assured me that if anyone can find the solution, it is you." He held her eye for a moment, a slightly manic gleam in his. "Now, we really must start our rehearsal."

He got abruptly to his feet and stalked off to give some instructions to a skinny man, presumably playing Svärd the Orderly, and then spoke to a striking, dark-haired woman, who came over to Kathy.

"Don't mind Stafford," she said. "We all have to put up with him. I'm Vicky."

"Hi, I'm Kathy."

"Yes, I saw you last week when you were here. You can use my book. We're here, in act two, this scene between Edward, the Captain, and his wife, Laura. That's me."

"Vicky, darling!" Stafford's voice cut in again, "Let us resume our struggle with the second act, if you please! From Bertha's exit."

"Don't you want Bettina for the moment, then, Stafford?" Ruth Sparkes spoke up from the doorway. "Can we have her next door for her fitting?"

"Yes, yes." He waved his hand impatiently, and Bettina stood up to follow Ruth out of the room. Kathy watched her go, out of place among the other actors, a generation apart, dressed in a black T-shirt and short black skirt with a frayed hem, below which a pair of sturdy legs ended in a pair of thick-soled Reeboks, also black.

"Silence, everyone!" Stafford barked. He pointed a bony finger at Vicky to begin.

"*Oh, am I as powerful as that?*" She spoke to Quinn with hands on hips, voice heavy with sarcasm.

"*You insulted Nordling till he went away; and then you got your brother to scrape up votes for this man.*"

Vicky stared at him blankly for a moment, then shook her head and turned away, dropping out of character.

"What's the matter, darling?" Nesbit said with exaggerated patience.

"That's not the line," she complained. "You jumped again, Edward."

"Did I? Sorry." He looked hopefully at Kathy.

"Do you think a father . . ." Kathy prompted.

"Ah yes," he nodded. *"Do you think a father would let ignorant and conceited women teach his daughter that he is a charlatan?"*

"It's less important to a father."

"Vicky, darling," Stafford said, kneading his domed forehead, "why don't you move downstage left at that point? We're getting awfully static. Although you seem to be hopping about a bit, Edward. Have you got an itch?"

"I'm trying to keep clear of Vicky. She's blocking me."

"You're upstaging me, Edward!" Vicky flashed back at him. "I can't talk to him when he's standing right behind me, Stafford."

"I'm trapped by this bloody sofa, for God's sake!"

"Children! Children!" Stafford thought for a moment. "Why don't we have the Captain sitting on the sofa for this part, Edward? You could sit down when Bertha exits. On the line *Leave us, Bertha.* All right? You sit down and fold your arms, the stubborn husband. Laura, on the other hand, the manipulative wife, paces back and forward, between down right and down left. Vicky?"

She nodded, and Edward arranged himself expansively on the two chairs standing in for the sofa.

"Prompt, Kathy," Nesbit said. "Can you give us the cue?"

"It's less important to a father."

"Right."

"Oh? Why?" the Captain said.

"Because a mother's nearer to the child—since it's been discovered that no one can tell for certain who is a child's father."

Kathy thought how good Vicky was in the part of Laura. She was delivering her lines with a confidence that was compelling, and Kathy had to force her eyes back down to the page to follow the script.

"Edward, you're looking a bit complacent, old chap. Begin to sit up as she says this. She's showing you the weapon she's got, the one she's going to skewer you with. You might note the warning signs."

"I thought it might be effective if I appeared a bit slow on the uptake, Stafford."

"That shouldn't be difficult," Nesbit muttered under his breath, so that only Kathy, sitting nearby, heard it and smiled.

"Try it my way, Edward."

Quinn nodded. *"What has that to do with it?"*

"Simply that you don't know that you are Bertha's father."

"Is this a joke?"

"Of course I know!" Kathy broke in.

They all looked at her.

"He skipped a line," she explained. *"Is this a joke?* comes after Laura's next line."

"Thank you!" Vicky smiled at her.

"Oh, look . . ." Edward threw up his hands. "We have a bit of latitude, Kathy, OK?"

"Sorry."

"Latitude!" Vicky exploded. "You're always doing this, Edward, mangling the lines. How can I get my timing right if I never know which line is coming next?"

They struggled on to the end of the scene, when Nesbit called a ten-minute break. Most people wandered off to get a drink from the bar, leaving Kathy, feeling rather shaken, alone with the Indian dinner which had arrived for her. Ruth Sparkes came in, and Kathy explained what had happened. "Every time I gave a prompt it seemed to make trouble."

Ruth laughed. "That wasn't your fault, Kathy. That's Edward and Vicky. They're always like that. Edward is notoriously slow learning his lines. And when the others nag him he sometimes deliberately makes mistakes, trying to corpse them."

"Corpse them?"

"Yes. Corpsing is where you do something to try to throw somebody else out of their character, like make them laugh in the middle of a death scene."

"That's terrible! But he wouldn't do it during an actual performance, would he?"

Ruth laughed. "*Especially* during an actual performance!"

"But that's vicious! No wonder Vicky gets angry."

"Well, it's a kind of game. Taking risks with the characters, testing how good you are at staying in character, even when you're struggling to work out what on earth is going on."

Kathy shook her head. "I don't know how they can stand it. It must be bad enough going out there, hoping you can remember your own lines, without having to worry about all that going on around you. And the emotion! Even at rehearsals. It was exhausting just to watch."

"Did we have an upstaging episode?"

"How did you guess?"

"It's one of their routines. Another form of corpsing, really. One manoeuvres to the back of the stage to upstage the other and make them turn their back to the audience. So instead, the downstage person counter-attacks by moving directly in front to block the upstager, turns their back on them and delivers their lines directly to the audience. It can go on like that for some time."

"You make it sound like a battle. I thought they were supposed to be on the same side."

"Well, really"—Ruth leant forward, a mischievous gleam in her eye—"it's a kind of foreplay. Stafford knows all about the chemistry. He's very good at creating it, making it work for him."

They didn't reach the end of act two that evening, and by the time Stafford released them, Kathy felt drained. Aunt Mary too was showing signs of exhaustion, and sighed wearily as she lowered herself into the passenger seat beside Kathy.

"They've certainly worked you hard today, Mary," Kathy said.

"That's good, pet. Takes my mind off things, thinking about the problems we've got."

"What sort of problems?"

"Well, bustles, for one thing."

"Bustles?"

"Aye. According to the books Ruth's been studying, bustles were back in fashion in 1887 when the play was written, and didn't go out of fashion again till 1890. But Stafford says he doesn't care—he doesn't want bustles. He says they look stupid. He wants a stark look, more modern. Vicky, on the other hand, thinks she looks quite becoming in a bustle. When she told Stafford this, he said, in a very sarcastic tone, 'becoming what?' "

"Ah. There's more to all this than meets the eye, isn't there?"

"That's true enough. But they're a grand crowd. I always thought southerners were cold, but they're smashing. You should do something like this, you know, Kathy. You should have an outside interest. Give you something other than your work to think about. Something less morbid."

"I don't think I could stand the excitement. The drama of the play is nothing compared to what goes on among the cast."

"Well, I don't know anything about that, but they do have a very active social life, with parties and outings and all sorts. And that's the kind of place you'd find a nice young man, like as not."

Kathy didn't rise to this.

"Well, anyway," Mary said, satisfied she'd made her point, "I shall be looking out for them in the papers when they come touring up north."

Kathy shook her head, getting a little tired of the subject.

"They don't go touring, Mary. They're not that kind of a theatre company. They're only amateurs."

"Oh yes they do!" the old lady said tetchily. "Last year they went to Edinburgh. Next year they're thinking of coming up to Scarborough."

"Edinburgh?"

"Yes, Edinburgh. They took part in the Edinburgh Festival." She closed the clasp of the handbag on her lap with a decisive loud snap.

Kathy said nothing for a bit. She almost let it drop, but that defiant little gesture with the handbag clasp had stirred some memory of her youth, and she was damned if the old girl was going to have the last word.

"No they didn't," she said firmly. "It just so happens I was looking at a list of all the theatre companies who were in the Edinburgh Festival last year, and SADOS was definitely not one of them. Someone's been pulling your leg, Mary. You shouldn't believe everything they tell you."

Having driven the point home, and getting no further response from her aunt, who just sat there in silence like a hunched teddy-bear in her furry hat and coat, Kathy felt a stab of guilt.

Mary said nothing for the rest of the journey, nor as they walked to the lobby of the flats, nor as they went up in the lift. Only when they were in the living-room did she speak. "I would like to make a phone call," she announced.

"Yes, yes, of course," Kathy said penitently.

"In private, if I may."

"Of course. There's a plug in the bedroom. I'll take it through for you."

As she retired from the room, leaving Aunt Mary sitting on the edge of the bed dialling, Kathy thought, *I've done it now. Hurt her pride. She's arranging to go home.*

A few minutes later the old lady opened the door again.

"Katherine," she said stiffly, "I would like you to speak to someone, if you please."

Apprehensively Kathy went through and picked up the phone, expecting to hear the irate voice of Uncle Tom, or the taxi company. Instead she recognized Ruth Sparkes.

"Hello, Kathy? Maryanne has given me instructions to tick you off."

Kathy smiled. "I'm sure she has, Ruth. Go on then, do your duty."

"She wants me to convince you that we really did go to the Edinburgh Festival last year. Well, we did, honest."

Kathy's smile turned to a frown. "Are you sure about that? Couldn't it have been the year before?"

"No, definitely last year. We've done it a couple of times now. We take up one of our productions and put it on for the Fringe. Last year it was *Equus*. Stafford staged it for the July production down here, and he took the same cast up north with it in August. It got a very good reception. I know, because I went up with them."

"Well . . . Looks like I got it wrong, then."

"Yes. It sounds as if you got yourself upstaged, Kathy."

"Totally corpsed. 'Night."

She replaced the phone and went out to make peace with her aunt.

ELEVEN

FIRST THING THE NEXT morning Kathy made another call to the Edinburgh police. "It's about that list you faxed me, of acting companies at the Festival last year. I've come across another group, not on your list, who say they were there."

"Really? What sort of group?" The Scotsman at the other end sounded young, somewhat harassed.

"A group of amateurs, from South London. They say they put something on at the Fringe."

"Oh, aye. I think the list we sent you was the official programme for the main Festival events. I don't think it included all the participants in the Fringe."

"Do you have details of those?"

"I'm sure I can get them."

Kathy gave him the information. "I'm interested in the dates they were there, and if the venue was anywhere near where Kirstie McFadden was found."

The incident centre at Orpington was almost deserted, everyone out collecting data. Kathy asked the office if Bren was expected, but no one seemed to know.

"That's not like him, is it? Would you check on that?"

She didn't wait for the answer, hurrying out into the bright morning sunshine.

At the library she found the assistant who had helped her the previous time. "I've got another request. A play called *Equus*."

The woman nodded. "Peter Shaffer," she said, and tapped up the call number on the computer. "Yes, it's in. Need a hand?"

"No, that's fine. I'll find it."

When she did, she sat down in a quiet corner and read. After half an hour she returned to the desk and signed another form to take out the book. Preoccupied, she turned to go, still holding the librarian's pen in her hand. "'Scuse me," the woman called after her. "My pen."

At first Kathy didn't know what she was talking about. "Sorry, I was miles away."

"You all right?" The librarian peered at her. "You look a bit pale."

Back at the office, Kathy phoned Ruth Sparkes.

"Hello, Kathy. Do you want your aunt?"

"No, it was you I wanted, Ruth. As secretary, you would have records, wouldn't you, of the activities of your theatre group over the past few years?"

"Yes, that's right, I keep all our records."

"Where are they?"

"Why, here, at home. One of your people has already been through them, looking for the membership list, and notes of ticket sales."

"Can I come over just now and have another look?"

"Of course, Kathy."

"The first time we spoke on the phone, Ruth, I asked you if Zoë Bagnall might have visited the National Theatre before she disappeared."

"Yes, I remember. I said not. Why? Was I wrong?"

"No. But you said that you sometimes went as a group to the National or the Old Vic."

"Yes."

Kathy took a deep breath. "Have you been recently?" It seemed to Kathy that her voice seemed absurdly flat and unemphatic, considering the significance of the question.

"Yes, just a couple of weeks ago, in point of fact. We went to see *Macbeth*."

As she hurried out, Kathy stopped at the front desk. "Has anyone heard from Bren Gurney, do you know?"

No one had.

"Where the bloody hell is he? Look, I'm going to this number. Get him to ring me there will you, when he gets in touch. It's urgent."

RUTH SPARKES KEPT THE records of SADOS, like her own person, in immaculate order. She lifted the glasses that hung from the cord round her neck, placed them at the precisely correct point on the bridge of her nose, and set the files out on her dining-table for Kathy.

"Productions, Social Programme, Members, Publicity, Bookings, Minutes. I don't keep the accounts, mind," she said. "Stafford is the treasurer, as well as the president, and claims to keep them, but . . ."—she raised her eyebrows—"I rather doubt if he does anything of the kind. What he actually does, I believe, is to spend what he wants and make up any shortfall out of his own pocket. Once a year he provides a statement for the AGM, but we hold that in the upstairs room of the Three Crowns, and by the time we get to the treasurer's report, everyone's slightly merry." She laughed, then saw that Kathy's face remained grim.

"It isn't the money I'm interested in, Ruth," she muttered,

turning the pages of the first file. "Just the details of productions and trips and so on. Could I have a look at these for a bit?"

"Of course. Are you looking for the productions that Zoë was involved in? I could point those out to you."

"I'd just like to have a browse. If I get stuck, I'll come to you."

"Very well." Ruth pursed her lips and removed her glasses. "Will the sound of our sewing-machine bother you?"

"No, no." Kathy saw the frown on her face and made an effort to sound unconcerned. "Mustn't slow down the war effort."

"Absolutely not. Your aunt is a treasure, Kathy. We simply wouldn't have managed without her."

Aunt Mary didn't raise her head from her sewing. Kathy thought she was looking extremely smug.

KATHY HAD BEEN WORKING through the papers for half an hour when Bren Gurney rang.

"Bren? Are you back at Orpington?"

"No, Kathy. I've got a bit of a problem."

There was a sound of a baby crying in the background, then a siren in the distance.

"Where are you? Can I help?"

"No, I just need a bit of time to sort it out. They told me you needed me urgent."

"Yes. I need to talk to you about the . . ."—she hesitated, aware of the two women at the table, heads down, busy at their work, listening to every word—". . . the case."

"What's happened?"

"I need to meet you, talk something over."

"Can it wait? Can you manage without me for a bit?" He was talking rapidly, anxious to get away.

"Could I meet you, wherever you are? It'll only take ten minutes."

"No, Kathy. Prefer you didn't. Look . . ." She heard the reluctance in his voice, not wanting to say more, then, "You remember I mentioned my mother-in-law the other day?"

"Yes, the one you wanted to . . ."

"Yeah," he cut in hurriedly. "Well, she's had an accident."

"Oh dear. Is she bad?"

"Yeah, pretty bad. I'm at the hospital, see."

"Right. What kind of accident?"

"Hit and run."

"Bren!"

"Kath, I gotta go." His voice had dropped to a rushed whisper. "Take care of things, will you?"

"Yes, yes, of course." She rang off, stunned.

"Bad news, pet?" Mary said quietly, after a bit.

"Er . . . someone's had an accident."

She dialled the Queen Anne's Gate number and was put through to Brock.

"Kathy! I've been wanting to catch up with you. How are things?"

"I need to see you, Brock."

"Of course. Later on this afternoon?"

"Now?"

"Well . . . why not? Where are you?"

"Shortlands. I'll be up in half an hour."

When she rang off she turned to Ruth. "I'd like to take some of your files with me. I'll keep them safe."

"That's all right, Kathy. Goodness, you do look serious! Is something terribly wrong? Can't we help?"

WHEN KATHY OPENED THE door of Brock's office she was taken aback to see Leon Desai standing at the desk with him, examining a stack of paper. She hadn't even heard that he was back from Edinburgh, and she felt a jab of resentment that Brock had wanted to put her off till the afternoon, when apparently he'd been meeting with Desai. Desai's expression didn't help, either, a cool assessment which made her feel that she should have checked herself in the mirror before charging in.

"Kathy!" Brock looked up and beamed at her, pulling the glasses off his nose. "Leon just dropped in with the latest collations on the audiences at the three venues." He lifted the thick sheaf of print-outs and let it drop back on the table. "Sweet F.A."

"The parameters are too wide," Desai explained, voice quiet. "We could go on for ever."

Brock shook his head grimly. "We haven't got for ever, Leon. He's going to do it again. That's one thing we can be sure of. Anyway"—he straightened and grinned at Kathy—"you gave me the opportunity I needed to cancel my grilling from our friends down the road this morning, Kathy. Something important's come up, I told them. Sergeant Kolla only consults me when she's made a big breakthrough."

A little smile formed on Desai's face. "I'll get going then, Brock. I need to show these to Bren."

"He's tied up at present, Leon. Probably be away for the rest of the day," Brock said. Kathy was relieved he knew.

"Oh, right. I'll get back to Lambeth then."

"Why don't you stay?" Kathy said, somewhat to her own surprise. Desai looked surprised too, Brock amused.

"You might be interested in this," she added.

"Yes, why not, Leon?" Brock said. "Have some coffee. You look as if you could do with it, Kathy."

Brock sauntered over to the percolator he kept continuously going by the window, leaving Kathy and Desai to seat themselves, scrupulously avoiding eye contact.

"Well, now," he said once they were provided for, "what do you have for us, Kathy?"

"I can narrow your parameters," she said.

"Can you indeed? Well, that would be very useful. How do you manage that?"

Kathy had rehearsed the story on the way up from Shortlands, but it seemed so obvious now that it told itself.

"I was struck—we all were—by the title of that play that Zoë had been in, *The Lady Vanishes*. It was such a beautiful and terrible coincidence, like a prophecy. But then I looked at *Macbeth* again, the play Angela Hannaford had been to see that night, and I realized that it too could be taken as a prophecy, of her death by stabbing, with a dagger."

Brock frowned and clawed at his beard thoughtfully. "Yes, that hadn't occurred to me, Kathy. It's certainly a thought."

"So then I wondered about the third murder that we knew was connected, in Edinburgh. I wondered what play could have suggested an attack on the eyes of the victim, stabbing them out."

"Mmm!" Brock's face had lit up with interest; Desai was still sceptical. "*Oedipus?*"

"Or *King Lear*. But I checked, and neither had been performed at the Festival."

"Oh." Brock sounded disappointed. "Pity."

"Only the list we'd got from Edinburgh was incomplete." Now Desai looked up sharply. "They hadn't included all the companies who took part in the Fringe festival. Among them was a group who did *Equus*."

"Oh my God." Brock stared at her. Desai didn't seem to follow.

Kathy turned to him. "*Equus* tells the story of a highly disturbed boy who loves horses, and who, after failing to achieve sex with his girlfriend, stabs out the eyes of his horses with a hoof pick. Apparently the author, Peter Shaffer, based it on a real case."

Kathy pulled the book out of her bag. "Look at the final speech of the play. The character describes how he stands in the dark with a pick in his hand, striking at heads. That's what Kirstie's killer did, isn't it?" she said softly. "He stood in the dark, striking at heads."

Desai nodded. "Yes."

"Well," Brock said slowly, "that does sound promising. If it really was more than coincidence, we could concentrate on the audience of just one out of the dozens of performances in Edinburgh that night, which would be a big help, wouldn't it, Leon?"

Desai nodded grimly. "It certainly would."

"There's more to it," Kathy said. "The group that performed *Equus* that night in Edinburgh was the same group that did *The Lady Vanishes*—SADOS, from Shortlands."

"What!" Brock jerked forward in his chair.

"It turns out they also had an outing to *Macbeth* at the National Theatre on the same Saturday night that Angela went."

For a moment Brock was speechless. Then he exploded, "How the bloody hell could we not have known that, for God's sake! We've been interviewing them for the best part of a week. None of them mentioned Edinburgh or the National Theatre, did they?"

"We didn't ask them. We decided not to raise the other cases with them—there's been no public announcement that they may be connected, or that we may be dealing with a serial killer."

Brock was out of his chair now, roaming round the room, his big feet narrowly avoiding sending flying the piles of documents dotted about the floor.

"Something else," Kathy said, and he stopped dead and turned to face her.

"During the week ending Saturday the ninth of June this year, SADOS put on a play at the Shortland Repertory Theatre. It was a comedy, by Neil Simon. It was called *Barefoot in the Park*. That

Saturday was the night that Carole Weeks was murdered in Spring Park. Her shoes were never found."

BROCK HAD STOPPED HIS roaming, and they sat around the low coffee-table on which the secretary, Dot, had put a plate of sandwiches. It was early for lunch, but Kathy's revelations had made Brock hungry.

"All right," he said, nodding his head, swallowing. "All right. Now what about that other murder we looked at? The woman in Blackheath. Any possible connection there?"

"Janice Pearce," Kathy replied. "That happened a couple of months before the Edinburgh murder, and it doesn't seem to correspond to anything in the SADOS calendar. Besides, the reason we identified that one was that it was the only unsolved murder of a woman commuter on the same rail line that Gentle uses. If Gentle is now irrelevant, there's no particular reason to include it in the series."

Brock nodded. "So, the proposition is what? That SADOS have a crazed fan who shadows them around the country, turning their make-believe into horrible reality. Is that it?"

"That would be one possibility."

Brock shook his head. "A sort of cultural Billy Spratt."

"Who?"

"Billy Spratt was a Chelsea fan. He used to follow the team faithfully to all their away matches, and whenever they lost the game he'd hang around the town in question afterwards, and kill somebody before he went home. Revenge. It was some time before anybody noticed the connection between the murders and Chelsea losing their away matches. But you wouldn't think of theatre people doing that sort of thing, would you? Or is that just me thinking in stereotypes? What would provoke it? A bad review in the paper?" He snorted dubiously.

"Another possibility," Kathy said, "is that one of the SADOS people themselves finishes off each stage run with a little private play of his own."

"That's even more bizarre. But it should be easy to check. The problem is that, even when we've narrowed the field of suspects down to people connected with this particular theatre group, we're still dealing with someone who takes a lot of care to cover his tracks. If he's as careful buying his tickets and keeping in the background as he is in cleaning up his traces at the murder scene, we may still miss him."

"The *Macbeth* murder shows that he's closer to them than just looking out for their play announcements in the local paper," Kathy said. "He must have seen their newsletter, or known someone who's a member, to know that they would be going to the National that night."

"True. Still, I think we need some help to get a clearer idea of what we're after here." Brock looked at Desai. "Dr. Nicholson again, I think."

Desai nodded.

"Is that the profiler?" Kathy asked. "The one who knocked my Gentle theory on the head?" Kathy had already formed a mental picture of a cranky old pedant.

Brock nodded. "Psychologist from the University of Surrey. I've worked with Alex a few times now. Very good."

"An academic," Kathy said doubtfully, her image confirmed. "Are you sure he's what we need, Brock? I mean, some old professor may be strong on theory, but . . . I don't know."

Desai smiled. "Alex Nicholson's a she. Our age. You'll like her." He nodded. "She's very good."

"Oh." Kathy coloured.

"Shall I get on to her?" Desai asked.

"Yes, please, Leon. See if she can spare us her weekend. OK with you, Kathy?"

"Yes, of course." Kathy nodded, chastened. "That's fine."

"Why don't you get that fixed up straight away, Leon?" Brock said. "There's one or two other things I want to go over with Kathy."

Desai nodded and got to his feet. Before he moved off he turned to her and said, "That was quite brilliant, Kathy."

"What?" she said dumbly, still thinking about her reaction to the psychologist.

"Your 'big breakthrough.' I'm very impressed."

Brock beamed at him. "Thought I was joking, didn't you, Leon? I knew she must have come up with something. I could tell. She reminds me of me, thirty years ago."

Desai grinned a broad grin, lots of perfect white teeth, the first time Kathy had ever seen them.

When he had gone, Brock said, "Don't let it go to your head, Kathy. What's all this about Bren?"

Kathy looked at him in surprise. "He's spoken to you from the hospital, has he?"

"Yes. What's going on?"

"Well, it seems his mother-in-law has had an accident."

"Yes, I know about that. She stepped out into the street without looking. They phoned Bren at work first thing this morning . . ."

"He was at work when it happened?" she interrupted, and felt a surge of relief when he nodded.

"Yes. Did you think he did it?"

"No! No, of course not."

"Shouldn't say it, but having met the lady once myself . . ." Brock stopped himself and grunted, looking uncomfortable. "My question was directed at you and Bren, Kathy. Are you two getting along all right?"

Kathy was puzzled. "Yes, I think so. How do you mean?"

"You're working well together? Teamwork is very . . ." He didn't finish the sentence.

"Important, yes, I know."

"Tricky, I was going to say. No personal difficulties?"

"Personal? Brock, I don't follow."

"No, no. I didn't think so." He sighed and spread his hands out on the table in front of him. "I should probably tell you that Bren's wife, Deanne, rang me not long ago. She was in quite an emotional state. I think I did mention, didn't I, that she lost her father recently, after a long illness?"

"Yes, you told me."

"He died, apparently, on that Monday evening, the day after we started the Angela Hannaford investigation. It was expected, by that stage, and Bren had promised to be home early. Only he got caught up in things at Orpington, with the result that Deanne was delayed getting to the hospital, and consequently she wasn't with her father when he passed away."

"Oh."

"In point of fact, at the moment Deanne's father passed away, Bren was with you, munching a hamburger in his car on the road back up to town, a fact which Deanne subsequently ascertained after prolonged interrogation of her husband."

"Oh dear."

"Yes. Unfortunately, Bren had earlier spoken about you to his wife, in glowing terms, she said, about how much he was looking forward to working with you again. His enthusiasm was quite childish, she said, an enthusiasm which clearly DS Kolla has manipulated for her own purposes."

Kathy winced. "I'm not her favourite person, then."

"I did my best, Kathy, but I think you can take it that you are one of the many dark clouds in Deanne Gurney's world at present."

"Should I go and talk to her, do you think?"

"I wondered about that. But when Bren phoned and told me about the latest blow this morning, I thought that would be the last thing the poor woman needs."

Bren was telling me the same thing, Kathy thought, recalling her offer to meet him at the hospital.

"I just thought I should warn you, Kathy. Go carefully, eh? Now." He sat up and rubbed his hands briskly. "Since you are effectively in charge of this investigation, where do we go next?"

"We'll have to interview the SADOS people again, try to compile audience lists for *Barefoot in the Park* and *Equus,* find out who went on the *Macbeth* trip. I thought I'd take a team down and catch them when they're all together at their rehearsal in the Three Crowns this evening."

"Good. I'll come with you if I may. I'd like to see what they're like, this crowd. Fancied myself as a bit of an actor once, as a matter of fact, long time ago."

TWELVE

BROCK BROUGHT THEIR REHEARSAL to an abrupt halt as soon as he came through the door of the upstairs room. He didn't need to say anything. There had been a light shower of rain, the evening was cool, and he had a black raincoat over his big frame. He stood, feet apart, hands deep in the coat pockets, considering them, and they knew that this was trouble even before he opened his mouth to introduce himself.

Stage presence, Kathy thought.

He apologized for interrupting them, but there had been a serious development. The police had been investigating a series of attacks on women in the south-east London area, and it was possible that they were related to the disappearance of Zoë Bagnall. It was possible that audiences at some SADOS productions might be able to provide useful information, and the police were therefore seeking the co-operation of the company to trace as many audience members as possible on the dates in question.

The message wasn't particularly threatening, but Brock's tone was ominous, and their faces showed that they were unsettled by him. The outside world was breaking in again, uninvited, to the Captain's half-realized living-room, demolishing its illusion in a few quiet words from the big policeman. Standing with another officer, a couple of paces behind him, Kathy felt Stafford Nesbit's eyes on her throughout Brock's little speech.

They moved to the room across the landing and began interviewing people in turn, while another two officers collected the information on ticket purchasers. Kathy and Brock began with Ruth, who was fascinated by these developments.

"Are you suggesting that someone in our audience at each of these performances is the person you are looking for, Chief Inspector?" she asked.

"Well, not necessarily, Mrs. Sparkes. But that is possible. Do you have someone in mind?"

"Oh no. I find it hard to imagine that anyone in our audiences would be capable of violence, really. Half of them are friends, work-mates and relatives of the company, loyally turning out to support their loved-ones' mania. The rest are people who for some reason decide to leave the box and come out for an evening of cheap live theatre. We have a core of regulars on our mailing list. Many are pensioners, who like the social occasion and have made a habit of it. There's a strong contingent who live on the Green Line bus route, but the only trouble with them is that they have to catch the last bus home, which stops outside the theatre at 10:27. So it is very important that we finish our performances by 10:25, or they all get up and leave. Edward tells a wonderful story about his grandmother, who was one of the Green Line pensioners. He was in something where he died on stage near the end of the play. Unfortunately they were running over time, and in the closing minutes he became aware of his grandmother in the front row getting to her feet. She came forward to the edge of the stage where he was lying, dead, and . . ."

She stopped suddenly. "Oh dear. I'm rambling on, aren't I? I'm sorry, Chief Inspector, where were we?"

"That's all right, Mrs. Sparkes. What did Edward's grandmother say?"

"Well, she said, in a loud whisper that the whole theatre could pick up, 'Good night then, dear. You were very good. Don't forget you're taking me to the shops tomorrow.'"

They smiled.

"It's all so innocent, you see. I can't imagine a *murderer* being interested in our shows."

"Among your regulars . . ." Brock pondered. "Suppose I paint a picture, see if it reminds you of anyone. A young or middle-aged man, rather quiet, solitary. Probably comes alone, maybe doesn't get into conversation with other people during the intervals. He seems to have an obsessive interest in the plays, perhaps comes to the same production several times. Hmm . . . anything else, Kathy?"

"Clean-shaven. Knows about theatrical make-up—Leichner spirit gum, for example. Probably a smoker. One possibility might be that he's obsessive about a member of the cast, one of the women."

"Nobody springs immediately to mind," Ruth said slowly. "Of course, we do get lonely, single people coming along to productions for the sake of some human contact, I suppose. The suburbs can be a very lonely place. But I've never really noticed anyone special— never been looking, I suppose. The really obsessive ones tend to end up as members of the company. They become addicted to the roar of the greasepaint and the smell of the crowd, as someone once put it.

"The idea of an insane admirer of one of the women in the cast is an especially terrifying one, isn't it?" Ruth's eyes widened with fascination at the possibility. "Like those mad fans who stalk Hollywood film stars, except that here he is attacking other women in her place. Is that what you mean? Of course, one would expect the woman he admires to have been a member of the cast on each occasion, wouldn't one?"

She jotted down some names. "There were several women in

both *The Lady* and *Barefoot* . . . Vicky is one of Stafford's favourites, and she played the lead, Corrie Bratter, in *Barefoot*, and a smaller role in *The Lady*. She was also in *Equus*. There were probably others too. I think you might have to eliminate me from that list, Chief Inspector," she smiled ruefully, "although the idea of one of the Green Line pensioners forming a murderous passion for me does have its appeal."

"What about the women in the present production—were they in those earlier ones?" Kathy said. "Vicky was. What about Bettina?"

"No, she only joined us at the end of last year. This is really the first production she's had any sort of part in."

"The Nurse?"

"Let me see . . . She was in *Barefoot*, I think, but she's almost as old as me, Kathy."

"Who picks the plays you do?" Brock said suddenly.

"The producers. Stafford in particular. We do four productions each year, and for the past few years he's been responsible for each alternate production, with someone else taking the ones between. He really shouldn't be doing this one now, because he did the last, *Barefoot*. But it suited both him and the next producer to swap their slots—I think Stafford is planning to go away later in the year. The other producer had intended to do *Blithe Spirit*, and it was scheduled in our programme, but Stafford was against having two comedies in a row, and so he made the change to *The Father*, much to everyone's despair, as you well know, Kathy."

"He's quite a character, isn't he?" Kathy said. "I imagine he usually gets his own way."

"Oh good heavens, yes! He *is* SADOS in many ways. Without him it would simply fall apart. He provides the focus, the drive. Everyone else just falls into line behind him."

"Why does he do it?" Brock asked.

"He loves the theatre above everything else. I believe he would have been good enough to be a professional actor or producer himself, and probably was persuaded to take the safe decision early on to become a schoolteacher, instead. A decision which he has no doubt regretted ever since."

"Like you, Ruth. A schoolteacher, I mean."

"Yes, like me."

"Does he have a family?"

"His wife died some years ago. Since then he has lived on his own. They had no children."

She hesitated. "We're his family, really. The theatre is his family." She blushed suddenly and for a moment looked acutely embarrassed.

"What is it?" Kathy said gently.

"No, no. Nothing."

"Come on, Ruth. Tell me. What occurred to you?"

"Oh . . ." She hesitated again, then said, "He told me, after Marjory died . . . I probably shouldn't be saying this, because I don't think he's told the others this story . . . but he's always been infatuated with the theatre, you see, and at some point he fell in love with a beautiful actress, who bore his child. They had it adopted, because he was married to Marjory at the time, and he never saw the actress or the child again. And then, as it turned out, Marjory was unable to bear him any children. It's such a sad story, you see, and so . . . theatrical. When he told me about it, I realized then how important we are to him. I suppose we are part of a sort of dream that he's had all his life, and has never really fulfilled, quite."

They spoke to Edward Quinn next.

"You were part of the group that went up to see *Macbeth* at the National Theatre three weeks ago, Mr. Quinn," Brock said.

"Yes, that's right. There were eight or nine of us, I suppose. Pretty much the people who are here tonight. Ruth organized it— she must have told you."

"Yes, she has. Would you have a good look at these pictures, please?"

Brock spread out photographs of Angela Hannaford on the table.

"Ever seen her before?"

"I don't think so. She looks sort of familiar, but . . . no, I don't think so."

"You might have seen her at the theatre that night, or on the train home."

"She was on the train, was she?"

"You caught the 11:08 from Waterloo, is that right?"

"I suppose it would have been, yes. But I don't recall her."

"You all got off the train at Grove Park, did you?"

"Er, one couple got off at Hither Green, I think, and then the rest of us at Grove Park, where we'd left our cars, or at least . . ."

"What?"

"Well, I hadn't actually. My wife, Rosemary, drove down to the station to collect me. She was waiting when we arrived."

He said it with a touch of embarrassment. *Checking up on you*, Kathy thought.

Brock looked at his notes. "The others were all couples, except Mrs. Sparkes, who got a lift home with two of them, and Mr. Nesbit, who picked up his car at the station and drove home alone, is that right?"

"Think so, yes."

As he got up to go, Kathy said, "How are the lines?"

He rolled his eyes. "Don't talk about it. I'm getting to the panic stage."

Kathy smiled. "They had me prompting for them yesterday," she said to Brock.

"Really? Getting a bit of a taste for it, are you, Kathy?"

After they had spoken to all the cast, only Stafford Nesbit

remained. They walked across the landing to the other room and watched as the rehearsal drew to an end.

"Grandmama doesn't tell lies."

The actress was the girl with the short blonde hair, Bettina, whom Kathy hadn't heard act before, playing the Captain's daughter, Bertha. She seemed clumsy and inexperienced compared to the older members of the cast, her movements wooden, voice flat, face expressionless.

"Why not?" Quinn smiled paternally at her.

"Because then Mama tells lies too."

"Ah."

"If you say that Mama tells lies, then I'll never believe you again."

Quinn seemed more confident in this scene, Nesbit less inclined to interrupt him.

". . . but when you come, Papa, it's like the spring morning when they take down the double windows."

For a moment Bettina seemed able to bring her character to life, her expression became animated, staring intently into her partner's eyes.

"My dear, darling child!"

Kathy watched Quinn move to her side. *Better watch your step, Edward*, she thought.

They trailed away, singly and in small groups, leaving Nesbit alone with the two detectives. He looked drained. "Well," he said, putting his long fingers to his temple, "have you found what you wanted?" He sounded mildly disdainful.

Brock murmured to Kathy, "Why don't you take him on?" and they drew chairs over to the small table where he was sitting. Kathy caught Brock's eye and he gave her a little nod.

"When Zoë Bagnall vanished last January," Kathy said, "immediately after starring in your play *The Lady Vanishes*, what did you think about that extraordinary coincidence?"

Nesbit seemed startled by her abrupt opening.

"I'm not sure I really took a view . . ." He took a deep breath and rubbed his eyes with his finger tips. "I mean, I suppose it didn't really register, not in the way you're suggesting. It was some while, several weeks I think, before people were saying that Zoë was missing. It seemed likely that she had simply moved on."

"Without saying a word to anyone?"

"Some of her friends seemed to think that wasn't improbable . . ."

"Your next play was *Barefoot in the Park*. On the night of the last performance, Saturday June 9, a young woman was murdered nearby in Spring Park. She was found the following morning, fully clothed but without tights or shoes—barefoot, in fact, in the park."

Nesbit stared at Kathy without reaction, his face registering nothing. She found it uncanny, as if the man's brain had simply been unable to find a suitable expression to paint on his face.

"You were aware of this?" she asked.

Nesbit swallowed, his Adam's apple moving slowly up and down his long leathery throat. "No . . . no."

"You don't seem surprised by what I'm telling you."

"I am . . . surprised. I am surprised . . ."

Kathy waited, but when there was nothing more she continued, "The play you did before *The Lady Vanishes* was *Equus*, which you took to the Edinburgh Festival. In late August last year, while you were there, a woman was murdered in a lane in central Edinburgh, not far in fact from the place you performed your play. She suffered massive head injuries. In particular, her eyes were stabbed out . . ."

Stafford Nesbit straightened in his seat, rigidly upright. He flinched as Kathy finished the sentence, ". . . like the horses in *Equus*."

The room was silent, Nesbit motionless.

"You must have read about the murder in the Edinburgh papers, Stafford. It was widely reported on account of the brutal nature of the attack. You'd have been taking the paper each day, wouldn't you, to look for reviews?"

Nesbit shook his head slowly in denial. "I'm sure you're quite wrong about this," he said eventually. "It's inconceivable." His voice was faint, without any of its previous conviction.

"What's inconceivable?"

"That . . . that what you're suggesting . . ."

"What am I suggesting?"

"That . . . there's some connection between a string of murders, and my plays!" He finally got it out.

"I'm really interested to know whether you noticed these coincidences. It would be hard to believe you didn't—not after Zoë Bagnall."

"I have no recollection of thinking any such thing. I rarely read newspapers."

"Really?"

"Surely, surely you must see that some other explanation is much more likely. Three coincidences . . ."

"Four, with the murder in Petts Wood three weeks ago. You must have heard about that. Angela Hannaford, murdered after going to see *Macbeth* at the National Theatre, just like you."

"You think . . ." Where before he had denied, he now seemed dumbfounded. "Do you really think that could also . . ."

"You travelled home on the same train as her. Pretty extraordinary, don't you think? Are you feeling all right?"

"It's so . . . hot in here." He was mumbling, dabbing with a handkerchief at his pale temples and attenuated, stringy throat.

"That's why we're so interested in everyone's movements that evening," Kathy continued. She spread the photographs of Angela Hannaford out in front of Stafford. "Have you ever seen her before?"

"No . . . Are you suggesting that one of us . . . ?"

"Well, that is possible. More likely, I think, would be the possibility of someone on the fringe of your group, following your movements and timing his own actions to coincide with yours."

"Good God," his voice a whisper. "Why? Why do such a thing?"

"It seems to date back to at least August of last year. Did you reject anyone from your group about eighteen months ago? Did you refuse someone a part in *Equus*?"

Nesbit's eyes widened in dismay. "No one, surely . . . they would have to be mad to do such things for such a reason."

"Could someone have developed a fixation for one of the women in your cast? Who was the female lead in *Equus*?"

"Vicky played Jill."

"She's the woman that the disturbed boy tries unsuccessfully to have sex with before he attacks the horses, isn't she?" Kathy asked.

"That's right." Nesbit abruptly turned away from Kathy and looked Brock in the eye. "You want me to cancel *The Father*, don't you? You're afraid it will happen again."

"That's certainly one possible course of action," Brock nodded. "I'd be extremely nervous come—what is it?—tomorrow fortnight, when you're due to put on the final performance of the play, if you went ahead with the killer still at large."

"You're wrong, quite wrong." He turned back to Kathy and fixed her with his large, piercing eyes, and for the first time the force of his feelings seemed to find genuine expression. "It isn't the way you imagine it at all. There will be no repeat of the pattern with *The Father*."

"How can you know that?"

Nesbit didn't answer at first. In response to Kathy's challenge the hoods came down over his eyes and he looked away. When he turned back they were expressionless again. "There are no violent deaths in *The Father*. Don't you see? The Captain has a stroke at the end, that's all. There is nothing to imitate."

"There's a scene with a gun . . ." she said, having wondered the same thing.

"But it isn't used," he snapped impatiently.

"There were no deaths in *Barefoot in the Park* either, if I remember right," Brock said. "It's a light comedy, isn't it? I don't think that's going to stop him."

Nesbit looked close to defeat. "Please," he whispered, and looked at Kathy, pleading. "It's important."

"Why?" she said.

"You don't understand . . . You don't understand."

AS KATHY MANOEUVRED OUT of the pub car park, she asked Brock, "You think they're in the clear, at least?"

"Hard to see how any of them could have murdered Angela. They were all together until they arrived back at Grove Park station, then Nesbit was the only one who wasn't accompanied home. If he'd spotted Angela at the theatre, say, or Waterloo station, and targeted her as a likely victim, he wouldn't have known which station she would be getting off at. Petts Wood was only one of seven possible stops after Grove Park. He couldn't have kept ahead of the train and checked the people leaving each of the stations."

"Are we going to stop them putting the play on?"

"Don't know," he replied, looking back over his shoulder. "Let's see what Alex Nicholson has to say, shall we? You told Ruth Sparkes back there that our man may be a smoker. How come?"

"The match in Angela's mouth."

"Ah, right." He looked back over his shoulder again. "Have you noticed a dark blue Cavalier on your tail at all?"

She glanced in the mirror and saw a pair of headlights following them out on to the street.

"It followed us into the car park when we arrived, and now it's leaving behind us."

"Maybe it's one of the SADOS crowd," she said. "I thought I saw a pale grey BMW a couple of times this week, then I thought I must be getting paranoid."

"Gentle," Brock muttered. "Still bothers you, doesn't he?"

PART THREE

FINAL STAGES

THIRTEEN

DR. ALEX NICHOLSON WASN'T at all what Kathy had imagined. She seemed very young, slight of build, with a thick mane of black hair worn with a low fringe over her eyes. She was wearing a black waistcoat over a white shirt, hanging out over black jeans and shoes.

Desai had brought her in and introduced her to the dozen or so people in the room, then went to fetch her coffee. He seemed to Kathy to be rather proprietorial in his manner, rather pleased with himself.

Brock came in, and the talking died away. "I want to thank Dr. Nicholson for giving us some more of her time. She helped us earlier in trying to arrive at a picture of Angela's killer, and the aim now is to develop the profile in the light of the new information we have. You got a copy of Kathy's report all right, Alex?"

She nodded, and directed a little smile in Kathy's direction.

"Later Alex'll spend some time with the forensic team, but I thought we'd start with some discussion about what this new information might mean."

He paused as the door opened. Bren stepped in, face flushed from hurrying. He nodded at Alex Nicholson as if he knew her and sat down.

"It might be worthwhile outlining the approaches you use, Alex, for those who haven't worked with you before," Brock continued.

She nodded and got to her feet. She spoke rather softly, apparently very calm. "We use four different approaches, based on four different psychological methods or theories. We use them simultaneously, because it's hard to anticipate which are likely to be the most productive in any particular case."

She turned to the white board behind her and wrote "1— Mental Maps."

"People develop mental maps of the places they're in. They need these to understand their environment and navigate their way through it. It's a particular interest of the department I'm in, overlapping geography and psychology. The relevance of it is that it's possible to infer characteristics of a person's mental map of a region from the way they use it. In this case, for example, it may be possible to reconstruct features of the perpetrator's mental map from the location of the attacks, and then suggest areas to look for where he lives, perhaps, or works. We did this successfully in the John Duffy case."

Kathy nodded, remembering Brock's obsession with the Southern Region rail system around Petts Wood.

Dr. Nicholson turned back to the board and wrote "2—Stats."

"In a large murder investigation like this, you accumulate a huge amount of information, much of which is subjective, qualitative, and unreliable. In the John Duffy case, to use that example again, we had statements from twenty-seven attacks, which gave his description as ranging from negroid to ginger-haired. We can use techniques called non-metric multidimensional scaling procedures, that have been developed to analyse statistically this kind of approximate, qualitative data. The idea is to reduce eyewitness statements to a matrix of items, and then use these techniques to discover statistically significant patterns in them. This is the second approach."

She wrote a third heading, "3—Offender Type."

"The third is based on work done in the United States by the FBI Behavioral Science Unit, now part of the National Center for the Analysis of Violent Crime. They have developed classifications of sexual offenders, following psychiatric taxonomies, and the idea here is to identify the appropriate type from the observed behaviours, and then predict his other characteristics. One problem for us is that we don't know if these American typologies are reliable in the UK, but we feel it's worth pursuing.

"And then, finally, the fourth approach." She turned back to the board and wrote "4—Crim. Career."

"In the case of a series of crimes, carried out by the same man over a period of time, the pattern is not constant, it evolves. This is the aspect that you gave that paper on in Rome, isn't it, Brock?"

He tilted his head in acknowledgement.

"Yes, well, to some extent you can read the offender's mind by studying the developing pattern of his criminal career. The FBI people have pointed out that in some cases the offender may become quite self-conscious and calculating about this, so that it becomes almost like an ongoing internal dialogue, which we are observing from the outside, from the evidence it leaves behind. And of course he may be very aware that that is what the police are doing, so that his pattern may be influenced by the knowledge that he has an audience."

She turned to Brock, who nodded. "Thanks, Alex. Questions? No? Well, which approach do we concentrate on here?"

"The first you did explore pretty well before, and it led you to the wrong suspect—Tom Gentle," Alex Nicholson replied. "I think the location of crimes seems to be so strongly influenced by the theatre locations that we may have difficulty separating out the individual's mental map."

"OK."

"The second approach, with statistics, you're pretty heavily into at present, I think. I could have a look at the data you're gathering from interviews and help set up a matrix with you, if you like.

"I'd prefer to leave the question of offender type for the moment, Brock. Which leaves the criminal career."

She sniffed and pushed some hair back from the side of her face. "This is the really spectacular thing you've come up with. I don't think I've ever seen anything like this before. The play provides the cue for the crime. Each crime seems like the next chapter of an ongoing drama. We can imagine that witnessing a performance— usually the final performance of the show—acts as the trigger for the violent act. But that act has been completely choreographed in advance. There's nothing spontaneous about the response to the trigger, yet the act appears uncontrollably violent to those who witness its results."

She hesitated. "It is like he's making a point, communicating something. But I don't think he's talking to the police, the people trying to catch him. It's so specific, being tied to this one little theatre group. It's more like a fixation, an obsession of some kind. And that's kind of supported by the other constant—the choice of blonde women as victims. So specific."

She came to a stop, reached for her coffee cup, and stood sipping it while they thought about this.

"Could he be imagining that they're one specific blonde woman, Alex?" It was Bren.

She nodded. "Yes, it could be that."

"You mean he's fantasizing that he's killing somebody else while he's attacking them? Acting out what he wants to do to her?"

"It could be more than acting out. It could be that he's deluded. That's where we get to the offender type. I wondered whether we might have a functional psychosis here. Maybe a form of schizo-phrenia. But I'm not really qualified to speak on that. I think it would be worthwhile to talk to someone in the clinical field, a psychiatrist who specializes in this area."

"But still, Alex, you obviously feel there are some indications here?" Brock pursued the point. "I thought schizophrenics suffered from disordered thinking, whereas this bloke seems pretty orderly in his attacks."

"It depends what you mean by order. There are many kinds of schizophrenia, and they don't necessarily have to hear voices in order to kill, though some do. Some rare crimes, like matricide, are almost only committed by schizophrenics, and the more bizarre the murder the more likely it was committed by someone with a mental disorder like this."

"Go on."

She was frowning. "Well . . . there is a very dangerous condition, allied to paranoid schizophrenia, but without the characteristic thought disorder of true schizophrenia. It's called the Othello Syndrome. That's why it occurred to me, of course, as soon as I read your report, with all the references to the theatre and plays, including the Shakespeare tragedies. The Othello Syndrome is a form of morbid jealousy, and quite well defined. The sufferer is usually a male in his forties, married or in a stable relationship for ten or more years, who has delusions of infidelity about his partner. These develop for four or five years, during which he becomes more enraged and more violent towards her. Nothing she can say or do will affect his delusion. In the end she must leave or he will probably murder her."

There was silence.

Then Bren said, "What happens then? After she leaves? Does he get over it, or what?"

She shrugged. "I don't know."

"So, let's say she's a blonde actress, and he goes on ticking away, after she's gone, like a bomb, until he's ready to blow. He goes to Edinburgh, to the Festival, maybe searching for her there, and he sees this amateur group put on this performance of *Equus*, and he thinks, my God, that's it, that's what I'm going to do to her, and after the performance he grabs the first blonde woman he sees, and stabs her eyes out."

Dr. Nicholson gave a little nod.

Bren continued. "Why does he then continue to haunt this same theatre group?"

"There must be some very strong association with the woman. Maybe she used to be in the group, or maybe one of them looks a lot like her. Maybe one of them *is* her. Zoë Bagnall, say."

"Her former husband? Christ, we never checked that."

"He would have to have been in a relationship with the woman for some time?" Brock queried. "And he'd be in his forties?"

"That's the typical case, Brock, but no, of course it might well be otherwise. Or she could have left some time ago. If it is this condition."

"Does he need an Iago to set him going, this Othello?" Brock said, scratching his beard.

"No." She smiled. "I don't think he needs a provocation. He does it all himself, inside his head."

"OK," Brock nodded. "Say you're right. The group has another play coming up the week after next. What do we do? Do we stop them?"

"I'm glad I don't have to make that decision," Alex replied. "Cancelling the play isn't going to stop him now—he's demonstrated that with the National Theatre outing, that he can use other things as a trigger. And if the play goes ahead, you'll know when to expect his next attack. But you won't be able to protect every blonde woman in south-east London, will you? I think if it were my decision I would cancel, yes, because I'd feel so bad when he did it on the day I knew about, even though I knew he'd have done it another time anyway."

The group erupted in argument and discussion about this.

When this finally died away, Alex Nicholson's quiet voice said, "If you do decide to let them go ahead, I'd do one thing. I'd get all the blonde women in the cast to dye their hair, for a start."

Later, as they were eating sandwiches for lunch, Kathy found herself next to Bren. She hesitated, then said, "How's it going? How's your mother-in-law?"

"She'll live. The driver that hit her said he did it in self-defence."

"That's original."

"Yeah. He says she leaped out at him waving her umbrella as he was driving along. His car was the same model and colour as mine."

"Oh, Bren! That's terrible." Kathy stared at her plate, then gave a little involuntary snort. Then she heard Bren do the same, and then they were both laughing.

THAT EVENING, SATURDAY SEPTEMBER 29, the whole production team for *The Father* gathered in response to phone calls from Ruth. There were many people in the rehearsal room whom Kathy had never seen before—stage-managers, set-builders, lighting, sound, props, stage-hands, publicity, ushers, and house-managers, as well as two members of the cast who were new to Kathy, Doctor Östermark and the trooper Nöjd, whose acting styles, as Ruth explained to Kathy, formed opposite extremes.

"Nöjd is the young man over there," she whispered as they waited for Brock to speak, "a panel-beater at a garage in Beckenham, and very useful if you ever have a bump with your car. The trooper Nöjd is the one at the start of the play who refuses to accept responsibility for the maid whom he's got pregnant, on the grounds he can't be sure the baby's his, and so gets the Captain wondering about his own daughter, and the uncertain position of fathers in general. His problem is that he over-acts terribly. He only ever gets small parts from Stafford, whom he worships, and he tries to throw absolutely everything into them. Östermark, on the other hand, has a tendency to turn to stone when he gets on to the stage. He actually is a doctor in real life, a registrar at the hospital, and terribly nice. In the play he is completely manipulated by the cunning Laura into believing the Captain is mad, so perhaps his rather robotic acting style is well cast. Stafford's problem is to try to animate him at the same time that he's trying to restrain Nöjd."

"We'll never keep tabs on them all," Kathy said, having already told Ruth something of the problem they faced.

"Well, I hope they decide to call a halt to the whole thing," the other woman replied. "We still haven't had a complete run-through of the play. Can you imagine, at this stage? It should have happened a couple of weeks ago. And now with this dreadful business, it's all become a nightmare. Mind you"—she nodded towards Kathy's aunt seated over by the wall, busy measuring the arm of the person next to her—"I don't think Maryanne would ever forgive us if we gave up now."

The murmur of conversations died away as Brock got to his feet. As he described the police theories linking SADOS productions to the murders, shock and disbelief froze the faces in the room. He asked them to consider again whether they might have noticed anything unusual during this or previous productions. He described the sort of precautions that could be taken against stalkers, and the kinds of assistance that the police could provide. The most obvious precaution, however, would be to cancel *The Father* immediately. This met with a stunned silence, then a babble of anxious voices. Kathy watched Stafford, head bowed, giving no indication of his feelings.

"Would that really solve anything though?" Edward Quinn spoke out, his voice strong and clear, just as on the stage, so that Kathy wondered if he and Nesbit had rehearsed this.

"I mean, the murderer would still be out there, wouldn't he?

He's not going to stop doing what he does just because we cancel a play!"

"It would avoid providing an obvious trigger," Brock said.

"But anything could be a trigger." Quinn echoed the argument that Alex Nicholson had put forward. "He's shown that. An outing to the National Theatre was a trigger. I think we should go on with it. At least then we'll know when the danger time is likely to be, and the police might have a better chance of catching him."

There was a murmur of approval for this.

"I'd like to hear what Stafford thinks," Vicky said. "It's his play."

All eyes turned to the producer, who took an interminable dramatic moment to raise his eyes to meet theirs. He let the tension build, then, softly, "Thank you, Vicky. But no, it is not my play. It belongs to all of us, equally. And it would not be for me to prolong it for one single second beyond its useful life. If it does represent, as the Chief Inspector so sensibly suggests, a danger to us, then we must bring it to an end immediately.

"Of course, Edward makes a strong argument against that view."

"He's doing Mark Antony," Ruth hissed in Kathy's ear. *"I come to bury Caesar, not to praise him."*

"Edward rightly points out that stopping the play doesn't really solve anything. But the Chief Inspector is a professional man, all his colleagues are professional men . . ."

"Oh Stafford!" Ruth hissed. "Shame on you!"

"The Chief Inspector naturally does not understand what the play means to us. For him it is no more than a social diversion. And this is entirely understandable and sensible. But the truth is that it is not for Edward, nor for me, nor even for the Chief Inspector and his colleagues, to say what we should do. They are not at risk. It is the women of the company who are at risk. For my part, I would not extend their risk by one second, if by killing the play stone dead now I could avoid it.

"Vicky, my dear. It is you and your sisters who must decide."

Before Vicky could respond, Ruth was on her feet. "It's perfectly clear what we should do. The police have given us their professional advice, and we'd be fools to ignore it. We can easily postpone the play until another time. There's no point in trying to take on a madman."

She sat down to cautious nods of agreement.

"Ruth, darling"—now Vicky took her cue, smoothly—"he'd have to be mad to take you on. But seriously, I for one think we've all invested too much of ourselves in this to give it up at the eleventh hour. And as a woman, I resent the implication that we should rearrange our lives and our priorities because some man decides to terrorize us. I suppose the police would be delighted if all the women in South London locked themselves indoors for the next six months."

Coming from Vicky, the most attractive potential victim in the room, it was an argument that Ruth couldn't easily counter. She shook her head in dismay as the company voted overwhelmingly by show of hands to continue with the play.

Stafford took control of the room immediately, asking non-actors to clear the floor. As the majority made for the door and the saloon bar below, he called out, "One other thing, everyone. To make us all feel much safer, Sergeant Kathy Kolla has kindly agreed to be our new prompt, since Hazel is clearly not going to be well enough to resume her duties."

To Kathy's embarrassment, there was a scattering of applause.

Brock ambled over, looking not at all put out by the decision.

"Don't you mind?" Kathy asked.

"Well, it was a bit stagey for my taste, but at least we got the right outcome."

"The right outcome?" Kathy looked at him in surprise, wondering suddenly if Brock had manoeuvred them all into this position.

"Well, Kathy, as Mr. Quinn so eloquently pointed out, at least we now have some kind of deadline we can anticipate and plan for. Was that your idea, about becoming part of their team?"

"Stafford asked me. I thought it might be useful."

"Did he? Did he indeed? He seems to be taking quite an interest in you, Kathy. But yes, it may be useful."

There was a loud rapping of keys on Stafford's formica-topped table. "End of act two, please. Let's get it right, finally, then on to the beginning of act three." The conciliatory tone had gone. People scurried off the floor.

"Laura and the Captain. Kathy, give Vicky the line, from the top of the last page of act two. Come along!"

It took her a moment to find it, during which Stafford drummed his fingers impatiently. *What do you mean by all this?*

"I realize that one of us must go under in this struggle." Edward picked up the cue.

"Which?" Laura asked her husband defiantly.

"The weaker, of course."

"And the stronger will be in the right?"

"Naturally, since he has the power."

"Then," she threw at him, *"I am in the right!"*

Not for the first time, Kathy felt an odd and elusive resonance between the lines of the play and the events shaping up around it. Her eye moved down the page, following the actors' words until they reached the end of the act, with Laura, backing towards the door at stage left, accusing her husband of insanity. At this point the Captain reached forward for a rolled newspaper, representing a lighted lamp according to Kathy's script, and tossed it at Laura's feet.

"NO! NO! NO! NO!" Stafford stormed forward, his face livid. He snatched up the newspaper and advanced on Edward, waving it in his face. "This is a lighted paraffin lamp, you ninny! You are not throwing a bunch of daffodils at the woman! You are hurling a Molotov cocktail at her, for God's sake! YOU ARE TRYING TO KILL HER!"

He glared at Edward for a furious moment, then turned on his heel and hurled the newspaper at Vicky, missing her head by inches. He then marched back to his table. Edward looked shaken. He glanced over at Vicky, who shrugged and rolled her eyes.

"Look, Stafford," he tried, "this scene is impossible. I simply can't see how that action is supposed to work. I know it's meant to be some kind of mid-point climax, but it just seems totally bizarre and unconvincing to me."

"Nobody gives a turkey's fart how it seems to you, Edward," Stafford retorted brutally. "We're not asking you to write a critique of the bloody play, only to portray one of the characters, and to do that as if you meant it. Not as if it were a way of filling in time until you can go downstairs for a glass of ale. My God, man! When are you going to start taking this seriously?"

Everyone was staring in shock at Stafford. Edward looked as if he might crumple. Yet he still found the words to come back one more time. "If I do as you say, Stafford," he said stiffly, with as much dignity as he could gather, "and throw it at the wall, it either *will* kill Vicky, or it'll bring the set down."

"Well, hooray! At least we'll get one performance where you're not all *half*-dead."

"It's extraordinary," Ruth said afterwards. "I've never seen him like that before. Normally he's the only one who keeps his head. I find it rather frightening. You'd think his life depended on it."

THE FOLLOWING EVENING, KATHY and her aunt were sitting in the flat, reading. Mary was studying illustrations of nineteenth-century costumes in the collection of the V and A, trying to decipher collar designs, while Kathy sat opposite her, reading collections of plays—Noël Coward, Neil Simon, Peter Shaffer, and August Strindberg.

The phone rang, and when she lifted it Kathy heard the mid-Atlantic accent of her cousin, Mary's daughter, on the line.

"Hello, Di," she said, watching the alarm appear on Mary's face. She raised an eyebrow at her aunt, who shook her head vigorously.

"Kathy, is my mother there with you?"

"Yes. Do you want to speak to her?"

"No. What I want you to do is put her on the next available train back to Sheffield. How long has she been there with you?"

"I think it must be two weeks now."

"Two weeks! What has she told you she's doing?"

"I rather think she's left your father, Di."

"That's utterly crazy! Is she out of her mind?"

"Actually, she's a lot calmer than when she first arrived. She seems quite sane to me."

"But . . . there must be something wrong with her. They've been together for fifty years. She can't walk out on him now. It's just perfectly grotesque."

"She's quite serious about it, Di."

"What about him? How is he going to survive?"

"Perhaps it'll be good for him."

"Don't be ridiculous!"

"How is he making out, do you know?"

"The cousins have been doing their best to cope, I understand, with the help of a neighbour—someone called Effie—and the Social Services people have been round. But that's no solution. You have to persuade her to go home, and make it up with Pop, and just stop being so . . . so absurd."

"She won't do it, Di. I'll tell you what. Maybe I could take her down to Heathrow tomorrow and put her on a plane to Toronto. I'm sure the airline would look after her for the transfer to Calgary."

There was silence on the line. Aunt Mary's eyes widened in consternation.

"Or would a Vancouver flight be better? It probably would, wouldn't it?"

"Kathy . . . that wouldn't do any good at all. I mean it isn't going to help her think any straighter. And besides . . . Don and I are going through a difficult time right now. I don't think having Mom around the place would be a good idea at all."

"Ah."

"Look, I'll give this some more thought. Please do what you can to make her see sense, Kathy. I mean, it's just all so . . . embarrassing."

Kathy replaced the receiver. "Di sends her love. She and Don are going through a difficult time right now, otherwise they'd love to have you over there."

Mary said nothing, returning her attention to her book, although Kathy noticed that the pages didn't turn. After several minutes the old lady said, "I've been imposing on you, Kathy. I'm sorry."

"Don't be daft. I've been eating better than I have for years. And Ruth and her friends would have been lost without you."

"Ruth thinks we'll have finished the costumes by Thursday," Mary said cautiously. "I would have liked to stay to see the play . . ."

"Of course you must."

"Do you mean that? Well, but when the play is over . . . I'll have to decide what to do."

"Do you miss him?"

"I feel numb, Kathy. I try not to think."

THE INDIAN SUMMER REFUSED to die. At the end of each hot, dusty day, after knocking at the doors of empty houses or interviewing women keen for a good chat, Kathy would look forward to her evenings at the Three Crowns. She would step thankfully into the cool of the saloon, order her half of lager among the last of the hot, homecoming commuters and the first of the freshly showered evening crowd, and then climb the stairs to the rehearsal room.

A change had come over the whole company since Stafford's outburst over the lamp-throwing scene. The earlier casual good humour was replaced by a mood of tense purpose. Edward had abandoned his temperamental games with Vicky along with his book. They were now having a full run-through every night, and since the Captain was on stage for about three-quarters of the whole play, the extent of Edward's lack of mastery of his lines was painfully clear, putting everyone else in a state of acute anxiety. Kathy, however, enjoyed it. She found she could pick up the hint of hesitation just before he was going to dry, and was learning to give him the minimum prompt necessary to get him started again.

A change had come over Stafford too. He seemed to have withdrawn from the company, standing apart from their conversations and gossip. Leaning forward over his table like a brooding vulture, he would rap out instructions and harry them until they complied precisely.

Kathy could see that Ruth was concerned for him, but he ignored her attempts to help him. Strangely, he was polite, almost excessively so, to just one person, Aunt Mary. Several times, during the breaks, Kathy noticed them in conversation, and the radiant expression on Mary's face as they talked.

"He's so caring," the old lady said as they drove home on the Tuesday night. "He thinks about every detail. Tomorrow he'll be coming round to Ruth's to help us make the strait-jacket."

"Is the battle of the bustle resolved?"

"Oh yes. Stafford won. He is the producer, after all. He explained that sometimes you have to sacrifice an attractive detail for the sake of the big idea."

Her euphoria evaporated when they reached home and discovered that she had lost her keys, including the key which Kathy had given her, to the flat. "I had them at the rehearsal," she moaned, as she emptied her bag on to the kitchen table. "I remember they were tangled up in the tape measure."

Kathy frowned. She had noticed the tape measure beside Mary's chair, but there had been no keys. There seemed no point in making a big thing of it, and she said lightly, "They probably fell out of your bag in the rehearsal room. We'll get them tomorrow."

BREN CALLED IN TO the rehearsal on his way home the following evening. It was late, and they were already well into the third and final act when he slipped quietly into the room. Kathy grinned at him, and he winked back and took the seat beside her, then frowned as he tried to make sense of the scene in the room.

Stafford had stopped them, and was standing clutching his forehead as if suffering some private agony. The Captain was lying across the seats which represented the sofa, his arms bound in the strait-jacket which his old Nurse had tricked him into putting on—another highly improbable action in Edward's opinion over which he and Stafford had almost come to blows. His wife stood over him.

"Go back to the 'all my enemies' speech, Edward," Stafford sighed. "It's coming apart at that point. It's not shocking enough. You should be raging against the world, and instead you're merely whining. Shock us, Edward! Chant the lines, the way I told you, for God's sake. This is your credo, your Nicene Creed. Do it like that. Kathy, give us Laura's line."

"*Do you believe that I'm your enemy?*" she said.

"*Yes, I do!*" Edward replied. "*I believe that you're all my enemies. My mother, who didn't want to bring me into the world because my birth would bring her pain, she was my enemy: she starved my*

*unborn life of its nourishment, till I was nearly deformed. My sister
was my enemy, when she taught me to be her vassal. The first woman
I took in my arms was my enemy, for she gave me ten years' illness in
return for the love I gave her. My daughter became my enemy, when
she had to choose between me and you. And you, my wife, you were
my mortal enemy, for you never let me be till you had me lying dead."*

Stafford stopped them again, moving Vicky further away from
the sofa, so that Edward would appear more isolated at centre
stage, an almost devotional figure in the crossed arms of the strait-
jacket.

"I know how that bloke feels," Bren whispered.

"It's not that bad, surely?" Kathy said, trying to sound as if she
thought he was making a joke.

"And I'll tell you what, I'll bet that's exactly the way our killer
sees it too."

Aunt Mary's keys were lying beneath the seat she had used on the
previous night, just as Kathy had predicted. Overcome with relief,
Mary babbled away on the drive home about their experiences that
day with Stafford.

"He's a difficult man, Kathy. I didn't like the way he spoke to
Ruth today. Quite rude, I thought."

"Yesterday you said he was very caring." Kathy immediately
regretted the comment, remembering the last time she'd tried to
argue with her aunt after a long day.

"Well, he is that too. You'd be surprised."

"Would I?"

"Yes, you would. He cares about you, as a matter of fact. We
had a long chat about you. He wanted to know all about how we
were related, and about your mum and dad. He was particularly
interested in them."

"What? Why on earth would he want to know about them?"
Kathy felt a flash of resentment.

"Because he's interested in people. He said that a theatre

producer has to study people, so he can make characters come to life on the stage. Ruth had to go out to buy some material, and Stafford and I had a good long yarn over a cup of tea. I told him all about us, and how you coped with your mum after your pa died."

"Did you tell him how Dad died?"

"I may have mentioned something."

"That's none of his business, Mary!" Kathy exploded. "I don't like you talking to him about our private lives."

"Oh nonsense! That's all in the past. You sound like a right southerner. There's nothing wrong with people being interested in each other's stories. That's what it's all about."

Kathy clenched her teeth, knowing what the answer to that was, knowing she should leave it alone, but unable to stop. "And did you tell him all about you and Tom splitting up?"

Mary was shocked. "I couldn't do that, Kathy!"

"No, well, maybe you should. Maybe it's time you started talking about it. Maybe it's time you started facing up to it."

Kathy saw the look on Mary's face, and her anger faded away.

"Anyway," she said, wanting to move the conversation away from dangerous ground, "he must be pleased with what you've done with the costumes."

"Oh yes." Aunt Mary was tight-lipped.

"Will you finish tomorrow, as you planned?"

The old lady nodded, accepting the truce. "Ruth can't wait to get them out of her flat. There's no room left. Stafford's taking everything over to his place tomorrow morning." She sounded desperately weary, her voice dropping to a monotone. "He stores all their costumes in his attic. He'll keep them there till next week." She sighed, then added in a barely audible whisper, "Ruth says he's got such a big spooky old house."

"Why was he being rude to her today?"

"That was something to do with you too. Something that Ruth

had told you, and when she mentioned it to him he was upset with her. I don't know what it was though, do you?"

"No," Kathy lied, slowly. "I can't think." *His ancient passion for an actress who had borne his child.* She couldn't imagine why it hadn't struck her before.

When they got back to the flat, Kathy rang Ruth. "Sorry to bother you so late, Ruth. I was afraid you might be asleep."

"No, no. I'm tucked up with my Horlicks, Kathy, reading the latest Mary Wesley. What can I do for you?"

"My aunt just mentioned that I got you into trouble with Stafford over that story you told me about his lost child."

"Oh, don't worry. He's a bit prickly sometimes. But he's got too much else to worry about at the moment to bother with that."

"Did you ever meet the lady—an actress, didn't you say?"

"That's right. No, I never met her. It was before I knew Stafford."

"So you don't know what she was like? Physically, I mean?"

"No . . . What are you after, Kathy? Why are you asking?"

"Just curious. Is Stafford religious, Ruth?"

"No, not in the least."

"He doesn't go to church? Ever?"

"I've never heard of him doing so. What odd questions."

"Sorry. One more. You said he was a schoolteacher before he retired. Which school was that?"

"Sundridge Grammar. Not far from Elmstead Woods station. He retired after his wife, Marjory, died, five or six years ago. It was understandable, of course, that he would feel depressed when she passed away, but it wasn't just grief. He's a perfectionist, an obsessive personality, I suppose, and he drives himself and everyone else mad with his single-mindedness. Marjory tempered that, kept him on an even keel, and when she was gone he had nothing to keep him in check. He just wound himself up until he snapped. He started having fights with the other staff at his school, bullying the children, outraging their parents. Then he had his breakdown, and took early retirement.

"It was a shame, because he used to get wonderful results for his kids. Sundridge used to regularly top the area A-level results in English because of him. He was always immensely thorough, and inspiring too. But then it all turned bad."

FOURTEEN

THE FOLLOWING MORNING KATHY rang the Hannafords. Basil Hannaford answered. He seemed startled to hear from her, then reverted to monosyllables in an uncomfortable, one-sided conversation. At the end of it Kathy was struck by the fact that he hadn't even bothered to ask her if there had been any progress. He did confirm, however, that Angela had been a pupil at Sundridge Grammar for eight years, finishing in the year following Stafford Nesbit's departure.

She rang to make an appointment at the school, then phoned Brock in London. "He claimed he didn't recognize her, but he'd been a teacher at her school. The point is, if he knew her, if he knew where she lived, he could have got off the train at Grove Park that night and driven straight to Petts Wood, to wait for her. I'm going to find out now if he actually taught her."

"And if he did, you'll bring him in?"

"Yes."

"Give me a ring."

Kathy put down the phone. *The other staff, the children, their parents—all my enemies.*

She met the headmistress an hour later, a determined-looking woman in a power suit, who winced at the mention of Stafford's name.

"Yes, I remember him very well. I hadn't been here long when he lost his wife, so that must have been, what, eighty-four or eighty-five? He had a reputation as an outstanding teacher of English literature and drama at senior levels. His A-level results were superb. Unfortunately the loss of his wife affected him very badly, to such an extent that eventually he was unable to continue here."

"In what way did his behaviour change?"

"He had always been meticulous, set high standards, both for himself and for his pupils. But he now became unreasonably demanding, and was extremely distressed when his goals weren't met. With his colleagues he saw any discussion of the course he taught as a personal attack upon himself. And with parents . . ." She shuddered.

"By the time I discovered how bad it had become he had alienated all of his close colleagues and driven a number of sixth-form pupils to a state of near-hysteria. I had a very painful interview with him, and we finally agreed that he should take a few weeks' leave and seek professional help. He never returned to school. After a week I received a brief note from his doctor saying that Stafford had asked him to advise us that he had been admitted to hospital as an in-patient. After about six months he requested early retirement on medical grounds."

"Can you give me the precise dates for all this?" Kathy asked.

"I'll have to send for his file."

"Thank you. And could you also get any information you might have on one of your former pupils, Angela Hannaford?"

"Angela . . . the poor girl who was murdered a few weeks ago? Oh no!"

The headmistress stared at Kathy in horror. "You don't think . . . ?"

Kathy saw the idea form in her mind, and saw her accept it immediately as being only too possible.

"He would have known Angela, would he?"

"Yes, there's absolutely no question of that. Angela was one of the bright girls who were very nearly knocked off the rails by Stafford's illness. She would have been in the lower sixth during his last year here. Fortunately she recovered her stride and did really quite well in her A-levels in the following year. You're still looking, are you? For whoever . . . ?"

"Oh yes. We're still looking."

KATHY DROVE BACK TO the Orpington station and collected a young uniformed constable to go with her to pick up Stafford.

The house was the oldest and largest in its street, a late-Victorian Gothic mansion which Stafford had inherited from his father, who had acquired it when it was still surrounded by farmland and woods. Now it was an anachronism, standing back darkly in its garden from the jostle of suburban red brick which had long since overwhelmed its rural setting. Its brooding character, reinforced by the outlandish figure of a giant monkey-puzzle tree in the front lawn, gave it a certain notoriety among the local children, which their occasional sighting of the formidably gaunt and abrupt owner had done nothing to dispel.

Ruth and Mary were at the end of the gravel drive, dragging armfuls of costumes out of the open doors of a Citroën parked next to Ruth's estate-car.

"Kathy! What a surprise," Ruth cried. "Are you after us, or Stafford? He's just popped round to the corner shop for a packet of tea. He told us to go on in."

Although she had been there many times before, there was a distinct diffidence about the way Ruth opened the front door and led them in, as if she wasn't sure how the empty house, cool and dark, would receive them.

"Stafford said he'd left us a rack downstairs," she whispered, and opened a door to one side of the large hall. She felt inside for the light switch, and an ancient pendant fitting came to life, throwing a dim amber glow over the interior.

"Ah!" She sounded relieved. The room was crowded with furniture, with barely enough room for the metal clothes-rack on castors jammed just inside the door. Kathy smelled the mouldering fabrics and her heart sank. *How could anyone live in this?*

They pulled the rack out into the hall and began loading it up with the clothes from the cars. When the last had been brought in Ruth rubbed her hands. "There should be an ironing-board in the kitchen. Maryanne and I will give them a bit of a press, Kathy."

"Can I do anything?"

"Well, we're short of hangers. There'll be some in the attic. And Stafford said we have some old army greatcoats up there. We need one or two to hang behind the door on the set. Black or grey, not khaki, if we have them."

Kathy nodded and made for the stairs. At the first-floor landing she took her time before going on up to the attic, looking inside each of the rooms. The first, heavy with the smell of mildewed paper, was piled high with stacks of books and boxes haphazardly stuffed with newspapers. The second was a large bedroom, crammed with three differently styled wardrobes and matching dressing-tables, as well as a high, quilted bed. Then came the bathroom, ancient fittings and cracked green tiles, from which Kathy rapidly retreated.

A geriatric, balding rocking-horse stood inside an alcove, guarding a narrow stair leading up to a panelled door above. The door was locked, but the key was in place. She turned it and stepped inside.

A ghostly department store filled the gloomy space beneath the roof. Line upon line of eccentric cast-offs donated by former members of SADOS and their deceased relatives hung from rafters and joists. Flares, plus-fours and tails were suspended alongside overblown ballroom gowns, A-line frocks, and flappers' beads.

Over to the side, beneath the two dormer windows and extending around the narrow eaves to left and right, were trunks and chests of various types. Kathy opened them one by one, discovering hoards of shoes, hats, umbrellas, and canes.

She was kneeling over a trunk whose lid had been stained by a leak in the slate roof above when she heard a sound behind her. She stood up quickly, almost banging her head on the joists, and turned to face the ranks of clothes. Stafford Nesbit was there, staring at her, something in his hand.

"Have you found what you're looking for?" he said, his voice harsh.

She said nothing, feeling her heart pounding from the shock of seeing him there.

"My nemesis," he said, as if to himself.

"What?"

"You, Kathy Kolla. My nemesis. Goddess of retribution and vengeance."

He raised the thing in his hand, and Kathy held her breath, trying to think which way to jump if he came for her, until she saw that it was only an old wooden coat hanger he was holding. He hooked it on the rack beside him.

"What are you looking for?" he demanded.

"Greatcoats."

"Ah. I thought you might be hunting for Zoë Bagnall."

"Is she here?" Kathy said lightly. "You seem to have almost everything else."

"I'm a hoarder. I keep everything. It's my way of coming to terms with the past."

"I'm the opposite."

"Yes, I know. You keep nothing, I understand. Not even memories. Equally pathological, I should say."

"Memories?"

"You wiped the memory of your father from your mind. I find that extraordinary."

"That's not true . . ."

"Is that because you felt so much guilt? They say that the people whom a suicide leaves behind feel tremendous guilt."

"Stafford, I'd like you to come back to Orpington police station with me now. There are things I have to ask you."

"Ah yes." He didn't seem surprised. He stared at her for a moment with his big, piercing eyes, slightly watery under the light from the dormer window. Then he stepped back and made a theatrical sweep of his arm.

"No," Kathy said. "You lead the way."

When they walked out of the front door on to the driveway, the uniformed policeman stepped forward and grabbed Stafford's arm. It was an unnecessary, clumsy gesture, which made Stafford suddenly appear awkward and humiliated. Kathy caught the expression on Ruth's face, horrified.

KATHY WAITED UNTIL BROCK arrived, reluctant to begin. She hoped, in fact, that he would take over the interrogation, but when he bustled in the first thing he said was, "I want you to question him, Kathy. Just you. I'll stay outside and watch."

"He respects you, Brock. Don't you think . . ."

"You have some kind of rapport with him, Kathy. I've noticed."

"You think it's because I look like them, don't you? Female, blonde."

"That could be. Play on that. Pitch it on a personal level."

Nesbit was clutching his temple in his long bony hands as if in intense prayer, and didn't look up when she came into the room.

She opened the file she was carrying and spread the photographs of Angela Hannaford out on the table in front of him, then sat down.

"We showed you these pictures a few days ago, Stafford, and you said you didn't recognize the woman. Do you want to change your mind?"

"No." His head shook, still protected by its cage of fingers.

"Look at them, please."

He pulled his hands away finally, and stared at the pictures for some time.

"I don't remember ever seeing her before." His voice seemed deeper, slightly hoarse, from a cold perhaps, or from shouting at the cast.

"Yet she was a pupil at Sundridge Grammar for eight years, and a student of yours from 1984 to '87. Throughout the first term of '87 she was sitting in front of you, in your classes, for five hours each week. Do you deny that?"

He frowned and lowered his eyes.

"You marked her essays, discussed the set books with her. She even took part in two school plays you were responsible for. It isn't possible that you don't know her, Stafford. Why are you lying to me about it? Why would you want to deny it now, now that we know?"

He kept his eyes lowered, avoiding hers.

"Where did you spot her, on September the eighth, that night you went to the National Theatre? Was it in the foyer? During the interval? Or afterwards, on Waterloo station? Where was it?"

He gave no reply.

"Stafford," Kathy said quietly, "this is no good. You have to say something. We can't let you go unless you explain yourself."

He looked up suddenly in alarm. "I shall have to be at the Three Crowns tonight, Kathy. You know they can't manage without me."

"That depends on you."

He shook his head slowly. "You may be right, about this girl. I don't know."

"How could you not know? You saw her almost every day for several years."

"When my wife died, I became depressed. My doctor gave me pills. As I got worse, he tried different things. Finally"—he sighed deeply—"they put me in hospital for several months. I was heavily sedated for a time, and they tried new forms of treatment. Afterwards, I found I had forgotten things, people, from that period. Sometimes a man or a woman stops me in the street and says 'You were my teacher' and I can't remember them."

"Are you on medication now?"

"Yes." He took a small packet out of his jacket pocket and handed it to her.

"How long have you been on this?"

"There have been various things over the years. I tried, a couple of years ago, to stop taking anything, but it upset the balance. We had to start all over again."

"Her name is Angela Hannaford, and her home is in Petts Wood. You knew that, didn't you, Stafford?"

He shook his head wearily. "No, Kathy, no. You're wrong."

Kathy glanced over at the mirror on the side wall, behind which she knew Brock was watching them. She sighed. "Just now, in your attic, you said you kept everything from the past, but now you're saying that isn't so. You're saying that you've been erasing your memories too, like me, is that right?"

"It's not the same. I had a breakdown, I was on drugs."

"What about before that? You had a child, by a woman who wasn't your wife. Is that right?"

He frowned angrily. "Ruth Sparkes's gossip!"

"She thought it was a romantic story, Stafford. A sad story. I think she's right. Tell me about it."

"I shall do no such thing! It's got nothing whatsoever to do with you, or your case."

"Have you kept a picture of her?"

"Mind your own business, young woman!"

"Oh, come on." Kathy smiled at him. "You were poking about in my business, weren't you? Pumping my aunt? And you were right, I have tried to obliterate my memories of my father. And perhaps I do feel guilty. Perhaps I still hate him for that. Do you hate her?"

"No . . . no."

"She gave away your child, didn't she? The only child you ever had. You must feel angry, and guilty."

Kathy was aware of a squeaking noise. He was rubbing his shoes together in agitation under the table. "I'm not going to discuss this."

"She must have been quite pretty."

"She wasn't *quite pretty*," he exploded suddenly. "She was very, very *beautiful*."

"Yes. What did she play?"

"Ophelia. She was a wonderful Ophelia."

"Ah yes. With long hair, I'll bet. Longer than mine?"

"Yes."

"But the same colour as mine. Fair."

"Yes."

"What was her name?"

"I am not going to discuss this further."

"If you told us her name, we might be able to trace her. We might even be able to help you find your son. That would be something, wouldn't it?"

"No! You have no right to talk about this. No right whatsoever."

"To see your lost child again, Stafford!"

He stared at her with pain in his eyes.

"But to do that, we would have to know how Angela died. You must tell us that, first."

"I . . . don't want to see her again."

"Did you kill her, Stafford? Did you kill Angela, and imagine that you were killing Ophelia?"

"NO!"

Kathy got abruptly to her feet and left the room. It was an uncalculated move which surprised her as much as Stafford. She simply felt an overpowering need to be out of his presence. She stood in the corridor outside, leaning back against the wall, feeling her heart racing unpleasantly out of control. Brock came around the corner.

"All right?"

"I'm not getting anywhere, Brock."

"Nonsense. You got the colour of the hair. You're doing fine. Bren's gone to arrange the search of his house. Change the subject. Talk about the play or something. Just keep him talking."

KATHY RETURNED CARRYING A tray with mugs of tea. She sat down and offered one to him, but he made no move to accept it.

"That speech of the Captain's, in the play," she said. "What you called the 'all my enemies' speech. Do you know the one I mean?"

He nodded, eyes heavy, so that she wondered if he'd taken one of his pills while she was out.

"It seemed to me that it was an example of . . . is it hyperbole? Is that the word?"

"Hyperbole . . ." He nodded, sluggish. "Yes."

"Completely over the top. Exaggeration to the point of caricature. I couldn't understand anyone feeling like that. Not really. My colleague, on the other hand—a man—seemed to find it perfectly understandable. I wonder if Strindberg would only make sense to a man?"

He gave her a thin smile. "Strindberg had trouble with the feminists," he said. "They disliked some short stories he wrote about married life, and he believed they were plotting against him. Perhaps he was goading them with an absurd caricature of how men are supposed to think."

"It's a speech about men's hatred of women, isn't it? My colleague said that the man who murdered Angela probably feels like that. Do you think so?"

"I haven't the faintest idea."

"Strindberg was quite disturbed himself, wasn't he? He had periods when he was consumed by insane jealousy. You can see it in that scene at the end of act two—a husband throwing a lighted lamp at his wife!"

Stafford gave her a secretive smile. "It's considered to be almost impossible to stage that scene convincingly, but we shall see. Strindberg got the idea from England. He understood that it was quite common for English husbands to throw lamps at their wives. In one of his letters he said that this wasn't surprising, considering what English women were like."

Kathy smiled, then said very quietly, "Whatever possessed you to put on this play, Stafford? What are you trying to tell us?"

"Do you find it disturbing, Kathy?" He leaned forward suddenly and hissed at her. "Perhaps the title is disturbing for you, if, as you say, you hate your father."

"I didn't say that . . ."

"Oh, but you did. And I know why."

"Do you?" She couldn't stop herself asking him, "Why?"

"Not because he left you and your mother bankrupt; not because you had to leave your comfortable big house in the home counties and go to live in that miserable little terrace in Sheffield with your aunt and uncle; and not because your mother died of shame within two years of his suicide."

Kathy stared at him, shocked. Aunt Mary had told him everything.

"No, the reason you hate him is because he left without giving you the slightest indication that he cared about you. He left without saying sorry."

For a moment Kathy was speechless. "That is ridiculous," she said finally.

He turned in his seat sideways to her, folded his arms, and said, "And now I should like to speak to my solicitor."

BREN RETURNED IN MID-AFTERNOON, looking flushed, sweat stains darkening his shirt around his armpits and down his back.

"That house is unbelievable. You could be in there for a week and still be discovering things. But we've had the dogs go through every room, from cellar to attic, and all through the garden, and we've come up with nothing. No Doc Martens, no bayonets, no condoms, and no Zoë Bagnall. Plenty of Leichner make-up materials, but you'd expect that."

"Did you come across a diary?"

"No, nothing like that. Seems like just about everything else, though. He's kept everything. *National Geographic* going back thirty years, scrapbooks of theatre programmes and reviews going back to the 1940s, his dead wife's clothing, everything."

"I spoke to some of our medical people about his claim of memory lapses," Brock said. "The general consensus is that it's possible he could be telling the truth. Depends on what they were giving him and whose opinion you asked."

"He could just have forgotten teaching Angela?"

"Especially if she was associated with the most painful period, at the end, just before he was admitted to hospital. Which seems to be the case."

Bren shook his head. "What do we do, then?"

Brock looked at Kathy. "You haven't said much, Kathy. What do you think? You know him best."

"I don't know." She was still burning from his words and from the knowledge that the others had been outside the room, listening, recording. "I really don't know if he would be capable of it," she said abruptly, but she thought of his rages at the rehearsals, and the look on the headmistress's face, and knew she wasn't being entirely honest.

"If we let him go, you'll be the one closest to him, Kathy," Brock said.

AFTER FINISHING WORK THE following day Kathy went alone to the Three Crowns, Aunt Mary having decided to stay at home and recover from her labours on the costumes. This was the final rehearsal before they moved to the theatre, and there was an atmosphere of suppressed last-minute panic, the cast wearing the preoccupied look of ill-prepared travellers about to set off on a desperate journey. They quarrelled over trivial details, and became impatient with each other's mistakes. Stafford was worst of all, constantly breaking into the flow of the speeches to make minute corrections of intonation and expression. And all the time Ruth watched him, shaking her head with disapproval and alarm.

"This is all wrong," she said. "He should let them run it through, and give them his comments at the end of each act. He knows that."

"Never mind," Kathy said, trying to calm her. "Soon be over."

"Sooner than you think! Have you seen that girl?"

"What girl?"

"Bettina!" She glared across the room at Bettina sitting smirking beside Edward. "She's wearing a ring in her *nose*! Stafford will go insane when he notices. I tried to warn her. Do you know what she said?"

"What?"

"She said he's a bully and a pain, and she doesn't give a stuff. Those were her precise words."

"I'm amazed. I thought she was a bit of a mouse."

"She's a surly, insolent girl. I've taught enough of them in my time."

It wasn't until they had ground their way into the second half of act three that Stafford noticed Bettina's gesture of defiance. It was after 11:00, and the landlord of the pub had just looked in to ask how much longer they would be. Stafford hurled a withering comment in his direction and turned back with a haunted look to the action in centre stage, between the Captain and his daughter.

"*To eat or to be eaten,*" he snapped.

"*To eat or to be eaten—that is the question,*" Edward said. "*Unless I eat you, you will eat me—you've already shown me your teeth. But don't be afraid, my darling child, I shan't do you any harm.*"

He reached across and picked up a revolver, meant to be hanging on the wall.

"That gesture is too weak!" Stafford roared. "The gun is a symbol, Edward. It represents your manhood. The women have removed the bullets, do you see? They have emasculated you. You must use the gun to tell us this."

Edward frowned, tired and tense.

Stafford rapped out the cue-line. "*Don't be afraid.*"

"*But don't be afraid, my darling child, I shan't do you any harm.*"

"Better."

"*Help! Mama, help!*" Bettina screamed, rather unconvincingly to Kathy's mind. "*He's going to murder me!*"

At these appropriate words, Stafford's expression underwent a profound change. His head jerked forward, mouth open, and he glared, astounded, at Bettina's nose. The Nurse, about to make her entrance, saw his look and hesitated. Like everyone else in the room she realized what Stafford had finally noticed. Eventually, after what seemed like several minutes of pained silence, she asked, "Shall I come on, Stafford?"

Stafford turned his gaze on her, raised his eyebrows in an expression of disbelief, and sank back on to his chair.

The Nurse waited, and when no instructions came, she moved tentatively forward and began her line. *"Mr. Adolf! What are you doing?"*

She got no further. From the producer's chair came a low growling sound. Stafford was talking, head down, apparently to himself. Everyone stared at him as the words became louder, and gradually more distinct. ". . . night after night . . . for no other reason than a joke . . . is that what you think . . . ?" His head was up now, his huge eyes wide, fixed on Bettina. "Nothing but a joke! Is that what you think?" Suddenly he was screaming at her, his whole body trembling violently, *"Is that what you think?"*

Bettina was stunned at first. She blinked rapidly several times as the waves of his anger battered her. And then, unbelievably to those who looked on, her lip curled up in a smile of contempt, her eyes bright, and she folded her arms.

"All right"—Ruth was on her feet—"we'll take five minutes, everyone. Edward!" She nodded her head at Stafford, then grabbed Bettina's arm and bustled her out of the room.

Edward and a couple of the other men hurried over to Stafford, who was slowly subsiding into his chair. He was very pale, and when they spoke to him he looked up at them, bewildered. His expression reminded Kathy of someone waking from an epileptic fit.

After a few minutes Ruth returned with Bettina, her nose unadorned. She was trying to maintain her air of defiance, but Kathy saw that her eyes were puffy, lashes damp.

Stafford remained seated, making no further interruptions to the rehearsal, which came to a rapid but irresolute end. It was left to Ruth to try to wind things up on a positive note.

"Well done, everybody," she said. "I'm sure you'll enjoy a well-earned break tomorrow, but on Sunday we need all the help we can with erecting the set. Can I have volunteers to help the set crew, please? Big strong men especially, and people who can use a paint brush."

A few unenthusiastic arms were raised.

"We start the technical dress rehearsal sharp at 7:00 on Monday. Don't be late. Everything will be ready for you at the theatre. We'll make any last-minute adjustments to your costumes then. All right? Well then, the last and most important thing, we still have lots of unsold tickets for Thursday and Friday nights, and a few for Wednesday and Saturday as well. Come on, everyone! One last big effort with tickets, please!"

There was a general groan, and the rehearsal broke up.

"When is Chief Inspector Brock going to call a halt to this, Kathy?" Ruth said as they watched the room empty. "Surely he's not going to let us go through with it?"

Kathy gave a weary shrug. "Special patrols are being organized for this coming week, and everyone will be taking extra precautions."

On her way out she met Bettina coming out of the loo, wiping her nose with a small, grubby handkerchief. Kathy smiled at her. "Hi."

Bettina sniffed and turned to go.

"Can I ask you something?"

"What?"

"Do you think I'd look better with brown hair?"

Bettina stared at her blankly. "I dunno."

"I think I wouldn't. Somebody suggested it. You'd look stunning, though."

"Eh?"

"With brown hair. There's a shade called 'auburn glow.' It'd suit your skin colouring, you see. But not mine. Too bad."

KATHY AND MARY DROVE back down to Shortlands on the Sunday afternoon, Kathy's aim being to check on any outsiders helping with the set construction who might not have appeared on their lists, Mary's to check on the delivery of her precious costumes to the theatre dressing-rooms. The front doors of the theatre were locked, and they made their way round to the stage door at the rear. A narrow, twisting corridor smelling of talcum powder led past the two dressing-rooms, toilets, and some crowded storerooms and finally came out at a black-painted door marked with a red sign, "Silence: Stage Area." Everything on the other side of the heavy door was painted black—bare walls, steel beams, an electrical switch-box, a steel ladder leading up into the black void above. The sound of hammering came from the other side of black curtains, which suddenly were swept aside as a large, sweaty man came striding through, brandishing a hammer.

"'Scuse us, ladies," he called, slamming through the exit door.

Beyond the black curtains lay a congested labyrinth of wooden braces holding up the backs of the canvas flats which formed the walls of the set. The braces were held in place by large iron weights on the floor, and care was necessary to step over these to get around the back of the set from stage right to stage left. Several gaps remained in the flats, painted on their audience side to represent the wallpapered walls of a late Victorian sitting-room. Kathy was amazed at how makeshift and flimsy it all seemed at close hand, yet when they found the steps in the front corner of the stage leading down into the auditorium, and took a seat to see the effect from the audience side, it looked remarkably convincing. What had seemed crude swirls of rough paintwork now came into focus as a decorative frieze, a marble fireplace, a panelled timber shutter.

"What do you think?" Ruth sat down beside Kathy.

"It's good. Are you happy with progress?"

"Oh, there are the usual problems with getting the doors in the flats to work properly, and the sofa still hasn't arrived, but on the whole it's going all right."

"Is Stafford around?"

"He came for an hour, had a row with the lighting designer, and stormed off. I think it's much better if he stays away. I was really worried about Stafford on Friday night, Kathy," Ruth went on. "He looked to me as if he might be heading for another breakdown."

"Yes. He looks very stressed, doesn't he?"

"You lot didn't help, dragging him off like that on Thursday. What did you want, anyway? He refused to talk to me about it afterwards."

"We just needed to check a few things with him. The constable got the wrong end of the stick."

"I think Stafford's house made him nervous, to tell the truth."

"Probably. Not surprising really. Tell me, you said that Stafford and his wife never had children, Ruth, but there were toys in the house—an old rocking-horse, and a clockwork train set in the attic."

"Those would be his own, when he was a child. He grew up in that house."

STAFFORD WAS ALREADY AT work in the theatre when Kathy arrived on the Monday evening for the technical dress rehearsal. He was standing down at the front aisle of the auditorium, the edge of the stage chest-high in front of him, talking to someone high up on a pair of tall stepladders. The man swore, and a blue spotlight filter gel fluttered down to the stage, to join half a dozen others.

Stafford looked gaunt and pale, but in control of himself.

"Are we really going to need all these blues, Stafford?" the man up among the lighting tracks called down.

"Yes, Peter, we are. We've been into all this weeks ago. It's winter. Their clothes are winter clothes, they have coats and hats.

In the first act, the daylight should be cold and wintry. After that, the lamplight needs to be warm, but claustrophobic, like a house snowed in at night. Right? Remember now?"

The set was finished, the furniture stacked to one side to allow the lighting designer to move about the stage. After an hour he was satisfied enough with the position and colour of his lights to begin the rehearsal. Two stage-hands arranged the furniture and the cast were called out on to the set. They moved awkwardly in their unfamiliar costumes, experimenting with gestures and movements to see how they might be inhibited by the heavy folds of fabric. Kathy was impressed. Even the recalcitrant Bettina had been transformed by Aunt Mary's handiwork into a Victorian innocent, in striped pinafore and hair ribbons.

"All right!" Stafford clapped his hands for their attention. "Quickly! I'm only interested in your movements, for the lighting, so we'll cut the static passages. Act one, Pastor and Captain, in position. Everyone else off the stage."

They shuffled away, those not required for a while coming down into the auditorium to watch, the rest taking up positions off-stage for their entrances.

"House lights! Curtain!"

As they worked their way through the active passages of the play, Kathy had the feeling that the cast were responding to Stafford as to an invalid, walking on eggshells. No one argued or did anything else remotely likely to provoke him. In fact they avoided speaking to him altogether, although they carried on endless nervous whispered conversations among themselves throughout the evening. Stafford was oblivious to them, entirely focused on bringing about the atmosphere of light and sounds he required to breathe life into his production.

The biggest challenge was the lamp-throwing scene, which involved the perfect timing and simultaneous actions of actors, stage-hands, sound, and lights. Edward was to hurl the lamp to a precise spot to one side of Vicky, where it would be caught by a stage-hand standing waiting behind the side curtain. At the exact moment when it would have struck the side wall, a sound effect of smashing glass would coincide with the abrupt dimming of the general set lighting and the switching on of an explosive orange light effect also hidden behind the side curtain, to simulate the burning paraffin. This would shine dramatically into Vicky's horrified face. The action would freeze for precisely three long seconds, then the set lights would fade to darkness, leaving only the paraffin light flickering over the set as the act two curtain came down.

It took almost an hour to perfect this single action. By the time they were finished, the flickering light had been tried in every position in the corner of the set, the breaking glass played at every level of volume and combination of speakers, and Edward had mastered both his lines and his throwing style. When Stafford finally allowed that it was good enough, the whole cast heaved a huge sigh of relief and relaxed.

Kathy drove back slowly, keeping an eye on her rear-view mirror for anything like a blue Cavalier.

"This is a new way home," Mary chirped. She'd had a good night, seeing her costumes paraded together for the first time.

"I just wanted to make sure Stafford got home safely," Kathy said. "He looked all in by the time we finished."

His old Citroën was parked against the garage doors at the end of the drive; a light was on in the hall window. Kathy imagined him returning alone to this place, discovering new little signs of disturbance made by the intrusion of the police searchers and their dogs as he moved around the silent interior.

As they watched, light appeared in the attic windows in the steep slate roof.

"I wonder what he's doing up there?" Mary said, and gave a little shudder. "Poor man."

THE DRESS REHEARSAL ON the following evening was a complete catastrophe. As it unfolded, one crisis lurching into the next, members of the cast muttered to Kathy with increasing desperation that this was exactly as it should be, that all the best first nights were preceded by disastrous dress rehearsals, though, admittedly, perhaps not usually on this scale.

The first problem was the doors. After weeks of low humidity, a thunderstorm during the night had created a damp atmosphere, causing the wooden frames of the canvas flats to swell. The result was that every entrance and exit was accompanied by a nerve-racking tugging and shaking of the canvas walls as actors struggled to open the doors while remaining grimly in character. For the small audience of technical people the effect was magnified by the apprehension which visibly grew on the actors' faces as their exit lines approached.

When the curtain came down at the end of act one, five minutes of feverish sawing and planing cured the problem of the doors, but the psychological damage was done. Kathy had never had to give so many prompts, with every scene in the second act accompanied by a major dry. People who had dependably rattled off their lines through weeks of rehearsal now had mental blocks over the simplest sentence constructions. At one point Vicky forgot the name of the Nurse, and came out with the memorable line, "*Yes, that would be better, then . . . old whatshername, the Nurse, can sit here,*" which corpsed the Doctor completely.

Kathy wasn't immune to the general panic, and caused a major difficulty in the second act by turning two pages together and giving a prompt from a wildly different scene. But the crowning disaster was the lamp-throwing episode over which everyone had worked so hard. Everything—the light and sound effects, the timing, the actors' moves and expressions—worked perfectly, except that Edward threw the lamp a couple of degrees to the right, so that instead of landing in the waiting hands of the stage-hand behind the curtain, it flew out in front of the curtain and bounced, loudly and unbroken, down the auditorium steps, while up above, the stage inexplicably reverberated with crashing glass and exploding flames.

Stafford sat silently through it all. From the safety of the wings, members of the cast peered through the tiny pinholes which earlier actors had made to observe the mood of their audience, and watched the solitary figure in the middle of row H observe it all, impassive, unflinching. At the end of act three he got to his feet, clapping loudly, and then instructed them as to how they should take their curtain call. They practised this, again accompanied by his solitary applause, and when the curtain dropped for the last time, and the house lights came on, he was gone.

FIFTEEN

KATHY FOUND IT DIFFICULT to deal with everyone else's complacency at work the next day. She had been able to sell a surprising number of tickets to her colleagues, so many in fact that she suspected that Orpington CID were going to be the financial salvation of SADOS. But for the rest of them this was just another working day; they moved around, chatting casually, taking problems in their stride, indifferent to the crisis whose approach she measured with every tick of the clock. She felt like a condemned prisoner whose cell looks out into a normal street, busy with oblivious people going about their ordinary lives.

Brock saw it. He passed her at her desk and noticed the hand automatically stirring a plastic spoon round and round in her coffee cup, and said, "Worried?" and she nodded. "Suppose he doesn't wait till Saturday, Brock? If he's close to someone in the company then he probably knows we're on to him. He may pull something different."

"I meant, are you worried about your prompting job tonight?"

She smiled ruefully. "Ridiculous, isn't it? I'm not even going to appear on stage. I can't imagine how the actors are able to deal with it. I feel sick just imagining what it must be like for them."

"This is your first time. When it's over you'll miss it, and the next time round it'll be this that gives you the buzz."

"There won't be a next time, Brock."

"How about our friend? How's he coping?"

"He was strange last night. There was one disaster after another, but it didn't seem to bother him at all. He sat through it all, clapped and left. It was almost as if he'd already moved on."

"I suppose he knows that there's no more he can do. It's up to you lot now."

Partly to take her mind off things, Kathy made a call to Effie, her aunt's neighbour in Sheffield. It had been more than a week since Di had rung from Canada, and there had been no further contact regarding Mary's flight.

"How's Tom?" Kathy asked cheerfully.

"Like death warmed up," came back the gloomy reply. "You should see him, you really should. Dr. Skinner's been three times now."

"Really?"

"Oh aye. Three times."

"What's the problem?"

"He's lost the will, love, hasn't he? The will to live."

It seemed to Kathy that Effie was laying it on a bit thick.

"Oh rubbish! He wouldn't give up his will for anyone."

"Don't be so sure, Kathy. Dr. Skinner's worried about a thrombosis. You tell Mary that!"

Kathy put the phone down with a groan. She could imagine Uncle Tom in his chair making a pitiful spectacle of himself, calling out the doctor at all hours, driving them all mad until they made Mary come back and apologize. Kathy was damned if she'd tell her.

STAFFORD WAS BACKSTAGE AT the theatre when she arrived that evening. He was wearing a dark-purple velvet suit, ruffled white shirt, and large bow tie, and carried himself with an air of such dignity and calm that everyone who saw him was inspired with confidence. He spoke briefly to each in turn, to the actors in the two dressing-rooms dabbing feverishly at their faces with make-up sticks and pencils, and the technical people checking the backstage arrangements for the last time, and the front-of-house ladies in their new frocks.

He spoke also to Kathy. "I dare say you think this will be a disaster," he said, "and that you will be responsible. Well, you're wrong. At the end of the day, you will look back and reflect that no one could have done the job any better than you."

She couldn't help being impressed as he strode off, head held high, and disappeared through the black door which gave access to the stage.

"Fifteen minutes, everyone!" Ruth bustled through.

Kathy took a deep breath and followed her down the corridor towards the black door. As she passed the women's dressing-room the door opened and Bettina stuck her head out. Her hair was auburn.

Kathy grinned. "That looks good, Bettina. It really suits you."

The girl gave her a grim little smile and closed the door.

Kathy settled herself in the bentwood chair they had placed for her downstage right, behind the side curtain. One of her nightmares in the small hours of the previous night had been that this rather elderly chair would somehow fall apart beneath her. She was reassured that it felt more solid than she'd remembered.

Taped music was playing in the auditorium, an excerpt from Grieg's *Holberg Suite* to establish the Nordic atmosphere. She watched the actors as they filed in through the stage access door, holding themselves stiffly, as if their faces, exaggerated like dolls by the make-up, might crack. A couple exchanged whispered remarks, but most preferred silence, breathing deeply, eyes unnaturally wide. Edward was close by, looking as if he faced execution. She smiled at him, smelling the spirit gum from his mutton-chop whiskers and bushy moustache. "OK?"

He nodded and swallowed. "Matter of controlling the heartbeat," he said. "Be all right once it starts."

"One minute," the stage-manager whispered. "Places openers."

The Captain, in cavalry uniform and spurs, paced silently on to the stage and sat himself carefully on the leather sofa. The black-clothed Pastor followed, sat beside him and began sucking on a pipe. To her left, offstage, Kathy saw Svärd the Orderly take up position behind the door.

The Grieg gently died away. The house-lights dimmed. There was silence, and then the curtain rose. Mouth dry, Kathy watched Edward lift the bell on the small table at his elbow and ring it loudly. Svärd counted to three, smoothly opened the door and stepped out into the light.

"You wanted something, sir?"

"Is Nöjd out there?" Edward replied, and they were away.

IT WAS A TRIUMPH.

Their performances were impeccable. Kathy had to give only one prompt, a soft couple of words to the Nurse, who picked them up and recovered before the audience realized that anything was wrong.

Above all, the lamp-throwing scene worked to perfection, and had the audience on its feet for a standing ovation at the end of act two, an unprecedented tribute.

After the final curtain the company was in a state of elation. Not only had the whole thing, incredibly, come off, but everybody had played their part without fault. They gathered on the stage, eagerly ploughing into trays of plastic beakers of champagne, whispering excitedly, for the stragglers of the audience were still in the auditorium on the other side of the curtain.

"Where's Stafford?" someone asked, and Ruth came on carrying bundles of envelopes and said, "He'll be here soon. Here are his cards."

This was a tradition, so Kathy learned. On the first night of each of his productions every member of the company would receive from Stafford a personal card, with a message written with his fountain pen in a flowing hand, along the lines, "Vicky darling, Wonderful as always. Thank you, Stafford."

Kathy noticed that the envelopes bearing their handwritten names were identical, except for Ruth's and, to her embarrassment, her own, which were both larger than the rest. She watched Ruth's face flush with pleasure as she took a large floral card out of her envelope.

Kathy stepped back from the throng and opened hers, and saw that the reason for its size was not a card, but a 7×5 black-and-white glossy photographic print inside. It showed the head and shoulders of a woman, whom she recognized immediately as the missing Zoë Bagnall, photographed under a harsh light. Zoë's eyes were open, but she could see nothing, for her throat was cut with a gaping wound from ear to ear. On the back of the photograph, written in the same flowing ink line, was the message, "Kathy, I am responsible. I am so sorry. Stafford Nesbit."

Kathy stuffed the picture back into the envelope before anyone else could see it, and stood for a moment trying to think, to clear her head of the unexpected shock of the picture.

"Are you all right, dear?" It was Ruth, beaming at her. "Excitement too much? You have visitors. They're waiting at the foot of the stage steps."

Kathy felt in her bag for her radio. "Ruth, where is Stafford?"

"Well, that's the odd thing, Kathy. No one seems to have seen him since the act one interval."

"Could you check again with everyone for me? It's important I find him."

Kathy hurried across the stage and came out at the head of the steps leading down into the auditorium. A group of people were standing talking, Bren among them. Aunt Mary was behind him, and another woman had her arm through his.

Bren saw her and winked, then, seeing her face, "You all right, Kath?"

She shoved the envelope into his hand, aware of the other people's curious stares. "Has anyone seen Stafford Nesbit?" she said, and for a moment her eyes met those of Bren's wife, who was examining her closely.

Mary said no, and then Bren in a low voice exclaimed, "Hell! Where did this come from?"

"I'm going to check the car park," Kathy said.

He caught up with her outside.

"His car's not here," she said, breathless. "Where's Brock, do you know?"

"Not far away," Bren said. "Half of Orpington CID was at the performance tonight."

"We've got to get them back. Nesbit's disappeared. We've got to find him before he kills somebody else."

There was no sign of him in the area of the theatre, and they returned to the Orpington station, taking Ruth with them because she seemed the one most knowledgeable about Stafford, and also Mary because Kathy didn't know what else to do with her.

They were sitting together in the canteen over a cup of tea when Brock came down to tell them that a Citroën BX with Stafford's number had been reported involved in an accident on the M25 two hours before.

"Or rather," he said, "not an accident. Eye witnesses in two following cars say the Citroën suddenly swerved across all three lanes and drove into the supporting concrete structure of a bridge crossing the motorway. They say it looked as if he aimed for it quite deliberately. He was killed instantly."

"Oh no!" Ruth gasped. *"Blithe Spirit!"*

"Sorry?"

"Originally we had been going to do *Blithe Spirit* this time instead of *The Father.* In the Coward play one of the characters is killed by an arranged car accident."

But Kathy knew otherwise. She stared at her aunt, who had gone very pale, and said nothing. Only later, when they were in the car and heading home, did she ask the question. "You told him, didn't you, Mary? When he was asking you about my past, you told him how Dad died?"

"Yes," she whispered.

"And he chose to do it the same way."

"But why? I don't understand, Kathy. Why would he do that?"

"THIS TIME THE GARDEN'LL have to come up." The following morning Bren was organizing the second search of Stafford Nesbit's home for the remains of Zoë Bagnall. "There are underfloor cavities in some areas beneath the house, and yet the house doesn't appear to have a cellar, and there's any number of places where there could be sealed cupboards. We're having plans drawn up as we work through."

The M25 crash had made the morning news bulletins, and a carefully worded press release had been issued, linking Nesbit's death with the investigations into the murders of Angela Hannaford and the other three women. Two photographs of the man had been provided, and these pictures accompanied a report in the afternoon and evening editions of the London evening paper on that Thursday, which also carried a police appeal for information from the public.

THE COMPANY SEEMED NUMBED that evening. Kathy sensed that they wanted to ask her questions about what had happened to Stafford, but they held back, and she didn't encourage them. They had discussed whether they should abandon the play, and had decided that Stafford would have wished them to continue. Edward was nominated to make an announcement at the start of the performance, paying tribute to Stafford and dedicating the production to his memory.

The performance was again faultless, but subdued compared to the previous night, as was the audience. In act two, Kathy was struck by some lines which made her think of Stafford's house. Bertha, the daughter, was speaking to the Nurse about the upper floor of their home.

"I daren't stay up there all alone, I think it's haunted."

"There now, what did I say?" the Nurse replied. *"You mark my words, there's a curse on this house. What did you hear, Bertha?"*

"Well, actually, I heard someone singing up in the attic."

"In the attic? At this time of night?"

"Yes, it was such a sad song, the saddest song I've ever heard. And it seemed as if it came from the box-room—you know, on the left, where the cradle stands."

From that point, Kathy kept hearing passages whose meaning seemed transformed by Stafford's death. Later in the same act, Laura was to say to the Captain,

"You say that you'll kill yourself. You'll never do that."

To which he replied,

"Are you sure? Do you think a man can live when there's nothing and no one to live for?"

She could imagine Bren's objections to attaching any retrospective significance to such lines, and yet her skin crawled as they were spoken, and she underlined them in her book.

One other thing turned her stomach that evening. Towards the end of the second interval she stood near her place in the wings and looked through the pin-hole in the screen wall facing the audience, watching them return to their seats. She was stunned to see Tom and Muriel Gentle working down the fourth row and taking seats directly in front of her. He was grinning contentedly, a basset-hound with a new bone. She assumed he had read the newspaper reports and had come to be seen and to gloat. Innocent or guilty, she still found him loathsome. She wondered if he might have his little Minolta camera up his sleeve, photographing them all.

BREN'S TEAM HAD FOUND nothing at the house on the first day of their search, which resumed on Friday. Kathy went to Orpington, and discovered on her desk a copy of the local weekly paper, which had come out that morning, opened at a glowing review of *The Father* from the theatre critic. It had been written immediately after the first performance and so made no reference to Stafford's suicide, a gaffe made more excruciating by references to "Producer Stafford Nesbit's brimming vitality" and his "underlying optimism."

As she was reading, a phone call came in from a solicitor at the city firm of Baker Bailey Rock. The name rang a bell, but she couldn't place it.

"I thought I'd better contact you," the woman said. "It's probably not relevant, but I read the report in the *Standard* last night about that crash on the M25, and your appeal for information about the man, and what with your officer calling on us a couple of weeks ago, I thought I'd better follow it up."

Kathy was lost, but didn't say so. "Oh yes? You knew Stafford Nesbit?"

"I met him, yes. He came here to our office. I spoke to him."

"When would that have been?"

"Well, that's the point. I checked in my diary. It was last year, July. Which was the same month that Janice was killed, you see."

"Janice?" Kathy felt at sea. *Who's Janice?*

"Janice Pearce. She worked for us. You remember?"

"Oh, of course. I'm sorry, I was lost there for a minute. Janice Pearce."

The legal secretary, the earliest murder, the one we decided had no connection with the others. "Maybe I could come up and see you?" Kathy said.

"All right. This morning?"

"That would be terrific."

Kathy put the phone down and realized that her heart was thumping.

She decided to take the train. It was almost five weeks now since she had first travelled on this line, following Angela's route home. The weather was almost identical to how it had been then, even though it was now early October, and she had an acute sense of time suspended, of travel without destination. Discoveries had been made, facts uncovered, people implicated, and yet she felt no closer to understanding the reality of Angela's death than when she had first settled back in a Southern Region compartment and watched Angela's London unroll outside the window.

As advised by the solicitor, she got off at London Bridge and caught the tube up to Moorgate. A couple of minutes later she was sitting in a small, cluttered, modern office with a cup of coffee and a chocolate biscuit.

"I wouldn't have contacted you," the solicitor said, "except for the way the newspaper report was phrased, linking Nesbit to the four murders. Was he a suspect?"

"Let's just say that, if he was alive, he'd be presently helping us with our inquiries."

"I see. I've never actually come face to face with a serial killer before. Family law is my area. Something of an oddity in this practice, which is mainly commercial. A spin-off really, for when our commercial clients' home lives run into trouble." She fixed Kathy with a penetrating smile, as if inviting her to confess that she too might need these services. "I should have thought that he might have been a bit old for violence. Though he was very intense, as I remember."

"He was a client, was he?"

"In a way, yes."

"Was it on a family law matter that he saw you?"

"It was unusual, actually. That's why I remembered his visit so clearly. Not at all the normal divorce business." The solicitor paused to smooth the immaculate sleeve of her grey linen suit. Italian, Kathy guessed. "He wanted to talk about an adoption."

"He wanted to adopt someone?"

"No. He wanted to trace someone. His own child, who had been put out to adoption at birth."

"Ah, yes."

"I rather gathered that his wife was not the mother. I had to establish that in order to advise him, you see. It affected the circumstances of the case. The reason why he came to us was that he had, over a number of years, had dealings with this firm concerning the child. I'd better explain this."

The solicitor smiled and eased back in her chair, holding its arms firmly in her slender hands, speaking the way she did to her divorcing clients when she had to explain a point of law that would be central to the outcome they wanted, and, incidentally, to their continuing faith in her. "The law stipulates that it is not lawful to make or give a person any payment or reward for, or in consideration of, adoption. However, the court may permit a scheme of allowances, balancing all the circumstances with the welfare of the child as first consideration against the degree of taint of the transaction."

"A scheme of allowances?"

"Yes. Let us say that a person had a child in circumstances where he could not openly acknowledge the child, but nevertheless wished to contribute to its well-being even after it was adopted. He could apply to the court to allow him to provide an allowance to the child or its family by some scheme approved by the court. In this case, Mr. Nesbit paid a monthly allowance into a special account held by a neutral third party—this firm of solicitors— who paid this money each month, less a small fee for service, to the adoptive mother. Neither the natural father nor the adoptive mother knew who the other was, thus avoiding taint. Their only connection was through this firm. At one time we specialized in this sort of thing. Mr. Bailey, one of the founding partners, was himself adopted, and had a close relationship with a number of the adoption societies and agencies that used to flourish in London.

"Mr. Nesbit's arrangement with us expired some years ago— presumably when the child reached its eighteenth or twenty-first birthday. He was coming to us again now because he wanted to establish contact with the child, and thought that we could provide a name from our records."

The corners of her mouth turned down. "It was out of the question, of course. I began to discuss with him what other options he, and indeed the child, might have available, if they wished to re-establish contact, and that was when the matter of the legitimacy of the birth came up. You see, the birth documents of an illegitimate child might contain no information whatsoever about the father. Under the present English law, any adopted person may, having reached the age of eighteen and paid the stipulated fee, obtain a certified copy of their birth certificate. This will tell them the date and place of birth, the name under which they were originally registered, the mother's name and possibly her occupation, the name of the person who registered the birth, the date of registration, and the name of the Registrar. But if the parents weren't married at the time of registration, it may well say nothing about the father. And if the mother withholds information about the birth from the father, we may have a situation where neither father nor child is able to establish contact with the other at a later date."

"Except, in this case, through your records of the scheme of allowances," Kathy said.

"Precisely." The solicitor smiled brightly at her once again. Kathy was becoming a little bit irritated by that smile, and wondered how it went down with the divorce clients when things got really sticky.

"Well," Kathy said, "those records may well be something that we would be interested in."

"Oh, do you think so?" The smile abruptly vanished. "Of course, you could apply to the court, if you could show an overwhelming public interest. However, even if you were successful, it wouldn't do you any good."

"Why not?"

"We don't appear to have them any more. It seems they no longer exist."

"YOU WERE SPOT ON," Brock said. "Absolutely spot on. He must have had a fit when you started asking him about the lost child during his interview. It's like some Victorian melodrama. You think he killed Janice Pearce in order to get hold of the records of the child?"

Kathy had tracked Brock down to the Bride of Denmark, to which he had descended in order to escape the phone while he prepared the final version of his overdue budget forecasts.

"That's what the solicitor was wondering. She said that Janice Pearce would have been the one person in the office most likely to track down old records. It's possible that Nesbit tried to cultivate her, get her to help him on the side, when he realized he would never get hold of the information officially. Then, when she refused to help, he became enraged and strangled her."

Brock stared up at the beamed ceiling and tugged thoughtfully at his beard. "A man in his sixties, no wife, no career, no family, going quietly potty in his big spooky house, developing a desperate, an overwhelming desire to see the child he fathered decades ago, and secretly helped to support for all those years. Without the co-operation of the child's mother, who might be dead herself by this time, his only way is through the records at Baker Bailey Rock."

He stopped. "Is that right? Surely there would have been some other way? Couldn't he have applied to the adoption agency that was responsible for the original placing?"

"If he knew which one it was. But what status does he have? Some bloke who suddenly appears, thirty or more years later perhaps, claiming to be the unregistered father of a child about whom he knows nothing. What are they going to give him?"

Brock shrugged. "All right. So he murders the legal secretary in his madness to get hold of the name. Why does he then go on to murder the other women?"

"He now has no way of ever tracing his child. His rage turns on the woman who gave the kid away, the mother."

She hesitated. *All my enemies.* Could Stafford really have been like that? "I suppose, when you think about it, he was the obvious person, because he was in control of the dramatic society. He specifically chose the plays to provide the death themes, each murder coming at the climax of one of his productions."

"Ironic that the file that he first murdered for no longer existed," Brock said. "What happened to it, I wonder?"

"They don't know. After Nesbit's visit, the solicitor asked one of the juniors to dig out the file. It should have been in a storeroom of old files, but after an hour or two they couldn't find it and gave up looking. They've moved office twice in the past ten years, and they went through a period of enthusiasm for microfilming old records that fizzled out half-way through, and another period of computerization. It's even possible that the file is actually there somewhere, but wrongly labelled."

"Couldn't they get at the information some other way? The bank account, for instance."

"The partner who set up the scheme is dead. The account was closed years ago, and they don't know which bank it was with, or whose name it was under."

"Well," Brock grunted, "that's all quite satisfyingly mysterious and theatrical. Somewhere out there is somebody who has absolutely no idea that his natural father has murdered five innocent women out of sheer frustration at not being able to find him."

He frowned. "Just as well the mad old bastard's dead, really."

"How do you mean?"

"Well, it's all conjecture, isn't it? I'd have hated to try to get a conviction against him on the strength of what we've turned up so far."

AUNT MARY, EXHAUSTED BY the drama of events, had decided to miss the performance that evening and have an early night at home. When the play was over, Kathy slipped away, driving back, as she had on the night of the technical dress rehearsal, by way of Stafford's house. It was a cloudless night with a full moon, and the ravages of Bren's excavations in the front lawn were clearly visible from the street. Kathy was reminded of another passage from the play: ". . . *we found ourselves sitting among ruins in bright moonlight.*"

She left the car around the street corner and walked back to the house, down the front drive through the moon-shadow cast by the enormous monkey-puzzle tree, and past the front door, draped by a police tape. When she reached the back garden she saw that it was in even worse shape than the front, with holes and mounds of earth everywhere. The back door swung open at her touch, the lock broken. She stepped inside.

She passed from the kitchen into the hall, dimly lit by moonlight rippled and tinted through the stained-glass panels above and to each side of the front door. The smells of disturbed dust closed around her as she climbed into the darkness of the upper floor, the massive banister cool to her touch. Along a dark corridor she saw that the door at the head of the attic stair must be open, for the rocking-horse was lit in a pool of moonlight from above. Its worn head was raised towards the light, and when Kathy went towards it and looked up, she saw that the roof space was filled with the glow of moonlight, bright in contrast to the darkness below. She climbed the narrow stairs and pushed her way through the dark ranks of hanging costumes towards the dormer windows.

She stood there for some time, looking out at the magical transformation of the suburban landscape in the moonlight, the foliage of the monkey-puzzle tree black against the silver of the drive. There was no traffic in the street, no sound but the clicks and creaks of old timber adjusting to the night air. At one point she thought she heard movement below, and went silently back to the head of the stairs to listen. Hearing nothing more, she returned to the dormer, looked down, and saw a car pull up at the kerb opposite. As its lights went off she saw that it was a Cavalier, dark in colour. The driver's door opened and a bulky figure got out. For a moment, the gesture it made, stooping to close the door carefully, made her think of her father. Then it turned and walked slowly across to the end of the gravel drive. It stopped and stood, dark and motionless, staring up at the house.

She held her breath, trying to judge its height, its weight. After several minutes it moved forward, gliding on its pool of black

shadow, the moon being now directly overhead. Half-way down
the drive it came, then stopped again. It seemed to be examining
the signs of digging to left and right, and then the head turned
and stared directly up at Kathy's window. She drew back, making
out a pale face framed in darkness. It seemed to hesitate, uncertain
what to do.

Kathy jumped to life, running rapidly through the racks of
clothes, dropping down the stairs in threes. She hesitated on the
landing, straining for any sound, and when none came moved
swiftly down the main stair and slid into the darkness of the
kitchen doorway. The outside door was exactly as she had left it.
Slipping through, she jumped across the gravel path and ran silently
along the grass verge until she could see the front drive. It was
deserted. She raced on, to the street, and found nothing, stopping
finally among shadows on the far side, catching her breath, checking
in all directions. In the distance the silent progress of a late train
was marked by flashes in the sky, like lightning, from its contact
with the electrical rail. She ran to her car and drove around the
deserted streets for a while, looking without success for the dark
figure of a man, or a blue Cavalier. Both had vanished, like ghosts.

SIXTEEN

SHE WOKE UP WITH a start, and for a moment couldn't think where she was because the pattern of pale light on the ceiling wasn't like that in her own bedroom. Then she remembered the temporary bed. Her mind went back to her dream, a dreadful dream. Stafford. Directing them, angry, pointing with his long bony fingers, but silent because he was dead. He turned to her, and he was telling her something, his jaw working silently, beard silver in the moonlight.

His beard. She sat up slowly. Why would a bearded man use Leichner spirit gum?

And there was something else. Something that had worried her less than it should. Stafford Nesbit had spoken to the solicitor two weeks *after* Janice Pearce was murdered.

"I SUPPOSE," BROCK SAID, "that you could find a perfectly plausible explanation for both things."

"Yes."

He noticed how pale Kathy had become in the last few days and said, "If he failed to get the information he wanted from Janice Pearce before he killed her, he might well have gone to see the solicitor openly two weeks later, as the only other option he had."

"Reckless, though. Unbelievably reckless."

Brock shrugged. "He was obsessed. Seriously, what other explanation could there be, if it wasn't Nesbit?"

Kathy took her time before replying. "After I finished interviewing the solicitor at Baker Bailey Rock, she gave me a book on the rules of adoption to look at, and I sat and scanned through it for a while. There was a section that talked about the rights that adopted people have to get access to their own birth records. Apparently, in exceptional cases, the courts can deny this right. The book referred to a particular case"—she looked at her notebook—"*R. v. Registrar-General, ex parte Smith* (1990), in which it was established that this information can be withheld where there's a fear that the person might use it to commit a serious crime. In that case the applicant was a thirty-one-year-old trying to trace his natural parents. At the time of his application he had already killed two people, the second being the prisoner with whom he shared a cell, and whom he strangled one night in the belief that the man was his mother. The court didn't think it would be a good idea for him to find out who she really was.

"I suppose what struck me about that was that Alex Nicholson had mentioned matricide briefly when she was talking to us about schizophrenia, do you remember? But there was no particular reason to think any more of it. Now, though, I wonder."

"You wonder what, Kathy?"

"I wonder if we could have been looking at the wrong side of the relationship. Suppose it was the child who approached and murdered Janice Pearce, trying to find out about his father. And suppose he was successful, and did get the file from her, and then contacted Stafford Nesbit."

She hesitated, and Brock said quietly, "Go on."

"He hates them both, but especially his mother, the blonde actress. So he kills her, again and again, littering his father's path with corpses, macabre messages only he would understand."

"Taking his cues from his father's plays."

"Yes. What would the father do, when he realized what was happening, when he received the picture of Zoë Bagnall with her throat cut? Would he tell the police, and betray his child a second time? Would the police be able to stop it anyway? The only other way would be to kill himself. He didn't actually confess in the note he left me, Brock. He just said that he was responsible. And then there's the play."

"*The Father?*"

"Yes. All about uncertain fatherhood and the way men and women torture each other through their family relations. And it ends with the impending death of the father."

They said nothing for a while, and then Brock grunted, "I must say that the lack of any incriminating evidence whatsoever at Nesbit's house is a bit of a worry."

"Yes. And if the murderer is still alive, he will have selected another victim for the last night of his father's play, tonight. He must be wondering whether to go ahead with it, now that his father's dead."

"Bren had been thinking about providing an escort for all the blonde women in the production for the next twenty-four hours at least."

"I think I may have solved that. The only one was Bettina Elliott, and I managed to persuade her to become a brunette."

"Ah. That just leaves you, then, Kathy."

Kathy nodded. "True."

"Seriously, I want you to pull out. They can get someone else to prompt."

"No!" Kathy startled herself by the force of her reply. "No, Brock. It's all the more reason for me to stay in there."

"Kathy, I can't afford to lose any more of my team. People will begin to say it's my fault."

"Don't worry. This is probably just a red herring."

"All the same . . . All right," he said reluctantly, "but I'm going to give you a side-arms authorization. I want you to go over to Broadway right now and get yourself a gun."

IT WASN'T THAT THEY had forgotten Stafford, but for their fourth and final performance on the Saturday night the cast had developed sufficient confidence in their ability to do the play on their own that a certain flair, even flamboyance, had crept back into their performance. Vicky was more frighteningly implacable, Edward more pathetically doomed, than they had ever been before. By the time they came to the final scene, the whole company was aware of the atmosphere of tense attention which told them that their audience was gripped. Not one Green Line pensioner twitched or looked fretfully at their watch as the Captain, still bound in the strait-jacket and draped with the Nurse's shawl and his own military tunic, made one final effort to rise, gave an agonizing cry, and fell back into the Nurse's arms.

"*Help, Doctor,*" Laura cried, "*if it's not too late. Look, he's stopped breathing.*"

"*It's a stroke.*"

"*. . . First death, and after that the Judgement . . .*"

The daughter Bertha ran on stage towards her mother. "*Mama! Mama!*"

"*My child—my own child!*" Laura cried, taking her into her arms.

The Pastor lowered his head. "*Amen.*"

The theatre erupted in thunderous applause as the curtain came down on this tableau, something which Kathy, on her first reading of the script, had hardly believed possible.

THE END-OF-PRODUCTION PARTY WAS held at the home of Vicky and her husband. He welcomed everyone hospitably but remained, as did all of the accompanying partners, in some indefinable way an outsider. The camaraderie generated from crisis transformed into triumph was, for the moment, too strong for more everyday relationships to compete. Edward, whose wife was preoccupied in the kitchen with the food she had provided, made a particular point of cultivating Kathy, and she enjoyed his attention for a while, telling herself that it really was all over, that Stafford had confessed and was dead, that the figure in his moonlit garden was just another suburban prowler, made curious by the police tapes and earthworks, and that, even if that weren't so, there were only a few more hours to go before the pattern of murders would have been broken, for good.

And when midnight came, and there had been no phone message about some girl found trussed in a strait-jacket, or immolated by burning paraffin, she finally did relax, and told herself she could have an alcoholic drink at last. She went into the kitchen where the booze was set out, and saw Ruth in a state of advanced inebriation, describing with dramatic gestures Edward's disastrous lamp-throwing rehearsal.

"Kathy! Where have you been? I've mished you!" she called out.

"Dancing, Ruth. Where's Mary?"

"Maryanne," Ruth corrected slurredly. "Her name from henchforth shall be Maryanne."

"Yes." Kathy smiled. "So where is she?"

"That man came to take her away. Someone's had a stroke . . ." She frowned. "Or was that in the play?"

Kathy froze. "It was in the play, Ruth," she said carefully. "Who came to take her away?"

"This big man, with a beard. Oh, I was supposed to tell you! Oops. Sorry. It was about the stroke."

A chill swept through Kathy. "Ruth! The stroke was in the play! Where did Mary go with the bearded man?"

"No, Mary had a stroke too—I mean someone did. Someone she knows . . ." Ruth was becoming confused. "He said he was taking her home. Yes, *home*, he said."

"Dear God." Kathy took out her phone. She first tried the number of her flat but got no reply. Then she rang the Duty Sergeant at Orpington police station and explained what had happened. "I'm going to try my home in Finchley first. See if they've gone there. Would you notify the Yard?"

It was only when she was in her car and driving that the significance of the message about a stroke hit her. The stroke was the connection to the play. Stafford's play. They had gone to Stafford's house, not hers. The message was for her to follow.

She stopped the car in the street next to Stafford's and ran the last fifty yards, seeing the top of the monkey-puzzle tree loom closer above the neighbouring roofs. There were no lights visible in the house from the front, but when she reached the back garden she could see a faint glow around the edge of one of the upstairs windows. The kitchen door was half open. She slipped her right hand round the grip of the Smith and Wesson in the small holster on her hip, eased it out, and stepped silently into the house, heart pounding wildly.

She crept as swiftly as she could up the long flight of the main stairs, crouching towards the top so that she could see over the edge of the landing. The door to what she remembered as the overcrowded bedroom was slightly ajar, a dim amber light seeping round the jamb. She flattened against the wall beside the door and tried to look in, but could see nothing. Taking a deep breath, she pushed the door open and entered the room.

The bed was a mess, bedding ripped, pillows shredded, mattress pulled half off the base. Someone in a black hooded jogging top was kneeling beside the corner of the bed, back to the door. The figure was engrossed in something on the floor and seemed unaware of Kathy's entry. She noticed the Doc Martens on the feet, blinked, and looked round quickly, checking the rest of the room, lit by one miserable bulb whose light barely made it through a heavy yellowed parchment shade. She took three paces into the room and aimed the gun at the centre of the back.

"Raise your hands," she said. "I'm a police officer and I'm armed."

The figure froze. Then the head very slowly began to turn. It was hard at first to make it out, the hood shrouding it in shadow. Then Kathy saw a pair of dark eyes, a ring in the nose.

The figure remained crouching and the face smiled up at her.

"Bettina?" she said, stunned. "What are you doing here?"

"It's all right," Bettina said. "I've found it." Her left hand came up, holding a photograph. "Look, I've found it."

Kathy, mystified, lowered her gun and started to walk towards the kneeling woman, whose face was glistening with tears. Only at the last minute did she see the right hand coming round, and the bayonet.

There was an explosion so loud, so devastating, that Kathy could hear nothing but a ringing in her head. Bettina could hear nothing in her head, for her head was gone. In its place was a red cloud, and scarlet rain spraying everywhere. The girl's dark body tumbled to the floor, leaving the red mist suspended in the air above it. Kathy gaped at the gun in her hand, wondering how the hell it had gone off, how a .38 could have taken off Bettina's head and shredded it across the wall there, beside the bed. She turned away, looking for an explanation, and saw the silhouette of her father standing at the door, solid, commanding, horn-rim glasses, a shotgun in his hands, and the thought came into her head, *No, no, I didn't need your help.*

She forced herself to look at him, to meet his eyes, and she saw Basil Hannaford, standing there, stunned by what he had done.

"IT SEEMS HE'S BEEN trailing you for a couple of weeks," Bren said cheerfully. "He'd been following Gentle without success, and reckoned he might do better shadowing you instead. Didn't you ever notice? Dark blue Cavalier."

Kathy was at the kitchen table, towelling her hair. The shotgun blast had taken the fragments of Bettina's head away from her, but she'd been drenched by the following spray of arterial blood from the torso. They had found her a change of clothes in the attic.

"He thought—he still thinks—that the person he shot was Gentle."

"I don't understand, Bren. I don't bloody understand."

"Yeah. Well, when you're ready, we've got the girl's home address. Not far away. Brock'll meet us there."

"What about Mary? Haven't they found her yet?"

"No sign. She's certainly not here, nor at your place. It couldn't be that someone up north really has had a stroke, could it? Could have sent someone down for her, urgently?"

"No . . ." She thought for a moment. "No, that's too . . . Her Sheffield number's in the address book in my bag. God, Bren, I don't know what's the matter with me, my arms feel like lead."

"Too much drama. Don't worry, I'll try the number."

"What was she holding in her hand, Bren? It looked like a photograph. She said she'd found it, as if she'd been searching."

"Yes, a photograph. Blonde woman, stunner, taken some years ago, from the hairstyle. The sixties."

He returned a few minutes later. "You're shaking now. I'm going to get the doc down here for you."

"I'm all right. I just need a minute."

"Are your shots up to date? Hep B?"

She nodded. "Nothing on the phone?"

"No reply, but I'll get Orpington to get on to Sheffield police. They'll be able to check properly for us. God, you are shaking. Hang on."

He left again, and came back holding a small glass brimming with golden liquid. "Get this inside you."

She sniffed the brandy fumes, nodded, and gulped it down. "Thanks, Bren."

WHEN THEY ARRIVED, BROCK was already there, in jeans and sneakers, rubber gloves on his hands, carefully working his way round the room with Leon Desai and a couple of men from Scene of Crime. Brock was so engrossed that he didn't notice her arrival, but Desai looked up immediately, and shot her an odd glance, relief or solidarity, it was hard to tell. He took a couple of paces towards her, and for a moment she thought he might have been going to put an arm around her, but Bren bustled in behind and Desai's gesture faded.

There wasn't a lot to see. Bettina's living arrangements were the precise opposite of Stafford's, a single room, almost devoid of furniture or belongings. In one corner a black duvet lay crumpled on a futon mattress. A built-in cupboard contained one rack of clothes on hangers, and half a dozen drawers.

"Did she really live here?" Kathy looked round the bare space. Two posters were taped to the wall, one a rock band, the other the tail of a whale over a dark ocean. It made Kathy's flat seem cluttered.

"Sir." One of the SOCOs held up a packet of condoms and a photograph he had found in a drawer beneath underwear. Zoë Bagnall's face again, eyes closed, throat intact, the lighting and format as in the one Kathy had received from Stafford.

"Leon," Brock said, "give Morris Munns a ring, would you? Ask him if he'd care to leave his nice soft bed and have a look at this for us."

SEVENTEEN

IN HIS DREAM, TOM Gentle was in an ambulance, siren howling, speeding through deserted streets, on and on towards a hospital which they could not find. He woke up with a start and realized he was hearing the persistent bleat of the car alarm in his BMW.

He swore softly and slipped out of bed, leaving Muriel undisturbed. Dressing-gown, slippers, keys, he padded down the stairs. The dog was as oblivious to the nagging sound as his wife. He opened the back door, and saw that it was dawn, but a dawn dimmed by black, threatening clouds stretching from horizon to horizon. It was unexpectedly cold outside too, and the gravel drive was wet from recent rain. It was over at last, the summer. Thin summer dresses would give way to heavier skirts, sandals to boots, lifestyles would adjust.

There was no sign of anyone around the car. He aimed the remote at it and pressed the button, cutting off the noise and the flashing hazard lights. He turned back and nearly jumped out of his skin, finding himself face to face with a woman.

"Shit!" he said, and then recognized her. "What are you doing here?"

"Get in the car, Mr. Gentle," Kathy said softly.

"What . . . Why the hell should I?"

"Just do as I tell you." She spoke without emphasis, and turned to walk round to the passenger door. She was dressed oddly, in a man's shirt and a pair of black trousers too big for her. And a gun in a holster on the belt, tucked up on her hip. He goggled at it in surprise, then fumbled the remote again to unlock the car.

They got in and closed the doors, and Kathy stared forward out of the windscreen for a moment before turning to face him. "Basil Hannaford killed Bettina tonight," she said. "He blew her head off with a shotgun. Two barrels at five yards. It was like hitting her head with a huge sledge-hammer. He thought he was killing you."

Gentle didn't say anything. His soft, rather full lips shrivelled a little and his puppy-dog eyes widened.

"I wanted to tell you this myself, so that you would understand."

"Understand what?" His throat was dry.

"I find it physically loathsome being so close to you," Kathy went on, "knowing what you did. For a moment, while I was standing there waiting for you to come down, I remembered Angela, and I thought the best thing, really, would be to sit like this, beside you here, and put a bullet through your head, and just end it.

"We know what you did, you see, but I'm not sure how long it will take us to prove it. Our photographic expert says that the two pictures of Zoë Bagnall that Bettina had—before and after her throat was cut—had a small area near one corner which was out of focus. This would be due to a flaw in a lens, either in the camera that took the picture, or more likely in the enlarger that made the print. The same flaw is present in some of the pictures we found in your attic. But is a flaw like that unique? It's not like a fingerprint. Maybe other lenses have the same flaw, those in the same batch as your enlarger lens, maybe all the ones the manufacturer made that year.

"This is only a detail, of course. The real reason we know what you did is the pattern of events itself. Without you it makes no sense. It's too coincidental. With you it comes, finally, into focus. But that wouldn't necessarily make an argument in court. We would have to rely on the forensic evidence, the flaw in the lens.

"You're wondering, aren't you, if I would try to stop you, if you were to run back into the house at this point, upstairs to your darkroom, and pull out that lens and smash it to pieces?"

Gentle was motionless, his back clammy with sweat against his pyjama top, although he felt icy cold.

"I don't mind if you do, because it would be the action of a guilty person. But, as I said, I don't think it will make much difference either way. In the end, I would guess you would be in the clear after three months, six months, even if it got to court.

"And by that time Hannaford would be free too. Oh yes, I think he would. Who could blame him for being driven to do that to the killer of his daughter? I know several journalists who will make a hero of him. And what would be the point of keeping him in jail if the court decided that Bettina acted alone?

"But he would know the truth.

"I saw the look on his face after he saw what he'd done to Bettina. He was elated. He had avenged Angela. I daresay you can imagine what will go through his head when he realizes that he didn't, not really. I was thinking about that as I drove over here. He's shown us what he's capable of. And he's surprisingly resourceful. He managed to tail me for two weeks without me knowing. I don't care on your account, but I worry about your wife. I think Hannaford might start with her, to try to make you suffer the way he suffered.

"I wanted to tell you all this, because I couldn't stand the thought of you listening to the news this morning about Hannaford and Bettina, and thinking that it was over, and that you were in the clear. I wanted you to understand what the rest of your life was going to be like."

Kathy stopped and took a deep breath. The dawn had got no

brighter, the heavy clouds suffocating the light. Ahead of them a car appeared on the lane leading to the house, headlights on. It came to a stop at the garden gate and waited.

"They've come to dig up your garden, Tom, and pull your house apart. It's purely a formality. They're angry because they can't find Zoë Bagnall."

They sat in silence for several minutes, and then he said softly, "What do you want me to do?"

She let the silence hang. Then, "I want you to give me the other photographs," she said. "The ones we didn't find last time."

"JANICE USED TO GET on the train at London Bridge." Gentle seemed remarkably relaxed, now that they were back at the Orpington station, the decision made. To Kathy it seemed as if he must feel no guilt, but Brock, later, suggested that guilt, the enjoyment of guilt, was his guiding principle, all his pleasures guilty ones.

"I noticed her because she looked so much like my sister." He smirked. "The same superior look, as if travelling in a rush-hour train was really beneath her. I noticed which part of the platform she always stood at, and I'd try to pick the compartment that would stop opposite her when we got to London Bridge. After a couple of times I got it right and she got in, and I gave her a smile and a look, you know, like what a trial this was, having to put up with all the riff-raff. But I never really had a chance to talk to her, because she got off at St. John's, where the train was still full.

"So I tried a different approach. I travelled in a different part of the train, and got off at St. John's myself, and followed her home, just to see what the set-up was. I found she lived in an old house, divided into flats—well, you've probably seen it. No? Well, when you go there, you'll see that she had the basement flat. The point was, the rear garden was heavily overgrown, terraced down to the back of the house, and was accessed from a lane. I found I could get into the garden, and sit in one of the bushes there and look down into her flat, completely unobserved. So I decided I wouldn't try to speak to her any more. Instead I'd make her one of my 'sleeping beauties.'"

He grinned mischievously. "That's the name I give the girls I snap without them knowing, without ever speaking to them. Well, it worked a treat. The basement was fairly dark, so she'd put the lights on, even in summer, and with a fast film I could get quite reasonable pictures with the telephoto lens.

"The third or fourth time, she had a visitor, another woman— Bettina. Janice fussed round her, very pleased to see her. She gave her a glass of wine, and they sat together on the sofa, and then Janice took an office file, quite thick, out of the shoulder bag she took to work, and showed it to the other woman. From the way she did it, offering it, then pulling it away, I could see she was teasing her. Bettina went along with it for a bit, then grabbed it and started to look inside. While she did this, Janice began stroking her and nuzzling her, and it was clear what she was after."

Gentle grinned, a naughty boy enjoying the full attention of his audience, and raised a glass of water from the table in front of him. A feeble ray of autumnal sunlight had crept across the ceiling of the interview room from the high-level windows.

"Janice was getting a bit carried away. She was trying to make Bettina put the papers down, and Bettina didn't look as if she was enjoying it one bit. Eventually she said something to Janice, who nodded and let her go. Bettina left the room, and Janice sat waiting for her, looking pretty pleased with herself. A couple of minutes later Bettina returned, Janice lifted her face up to her, as if for a kiss, and Bettina bent over her, wrapped something—her tights it looked like—around her throat and then hung on for grim life until Janice had stopped thrashing around."

He blew through pursed lips, a small percussive sound to

emphasize the raised eyebrows which said, "Well, how about that, chaps!" Brock stared impassively back at him. "She killed Janice?"

"She was bloody strong for a girl, I could tell that. She pulled Janice half out of the seat, and she held her there with the tights around her throat until she stopped struggling. Then she let go, and Janice just crumpled down, like a sack of potatoes.

"I was stunned, as you could imagine. I mean, sometimes when I'm taking my pictures I get a glimpse into people's private lives, but never anything like this! I'd got it all on film, the whole bloody lot. I was just hoping my grip had been steady enough. I watched while Bettina cleaned up. She was very cool. She wiped everything, put away the wine glass she'd had, arranged Janice in the chair as if she was asleep, and found a plastic carrier bag for the file of papers Janice had brought for her. She also took some money from Janice's purse. As she was getting ready to go I nipped out to the lane, back down to the street, just in time to see her come out of the house. Then I followed her, back to St. John's station, up to London Bridge, then the tube, northbound as far as Kings Cross, then the Piccadilly line north to Wood Green, where she lived."

"She lived in Wood Green, did she?"

"At that time, yes. I can find you the address if you want."

"Thanks."

A model of co-operation.

"I discovered her name too, from the label on her front door. Well, I went home, in a bit of a daze. I wasn't sure what to do. I certainly didn't want to put myself in the situation of having to explain what I'd been doing in that garden. I decided not to do anything until I'd seen how the photographs came out. Well, as you saw, they came out pretty well."

"Yes," Brock nodded. "Remarkable."

"Thanks." Gentle smiled, modestly pleased with himself. "I thought I should send them to the police or something, but I didn't want them tracing them to me, and anyway . . . the longer I looked at the pictures . . ."

"What?"

"I don't know, Janice looked so incredibly like Nora—my sister. Seeing her being throttled like that . . . I mean, it was shocking, but . . . I didn't really see why I should spoil it, by turning Bettina in."

"Sorry," Brock broke in. "I didn't quite follow that. You're saying that you liked the idea of someone strangling your sister? You wanted to help the person who did it?"

Gentle shifted uncomfortably in his seat. "Not exactly. No, that's not important. I shouldn't have mentioned it. You'd better take that out of the record. I just thought . . . it was an accident me being there. I was just a chance observer. Why should I get involved?"

Brock didn't pursue the change of tack. "Go on then."

"After some time, several weeks it was, I thought I might contact Bettina. Just to talk to her."

"To blackmail her?"

"Oh no!" Gentle was shocked. "Nothing like that! I just felt . . . this thing had happened, and I'd seen it, and . . . I wanted her to know."

"I'm afraid you've lost me again. What were you hoping to gain?"

"Not gain. Not exactly *gain*." He raised his eyes to the ceiling, trying to find a way to put it, an artist trying to explain to a philistine that if you can't *feel* it, how can I possibly explain it to you?

"You've seen those photographs, Chief Inspector. We see much worse, much more violent images every time we go to the cinema, or switch on the TV. These weren't as good, actually, in terms of clarity, photographic quality. But the fact that they were recording something *real*, not pretend! That makes them so incredibly compelling, doesn't it? That woman in the picture really is on the point of dying! My God, that makes a difference, doesn't it?"

The more Brock looked bemused and uncomprehending, the more agitated Gentle became.

"Don't you see? Those were the most incredibly compulsive pictures I'd ever taken. I couldn't stop looking at them. I couldn't just put them away in a drawer and forget about them! I had to see her again, speak to her, the person who'd performed that act.

"I called on her, after work one day, but she wasn't there. I left it for a week or so, then tried again. This time she was at home. I said I had some information for her, about Janice Pearce, and could I talk to her about it? She was surprised, as you'd expect, and she let me in. I'd decided to hit her with it, so to speak, straight away, before she had a chance to prepare herself. She said, what sort of information? and I gave her two photos, the first of Janice trying to cuddle her while she was reading the file, and the second of her strangling Janice."

He suppressed a snigger. "You should have seen her face! I explained to her that I was a keen amateur photographer, an observer of life, and I thought she would be interested in some of my work. I told her these were only a few of the pictures I'd taken of her and Janice. She asked what I wanted, what I was going to do, and I said, nothing; for me it was enough to watch and record. But I said I would be interested to know what it had all been about. Well, she thought about that, and then she started telling me this story about her being a poor orphan, trying to trace her long-lost parents, and I thought she was trying to have me on with some kind of sob story. But when I said as much, she got this look in her eye, the same as she'd had when Janice was trying to grope her, and it was pretty scary close up, I can tell you. So I apologized, and said I was really interested to hear her story, if she would tell it to me.

"Whoa"—he puffed his cheeks—"any chance of a cup of tea?"

"Of course. How do you take it? We'll organize some breakfast shortly."

"That'd be nice. White, two sugars, please." He gave an apologetic little smile to the WPC, who made for the door. "Sweet tooth."

Kathy hated the way Brock was humouring him, playing the rather dim but sympathetic interviewer. In his place she would have ripped the bastard apart, wiped the stupid smirks from his face, *made* him see what a grotesque little pervert he was. Which was why Brock was doing this interview and not her.

"So," Brock said, "Bettina's life story."

"Yes. She was adopted at birth, apparently, by a couple from Walthamstow. Sounded like a reasonable home to me—he was the manager of a hardware shop and she did cleaning—and Bettina didn't suggest that she was abused or anything like that. But she said she hated them anyway. She must have been a very difficult child. They told her, when she was five, that she'd been adopted, the way they'd been advised to do, and from then on she had these fantasies about her real parents, which would be natural, I should think, for anyone in her position. Sometimes they were poor but good people who had had some terrible misfortune which forced them to give up their daughter, and sometimes they were monsters who'd rejected her, and she'd dream of having revenge on them one day.

"Ah!" He beamed appreciatively at the WPC, who had returned with plastic cups of tea. "Just what the doctor ordered."

He stirred and sipped and sighed and relaxed back in his chair. "Her adoptive parents didn't really know anything about her real mother or father, so when Bettina reached eighteen, the first thing she did was to apply for her birth certificate. She said she was offered counselling about it—apparently they do that to everyone—but she told them to get stuffed. By this stage she'd already been in trouble, at school, and with the police. That's why she was so partic-ular about cleaning up after Janice, she explained—she reckoned you had her fingerprints on your computer.

"Well, the birth certificate told her the name of her mother, and described her as an actress. But it said nothing at all about her father, meaning they weren't married, and possibly the mother didn't even know who the father was. Bettina tried to find the mother, but all she had was a name, and an address which turned out to be a rented flat where nobody had heard of her. She didn't have a date of birth, or any kind of description apart from the one word, "actress," and the fact that her adoptive mother had once said that she'd been told that the natural mother had been blonde, like her. She tried for a while, contacting people with that name in the telephone directory, and acting agencies, but got nowhere. So she gave up, and got into worse trouble. I understand she got involved with a married man who wasn't very nice to her. She attacked him with a breadknife, apparently, and put him in hospital. He hushed it up.

"Her adoptive parents, who had no other children, both died last year, and it was when she was clearing their house that Bettina came across an old envelope marked with her name. Inside was a record of regular monthly payments to her mother from a firm of solicitors, together with a copy of the original court order setting out arrangements for her natural father to contribute to her financial upkeep, and a letter from the solicitors explaining that under no circumstances could the names of the parties be divulged to one another. So she went to those solicitors, ostensibly for help with her current troubles with the law, but hoping to find someone who would help her trace the name of her father. She found Janice Pearce."

Gentle yawned suddenly and stretched. "Do you know," he said, "confession makes you terribly hungry. Any chance of that breakfast now, Chief Inspector?"

"Fair enough. We'll suspend the interview." Brock looked affably at the clock. "Reconvene in forty-five minutes. OK, Kathy?"

Gentle turned and smiled at her as if they were making arrangements for an agreeable day out together.

BREN WAS WAITING OUTSIDE for Kathy. "How's it going?"

"He's just getting into his stride," she said wearily.

"Yeah, well, we've solved the mystery of your aunt, anyway." He said it warily, the messenger of bad news, and she felt a jolt of alarm.

"What's happened?"

"No, she's just fine. It's your uncle. He had a stroke yesterday lunchtime. He's in the Royal Hallamshire Hospital in Sheffield. She's there now, with him. The relatives sent a nephew down to fetch your aunt last night. You can ring her on this number at the hospital."

Kathy nodded, smiling her relief. "Thanks, Bren. God . . ." Fatigue and a sudden resentment at all the shocks and anxieties of the past twenty-four hours swept over her. "You'd have thought she'd have left me a message or something! I'll wring her bloody neck . . ."

Kathy dialled the number Bren had given her and waited while they put her through, too tired now to feel impatient.

"Mary! How are you? How's Tom?"

"Hello, pet. He's not at all well, I'm afraid. He's on the life support. They're not . . . They don't think . . ."

"Oh . . . I'm so sorry, Mary."

"There's nothing can be done, love. We'll just have to wait and see." Her voice sounded faint, exhausted. "And I was sorry to rush off like that without saying goodbye. They sent Tom's nephew Colin down to fetch me, and he had a terrible time finding me. Your nice neighbour, Mrs. P, heard him ringing your front doorbell and told him we were at the Shortland theatre. He got there after we'd all gone on to the party, but someone locking up thought they knew where we were, and then he got lost, and anyway he found it eventually. Did you get my note?"

"Note? No. Where is it?"

"In your flat. We called in there to get my things on our way back up north. I am sorry to leave like that, love. Have you been busy?"

"Sort of." Kathy almost mentioned Bettina, but immediately thought better of it.

"Did you see Bettina?" Mary said. "I asked her to tell you what had happened. She said she had been planning to see you later last night, but the arrangements had been cancelled. I didn't understand. She was a bit drunk, I think."

GENTLE HAD BEEN TO the bathroom after his breakfast; his soft brown hair was neatly combed back, his face fresh and pink.

"We'd got to the point where Bettina had got Janice to help her trace her father," Brock said mildly. "I don't really understand why she killed Janice, though. Had she planned to do that?"

"I asked her about that. I'm not sure that she'd planned it exactly, but she said she got very uptight where her real father was concerned. Janice had read the file, and knew the name. Bettina didn't like that. She didn't want anyone else to know it but her. She said it made her very angry. That and the way Janice was trying to get on to her."

"I see. So, now she had his name. What then?"

"His name and his address—he was still living in the same place. But suddenly she wasn't sure what to do. I mean, she'd had this big quest, she'd murdered for that name, but what was going to happen now? What if he didn't want to know her? Suppose he rejected her for a second time? So she was cautious. She went to see his house, like something out of the Addams Family, she said, and spied on him, seeing what he looked like, this weird old cove.

Then she phoned him up, several times, before she said anything—at first she just dialled the number and listened to him saying hello.

"Eventually she worked out what she would do. She pretended to be from some kind of agency, and said she could arrange reunions between adopted children and their natural parents, was he interested?"

"What did he say to that?"

"He said, yes, he would do anything, anything at all to meet his son."

"His son?"

"That's right, his *son*. She didn't understand. She said, was he talking about the child mothered by whatever the actress's name was, and was there more than one? and he said no, that was the one, his son, the only child he'd ever had. Well, apparently she was devastated. She rang off. She'd been prepared for him to say he wasn't interested in finding his child and then she'd have just got mad, but this threw her. Oh, she was really thrown by that, I can tell you. She went on and on about it. Her theory was that he must have wanted a son, not a daughter, and he'd somehow convinced himself that that's what he had. As if he'd rejected her twice, you might say, as a person and as a woman."

Gentle paused and drew a deep breath, shaking his head.

"You had another idea, Tom?" Brock asked.

He raised his eyebrows. "Seemed obvious to me. He hadn't dreamed up something like that. It was the mother who'd told him she'd had a boy, so he'd never, ever, be able to find his daughter."

"Ah. And how did Bettina react when you told her that, Tom?"

"She hit the bloody roof!" He cackled. "God, you should have seen her! Her mother hadn't just abandoned her, she'd obliterated her, wiped her off the face of the earth so she'd never have a real father!"

"And you helped her to see that, Tom," Brock said, nodding. "Iago. Motiveless evil."

"What?" Gentle looked at him in surprise.

"The part you played. Don't worry, a theatrical reference. Carry on."

"Well, anyway, she didn't like it. And she wanted to get back at them, especially her mother. She started following Nesbit around, finding out about him. She found out about that theatre group of his, and about this play they were doing at that time, in Shortlands."

"Which one was that?"

"It was called *Equus*. I was interested to see her father, so I said, why didn't we go along and see a performance, which we did. This would have been late in July last year."

"Yes."

"Afterwards, we talked about it. I thought it was pretty amateurish, myself, but she said it was really good, very moving. She particularly identified with one of the characters, a boy who stabs out the eyes of these horses. She said she came out of the theatre feeling that she could do that to her mother. She understood why the boy had done it, and she knew she could do it too. Then we saw that in the programme it mentioned that they were going to take the play up to the Edinburgh Festival, and she got the idea of following them there."

"Did you plant that thought in her head too, Tom?"

"Maybe. Anyway, she went. Muriel and I were away on holiday at the time, in France, and when I got back Bettina told me what had happened. She'd gone to see the play again, and afterwards she went into the alleyways behind the theatre, and when a blonde woman came by on her own, Bettina grabbed her, and stabbed out her eyes with a screwdriver, like the boy had done."

Gentle paused for a drink of water and Kathy noticed that his hand was shaking, although his voice had shown no emotion as he had described this.

"Well now, what was your reaction to that, Tom?" Brock asked neutrally.

"Oh, hey . . ." Gentle grinned. "Pretty damn surprised!"

"Surprised, were you? . . . But what else?"

"Well, impressed. Yes, impressed. That she had the nerve to do something like that. Christ, I never could! Could you?"

"Did you find it scary?"

"Yes, yes, it was scary. She was a scary sort of person, when you knew what she had done. Hell, I'd seen her in action!"

"But you were impressed, fascinated."

Gentle nodded vigorously.

"I'll bet you wished you'd been up there with your camera, eh?"

Gentle hung his head coyly, conceding the point without agreeing to it.

"Did you understand that she'd deliberately killed the woman in Edinburgh in that particular way in order to send a message to her father?"

"No, that came later I think, with Zoë. In Edinburgh it had been the play itself that had inspired her. Afterwards she wondered if her father would have seen the connection, and she said she hoped he would, and that's what gave us . . . gave her the idea for making Zoë Bagnall disappear."

"How was that?"

"Oh well, we were talking about her father, and she was saying about his acting thing, and how her mother had been an actress, and how she hated them both for it, pretending to be characters in a play when they hadn't been able to play their own lives properly, abandoning her, and how she felt they should be punished for it. And she mentioned that according to the programme of the theatre company, her father was planning on doing another play in the new year, called *The Lady Vanishes*. And we were kind of joking, you know, about the title, and then the idea just came up that she could make one of the women in the play vanish, and that would spook her father for sure."

"That sounds like your idea again, Tom," Brock said. "I mean she wasn't all that bright, was she? She needed a bit of help with the creative side, didn't she? Not much point being bashful now."

Gentle rocked his head in a self-deprecating little show of humility, his mouth squirming with guilty pleasure.

"So you decided on Zoë Bagnall."

Gentle nodded. "Bettina decided to move down to the Shortlands area, and join SADOS. It gave her a buzz to see her father at close hand, and know that he had no idea who she was. She helped backstage with *The Lady Vanishes*, and we decided that Zoë should be it, her being blonde and in the play."

"You started following her, did you?"

"I began travelling up and down to Victoria, the line she used, and getting the tube across to the office. I took photographs of her, and from time to time I met with Bettina and we discussed them."

"Were you lovers, you and Bettina?"

"No, no. Nothing like that. Our relationship was different."

"More like father and daughter, you mean? Or brother and sister?"

Gentle gave a little frown, as if to warn Brock against making jokes about this.

"Sorry, Tom, I'm getting tired," Brock said. "Why don't you tell us what happened with Zoë, and then we might take a break and finish off your statement later."

Gentle shrugged. "The factual things, do you mean?"

"The factual things, yes."

"I approached her in December sometime, coming home on the train. I let it out that I was a wealthy man, bored, looking for a new direction in life. After a while I asked her if she'd like to spend a weekend with me, and she was quite agreeable. I nominated

January the twentieth, and she told me she had the last performance of her play that night. She'd have to put in an appearance at a party afterwards, and we agreed I'd go to her flat and pick her up at the appointed time, and take her somewhere nice. I took her to Bettina's place. She said, what's this? because it wasn't exactly a luxury hotel, and I said I had a surprise for her inside. And when we went in, Bettina was waiting for us. She killed Zoë there."

"How, exactly?"

Kathy felt numbed by Gentle's matter-of-fact description of scenes of horror, of him calmly taking pictures while Bettina cut the woman's throat and mutilated her. She wanted Brock to hurry it up, to finish, although she knew he would have to go through every detail of it.

"What about your role, Tom?"

"Oh no, she did everything. I told you, I'd never have the nerve. I just recorded the event. I was always only an observer, not a participant. I'm not a murderer, Chief Inspector! Good lord, look at me! I only watch, take photographs. It seemed, well, obscene to me that such things might go unrecorded, unwitnessed. I felt I had to be there."

"The audience for her starring roles, Tom. The official photographer. But you were more than that, surely. Actors need producers too. You were her producer, weren't you? Preparing and planning, selecting the cast. Angela, for example. That was entirely your choice, wasn't it?"

Gentle conceded the point. "Bettina was getting very agitated at that stage. Nesbit seemed to be oblivious to her little messages. When he didn't react to the murder of the Weeks girl, in the park, Bettina insisted that we send him a picture of Zoë, with her throat cut. She attached a note with the message, 'from your only son.' But nothing happened. She expected him to go to pieces, but instead he just announced that he was going to do *The Father* instead of *Blithe Spirit* as his next play, which we thought was a bit rich. We didn't know, of course, what he was planning. So Bettina insisted we do another one, to wake him up. She was getting very twitchy. She wanted to grab someone after a rehearsal, Vicky probably, and I thought that was getting too dangerous. But then they arranged the trip to *Macbeth*, and I thought we might do something less obvious."

"Was it a coincidence, then, that Angela was going to the same performance?"

Gentle looked quizzically at Brock, wondering how someone so slow could be in this line of work. "Hardly. I arranged for her to go. I was the one who got her the ticket in the first place. I had been pestering her a little, and she'd taken offence. It was my way of saying sorry." He pursed his lips: what a naughty boy am I.

"Actually, it was more than that," he went on. "She had been threatening to make a complaint to Clive Ferry, the Head Office Manager, about me following her home. So I peeked in her office file, just to see if there was anything there I could use to persuade her to keep quiet. And I noticed that she'd gone to the same school as the one that Bettina had discovered her father had been a teacher at—Bettina had a whole file on her old man by this time. I thought what a wonderful twist that would be, when he recognized Angela's face in the paper. Bettina thought it was brilliant."

"Yes," Brock said, looking at him thoughtfully. "That was a very clever bit of stage management, Tom. But then why the hell did you end up buying her spare ticket, drawing attention to yourself?"

"Well"—Gentle looked up at the ceiling, shook his head, the great artist tripped up by the trivia of everyday life—"because unknown to me she'd gone back to the theatre and exchanged her ticket for two cheaper ones so her friend Rhona could go with her, and when that fell through Rhona was on the point of selling it to the young lad in Marketing who's had his eye on Angela for some time. He'd have wanted to see her home. He might have stayed the night—he might have spoiled everything. So I had to step in and buy the ticket myself. I thought, as long as I didn't actually go that night, I'd be in the clear. I knew Muriel would never let me go."

He shook his head sadly. "I really messed that up, didn't I?"

"So you were the producer and casting director," Brock said. "And stage-manager too, I shouldn't wonder. The disguises, for instance."

"Bettina had already started that in Edinburgh. She told me she'd bought a pair of size nine shoes up there so if she left any footprints the police would think it was a man. I just helped her develop it, with the beard and everything. We were creating a character."

"And the trick with the condom, was that your idea?"

Gentle nodded. "I did quite a bit of reading about police forensic methods. There was an account of a rapist who was using a condom so that the police couldn't get a DNA profile from his sperm. But the police were able to identify the make of condom he used from traces of the lubricant in the woman's vagina. It appealed to Bettina, to make it look like a man was doing it—her father's *son*. She enjoyed playing the part. You should have seen her performances! She was really scary. She tried the condom thing first with Zoë, even though the idea was that she would vanish without trace. She put the condom on the end of a broomstick, to cause bruising."

"And where is Zoë now?"

"When Bettina was finished, we cleaned up as best we could, and wrapped Zoë in plastic. We lifted her into the boot of my car, and next day I took her to the dump, along with a pile of junk we wanted rid of. She's in the Sevenoaks municipal refuse tip, I'm afraid." He gave a little apologetic shrug of his shoulders. "I was due to change my car soon after, anyway."

Brock glanced at Kathy, pale and drawn, over Gentle's shoulder, and said, "I think we might take a break at this point, Tom. Give us a chance to check up on one or two things, and I dare say you might want to contact your solicitor."

"One thing," Kathy spoke for the first time. They looked at her in surprise. "You didn't know that Stafford was planning to kill himself. So presumably you had another killing planned for last night."

A crafty look came over Gentle.

"Who was the victim going to be?"

"You've got me there, Sergeant." He gave a sly little smile. "Bettina had a key to your flat. She made a copy from the ones she pinched from your aunt. We were going to pay you a visit when you returned from the cast party."

"What about my aunt?"

He shrugged; a matter of no concern. "When Nesbit killed himself, Bettina was completely thrown. In an odd sort of way I think she grieved for him. We decided to abandon our plans for Saturday. I really think she might not have done it any more."

"What was she doing at Stafford's house?"

"She thought he might have a picture of her mother. Maybe information about her. Where she lives . . ."

Kathy thought of a line she'd read from the closing passages of *Equus*, the voice of the horse asking why.

"Why did you pick me, Mr. Gentle?"

He smiled at her. "Bettina didn't like you. She said she didn't like the way you got on with Nesbit, the way he looked at you as if you were his daughter instead of her. She was jealous. And then, of course, you had the right coloured hair."

EIGHTEEN

THE MOTORWAY PATROL SPOTTED the car parked on the hard shoulder just short of the bridge, and pulled to a stop behind it.

"Go on," the driver said to his mate, "your turn." Neither wanted to get out, with the rain sluicing down and great waves of spray buffeting the car with every truck that passed.

Reluctantly the other man put his cap on his head and turned up his collar. "Maybe it'll ease off in a minute."

"No chance," the driver grinned. "And it'll be dark soon."

The officer got out and ran forward to the window of the parked car. He had to peer through the streaming glass to make out that the car was empty. He straightened and looked along the hard shoulder, trying to see if he could catch sight of the driver. It took him a moment to spot her, standing motionless in the darkness under the bridge. He called out, but she had her back to him, and with the roar of the traffic and the rain he wasn't sure she would have heard, so he began running towards her. At least it would be dry under the bridge.

She turned at the sound of his footsteps and he saw that she was soaking wet, fair hair plastered to her head, face glistening with water.

"You all right, madam?"

She nodded. Her face seemed unnaturally pale in the evening light, catching the glow from the headlights rushing past.

"Trouble with your vehicle?"

She didn't react at first, and he repeated the question, louder. Then she shook her head and muttered some reply which he didn't catch. The underside of the bridge was magnifying the traffic noise. He made to move towards her, but she backed away, like a nervous pony, he thought. Then she turned and started walking back to her car. He followed after her, and stood watching as she got in, started it up, and drove off into the traffic stream.

"What was all that about?" the driver asked as he got back, dripping, into the patrol car.

"Who knows?" he said wearily. "Some melodrama."